O9-ABI-875

Cattery Row

Also by Clea Simon
Mew Is for Murder

Cattery Row

Clea Simon

Poisoned Pen Press

Poisoned
Pen
Press

Copyright © 2006 by Clea Simon

First Edition 2006

10 9 8 7 6 5 4 3 2 1

Library of Congress Catalog Card Number: 2006900731

ISBN: 1-59058-306-X Hardcover

Poisoned Pen Press
6962 E. First Ave., Ste. 103
Scottsdale, AZ 85251
www.poisonedpenpress.com
info@poisonedpenpress.com

Printed in the United States of America

For Jon

Introduction

They came in the night, quiet and professional. Two of them, dressed in black, their faces shielded by nylon ski masks and their hands gloved. They didn't have to be so careful. The head of the house was away, and the residents watched, wide eyed, as the team went first to one and then another, looking for their prize. When they found her, she didn't cry out. Bred to be regal, relaxed and calm, she only exhaled, giving up a sigh of discomfort as they hefted her soft pliant body out of her bed and into the waiting cage. As an afterthought, they grabbed three of her offspring, who had settled nearby. These were as wellborn as their mother, but a little more high strung, feisty with youth. One, then two went into the cage, but the third struck out, sinking her sharp new teeth into the hand of her abductor. "Ah!" The hand drew back. The cry had been muffled by the double thickness of the mask, but still the other looked around, anxious and angry with the fear of discovery. And then, fueled by nerves, the invader lunged for her again, grabbing for her more roughly this time as she cowered helpless in her rage.

Chapter One

Musetta pounced and her prey went flying. All across my kitchen table, the once-neat pile of overdue notices, envelopes, and vaguely threatening letters scattered into disarray.

"Kitty!" I grabbed at a phone bill that balanced on the table's edge and retrieved a final notice from the floor. October still had two weeks to go, but the paperwork had been piling up for over a month—to my discomfort but, apparently, my pet's amusement. I watched as my athletic little cat settled in on top of an auto insurance form and began licking an envelope. Beneath her white boot I could make out the words "Second Notice."

"Never mind." I reached over to stroke her sleek black head. "It's no good anyway, kitten. We're broke."

Pushing aside an envelope edged with ominous red lettering, I let my other hand settle into her thick neck ruff. I called her "kitten," but it was only a term of endearment at this point. My young cat had reached her full growth, developing into a full-bodied beauty, and as the weather cooled into a New England autumn, that included a dense coat as glossy as a seal's. Unconcerned by our looming financial disaster, the round face that looked up at me could have posed for Currier and Ives, were it not for the off-center white star on her nose. That made her look slightly cross-eyed and goofy, but eminently squeezable. And after an early kittenhood on the streets she suffered fools of my sort gladly, letting me rub her neck and the base of her ears until her green eyes closed and she purred to the point of drooling. To strangers, especially those who didn't appreciate simple healthy beasts, I skimmed over her stray youth, introducing her as a medium-haired random-bred Jellicle, after T.S. Eliot's fanciful naming of "tuxedo" cats, and let them make of it what they would.

It was harder, I had to admit, to come up with such attitude when describing myself. Thirty-three and feeling it, these days I was lacking the fire my red hair was supposed to signify. Partly that came from being a rock fan in a college town, a longtime habitué of the nocturnal world where the denizens all tended to look younger as I grew older—a shift particularly noticeable as each fall brought a new crop of students to flash their fake IDs and flood my favorite clubs. Partly that came from being a freelance writer, a free agent who had lacked the good sense not to alienate my one reliable source of income.

"It wasn't my fault, kitty." Musetta had laid back on the pile of paper, lulled into near-sleep by my constant petting and the taste of glue. "Well, not totally." Something about a cat compels honesty, and her green eyes, half-closed, demanded the truth. "I mean, you'd have bitten him, and that's what I did in my own way." She didn't respond, but that didn't stop me. I've always talked to cats. Who knows what they understand? And besides, nobody else would believe me.

When it happened, two months before, I hadn't thought it would be such a big deal. It had been one of those humid late August afternoons that make you either sleepy or mad. I'd been leaning toward the latter when I'd gone down to the offices of the *Boston Morning Mail,* the newspaper where I'd toiled as a copy editor for close to seven years and for which these days I did the majority of my freelance writing. I went as much for the air-conditioning as anything else, since the cavernous plant tended to be chilled to the point of absurdity all summer while my third-floor Cambridge apartment held heat like an oven. I figured I'd pick up the accumulated fliers and other junk that tended to fill the mailbox that still bore my name. Maybe say hi to some of my former colleagues, and just cool off. I hadn't looked for a run-in with Tim, the features editor. But when I saw him gesturing from his glass-fronted office, I'd put on the best friendly-eager smile I could conjure, pulled at my still-damp T-shirt to erase some of the creases, and made my way over to the messy little room, waiting until he sat behind his desk before lowering myself gingerly onto the pile of press releases that covered his one guest chair.

"Krakow," he barked by way of greeting, his gruff voice cutting through the air-conditioner roar. Most of my friends call me by my first name, Theda, but Tim had affected a Lou Grant-style grumpiness recently to match his expanding waist and receding hairline. Despite the chilled air, his button-down shirt looked rumpled and his neck was chafed red. I assumed the weather had gotten to him too, if not the constant noise. "That idea you had? You wrote me a note? I've been thinking about it."

I'd been a regular music stringer for a while by then, filling in for the staff pop and rock critics whenever one of them felt like a night in or a night off. Writing about live music, trying to translate those one-of-a-kind moments for those who missed them while also adding some perspective for fans who caught the show was the best, and I loved the rush of reviewing on deadline for the next day's paper, too. But such assignments were still few and far between. So to augment the reviews, I kept a steady stream of feature story pitches in circulation, ranging from two-paragraph outlines to a page or two from actual stories that I'd started writing.

Not having any clue as to which of a dozen such pitches Tim was referring to, I sat waiting as he shuffled papers. He cursed under his breath, and I fought a growing urge to shiver or at least roll my eyes at his disorganized ways. I had to. Being a freelance writer—I preferred the term "hired gun"—had its high points: the freedom to explore any topic that caught my fancy, the ability to research and conduct interviews the way I thought they should be done, the opportunity to structure my days around my writing. Even though I was paid by the piece, and not much at that, quitting my editing job the previous winter seemed like the right move for me as a writer. *Selling* my work, though, that's what tended to trip me up, and sitting there, waiting for Tim to find my proposal made me all too aware of what I lacked. As much as I believed in my stories, I found it hard to muster the marketing part, the smooth sell—hell, the sheer effrontery to pitch properly, effectively to the powers-that-be. Thirty words or less: that's what editors wanted to hear, and god help you if you didn't have a hot hook in there somewhere. Sex or drugs, these were needed to sell even rock 'n' roll these days, and what any of that had to do with writing a good story I never could tell. But at least I could keep a lid on my impatience. As I stared at Tim and waited, I could feel goosebumps begin to rise and crossed my arms. If only I still had my office sweater. Or a book.

"The behind-the-scenes piece at the cat show?" I knew I was shooting in the dark. I didn't think Tim would care for a story about high-end breeders and their cut-throat competitions no matter how into it I was, but I couldn't remember what else I'd tried to sell him recently.

"No, no more cats, Krakow. You're getting obsessed." He waved his pencil at me and started working through the papers piled in his "In" box. Yes, he was right that I liked to write about felines. But people liked to read about them, too. Tim paused, running his finger inside his collar, but I knew better than to jump in. "The club thing." He pushed aside a coffee-stained napkin, which landed neatly in "Out." "Oh, here it is."

"'Night Lines,'" I said aloud, nodding as I recognized the query letter I'd dropped off months earlier. This idea was special to me. A weekly column covering the music scene in the Boston area, I proposed it as half review and half preview, with news about local happenings—which band was breaking up, who was drawing record-label interest—for spice. I'd been hopeful about this one when I'd typed it up. With more than a decade's worth of nocturnal wanderings to draw on, I had the contacts to make it work and felt confident that my reporting chops would help me to ferret out the doings of those who made the

Boston clubs thrive. I knew and loved the music scene and by now had written enough critical pieces to be able to describe what I listened to in a way that would help readers hear what I heard, maybe even love what I loved. As the weeks went by and the pitch had gone unnoticed, I'd almost forgotten about it. But the timing made sense. I'd heard the same rumors as everyone else in the newsroom: The *Mail*'s circulation was sinking, especially among younger readers. Tim would have to start making some concessions to the thousands of students and recent grads who called the city home. What better way than running a new weekly column on the clubs?

"Yeah, 'Night Lines.' I like that. It would be regular, too, so we could get rid of some of those damned reviews. I mean, the show's over. Who cares? But I'm thinking of calling it something different." He tapped the paper before him with a pencil. I could see that at least two different hands had scrawled notes on it, and leaned a bit closer to decipher them.

"Something younger. More hip." Tim flipped the page over, so I sat back. "'The Boston Beat'?"

I bit my tongue to stop a groan. "Um, I think that might have been used before." At least a dozen times.

"Anyway, younger. That's the point, Krakow." I waited. "You've probably heard about the focus groups we've been hosting?" He didn't pause for an answer. "Younger, that's what they found. Our demographics are skewing too old. Too many soccer moms in the suburbs with their minivans and groceries." His voice took on the disparaging tone of someone who'd always had someone else to do his errands. Who brought his groceries home? My tongue was starting to bleed.

"So, we're going to go with it. At least for a trial run." He must have heard my intake of breath, seen my eyes light up, but he stopped me with a raised hand. "But we're giving it to one of our new hires, a bright young thing named Jessica." His eyes wandered to the glass wall and I collapsed back in my chair, deflated. "Real bright, that girl." With an effort I closed my mouth and followed his gaze out the window. A buxom young woman, made to look even younger by the long braids that held her dark hair, was smiling in at us. She waved, one of those cutesy little finger wiggles, and the flush on Tim's neck rose to his face. My smitten editor waved back and with a visible effort swung around toward me again. To do him credit, he didn't even try to meet my eyes. Instead, he started shuffling through the papers on his desk.

"Anyway, we want you to show her the ropes. You've been around. Get her up to speed on what's going on. We'll pay you for your time." He started stacking things, my silence coming through loud and clear. "How about, oh, I don't know…maybe a hundred bucks a week for three or four weeks until she figures out which end is up?" More silence. "We could maybe squeeze out a hundred fifty." He dared a glance up at me. "We really value your expertise and you'd be a great source for this column, Krakow. Give it a real sense of perspective. You know, give it some history. You're old enough."

So that's when it happened, and when I looked back on it two months later, I didn't see any way I could have played it differently. Sure, I could have watched my language. I didn't have to tell him to screw himself, the paper, and any willing portion of the focus group. I could have declined his offer with a polite "no, thanks" and made my exit without slamming the door so hard those glass walls shook and at least one shelf collapsed behind me. And, yeah, I didn't have to explain my displeasure quite so loudly when Ralph, the staff pop music critic, and Shelley from the copy desk both came over to inquire about the noise. If I'd voiced my frustration in a more modulated tone, the rest of the department might not have heard me. And then I probably wouldn't feel quite so shut off from ever going back into that chill warren of cubicles and glass. But my tongue hurt, as did my ego. And what would I have done if I'd stayed? What would my future assignments have been, now that I'd been relegated to the has-beens, the too-old, and the unhip? An endless series of smaller and smaller service features, undoubtedly. The kind they give to those suburban moms, or any writers they perceive as such. Friendly little stories on rainy-weekend tips or child-care-on-a-budget. A dozen things to do with paper bags. The kind of assignment that had broken the spirit of better writers than I and sent them scurrying from the newsroom into public relations jobs.

Well, I wasn't going that route, not that any big publicity firms would be courting me in the current economic climate. But I wasn't going back. I didn't blame Baby Jessica, as I'd taken to describing her to my friends. I couldn't in all good conscience. The job market was tough these days, you did what you had to, or at least she had. Although when I tried this line out on Bunny, my best friend, she started to argue that neither of us would have taken a gig out from under a sister. Since leaving her childhood Catholicism for the nature-based Wiccan religion, Bunny had become both more ethical and more stringently feminist. Maybe in part because she still worked at the *Mail*, where we'd met, and seen how the paper was changing. And I'd thought I'd be okay. I mean, all the whole Tim debacle had proven was that my ideas were commercially viable, right?

But then *I Do* magazine had stopped calling. I didn't know what I'd done to fall out of favor at the glossy wedding magazine. I didn't think I'd cursed out any of their editors. All I knew was that the big features—a grand or more for articles on shoe dying or whether to have a plated or buffet meal—dried up, leaving me without my other major source of income. And the bills kept coming, until I'd ignored them long enough to scare myself. Which brought me up to my morning of penance and thoughts of penury, as I finally opened all those piled-up, red-bordered envelopes and watched my calm kitty lick the sticky bits.

"What's with the adhesives, Musetta? Are we going to have to get you into a program for this?" Lying on her side, she turned her head upside down to look at me. I could see her petite fangs peeking out of her half-opened mouth and chucked her fuzzy chin. The glue seemed to have left her slightly stoned. "Leave some on the envelopes, okay?"

I slid an envelope out from under her and extracted the enclosed notice as she made a half-hearted grab at it. It was for sixty bucks, to our vet Rachel, for the spaying operation Musetta had had the month before. I looked over now at her exposed belly, the pink of her skin still showing through the growing fluff of white fur. I'd have to pay this one right away; Rachel was a friend as well as our vet, but I couldn't disturb the resting feline further.

"Keep the bills. But I get the newspaper." I started to slide the *Sunday Mail* out from under her hindquarters, spurring another flurry of pounces and paper. "Meh!" My feline colleague protested as I finally got the news section away from her, but then sat back on the rest of the paper to begin washing one white-stockinged foot.

Taxes, war, death, and more taxes. I leafed through the pages, looking for something that would distract me from my own mess. That's when I saw her: Regina's Princess Furbottom of White Eagle, a grand champion queen, that is, a breeding female cat. The star of her cattery, the aptly named Regina Ragdolls, the Ragdoll queen merited her own quarter-page photo with a big, furry body and the face of a startled Siamese. I'm not much on pedigreed cats, preferring instead the random shuffle of nature. But I do like generous animals and Botty, as the caption said she was known, looked like a puss you could seriously cuddle. Except, I read on, that she was missing.

I laid the paper flat and looked for the beginning of the story, which had jumped from the Metro front two pages earlier. There it was: "Cattery Robbed" read the headline. "$25k Queen Stolen" said the subhead, which proved to be misleading. Botty was a lovely beast, but valued at only eight thousand, according to the reporter's research. It was the other cats—a second Ragdoll female and three champion-bred kittens—who brought the total up to twenty-five grand. Some copy editor would catch it for that headline, I thought as old instincts kicked in, and then turned back to the story. The thieves had been smart. The cattery owner, who lived in the nearby suburb of Newton, was a well-known judge. So well known, in fact, that she had been the star attraction at a well-publicized national show held over the previous week in Chicago. She'd probably been judging the all-breed finals when the robbers had struck, according to the police source, cutting the alarm system and making off with the two best known cats in the building. And the two with the most potential for profit. Both Botty and her sister, Regina's Princess Ida, were relatively young and proven fertile. They'd both continue competing at shows, thus increasing their value, and producing healthy litters for years to come.

But why would someone steal pedigreed show cats? Without their papers or the history of their wins in the show ring, the cats' monetary value dropped to nearly nothing. Without proof of their breeding, they were just big, beautiful pets, and if that was the case, why grab the females instead of the larger, even fluffier males? I flipped to the jump again and read down the column of type that flanked the photo of the missing kitty. Underneath her mitten-like paws was the scariest news of all. This break-in, said the cops, was not unique. It fit a pattern of cattery thefts that had been occurring throughout the region, eight in four months, and for which, the source admitted, the authorities had no leads.

I looked over at my own prized pet, now emitting soft snores, and felt grateful for small things. Musetta was a beauty and I loved her, but objectively a random-bred (or, okay, stray) had no resale value. Still, I'd be bereft if anything ever happened to her. That's why I'd taken our vets' advice and had her micro-chipped, the small computer tag inserted into the loose skin at the nape of her neck when she'd been under anesthesia for her spaying. Though the idea of scanning cats like the checkout girl scanned groceries seemed more than a little futuristic, a number of the larger urban shelters were now doing just that when animals were brought in. It beat the "Lost Cat" posters that were constantly stapled on the lampposts of my city street, leaflets all the more heartbreaking because of the detail ("a little shy" or "slight left limp") included. If Musetta ever got out, if she ever got lost, I'd have a little more chance of reuniting with her because of that chip, that tiny nub, which I could feel when I pet her just right.

I did so now, reassuring myself by finding the pea in my princess' fur. "Nuff," she snorted, stretching one white forepaw into a yawn and shifting on her bed of mail. "Eh." She stared up at me. I was disturbing her, the overanxious mother my own mom had often been. I was getting too much into my own head, my debt and the news both contributing to a major funk. It was time to get some air. I stuffed a check in with the vet's bill and wrote out one more that I thought I could cover, then tromped down the stairs and out into a ridiculously beautiful autumn day.

Chapter Two

Autumn is supposed to be New England's best season, and true to form even my urban street had taken on a technicolor vibrancy in the clear, bright light of midmorning. My apartment building and its next-door twin, with their weathered brick and institutional trim, didn't look like much. But all down the block a variety of houses—some restored Victorians resplendent with lacy woodwork, some with sagging porches, and a few newer boxes that seemed entirely constructed of concrete—completed the urban patchwork that I'd come to love. This was Cambridge, a city of poets and students and working people, where I'd settled after college and which I now called home. A hodge-podge enclave, part counter-culture and part working-class where, despite the skyrocketing housing prices, the average IQ still far outweighed the average income, at least in my neighborhood, funky Cambridgeport, tucked between the bustle of Central Square and the river.

We had our version of fall foliage here, too, despite the congestion that lined commuters up at each traffic light and had divided most of those grand old houses into apartments. Stranded in the sidewalk, its patch of earth surrounded by uneven red brick, the sugar maple out front of my place was doing its best, flaunting crayola-red leaves against an insanely blue sky, while half a block down I could see the bright yellow of a birch, set off by a peeling green wall. The U-Hauls of the previous month had disappeared, and most of the students had found their way around, settling into the city life with only the occasional interruption from suburban parents. Even the weather was cooperating: cool enough to not leach the color from that Kodachrome sky, but warming as noon approached so that my light sweatshirt felt just fine. Debts or no, I should have been happy as a clam with myself, my city, and my kitty as I strolled to the corner mailbox.

The truth was, I was lonely. Elsewhere, all across the Northeast, a weekend like this was an invitation for a romantic getaway. While we New Englanders might scoff at the leaf peepers, tourists from New York and farther south who clogged the highways for weeks around Columbus Day, in fact we were not much better. We know that the crisp days of October are our last gasp before a winter that can slog on endlessly, and we too fill Boston's Common and Public Garden with last-chance picnics and frisbee games, or spend our spare hours biking along the river dividing Boston and Cambridge. But instead of heading out for the path along the Charles or a day on the Cape, I'd been closeted alone in my apartment pretty much since Friday. That's when Bill Sherman, my sometime beau, had driven off to Connecticut for a family function, the wedding of a cousin that I too had been invited to attend and had decided to decline.

It wasn't the wedding exactly. I've got nothing against an evening of free food and dancing, even if the music has been chosen by a committee of the relatives and the chicken breasts are guaranteed to be rubbery. It's just that at this point in our relationship, I wasn't sure I wanted to make the statement that showing up with Bill would be. We'd been thrown together by circumstance, as much as choice, and we came from very, *very* different worlds. For a while, our differences had fueled our passion. But recently? Well, we'd gotten together in May, six months ago, and I had a theory about relationships that had made me drag my heels when this invitation had come up.

Call it the theory of threes: Now, maybe this didn't hold for really solid long-term romances; at thirty-three I had scant experience with these. But for those emotional entanglements that I and my girlfriends had stumbled through, there seemed to be distinct markers in the run of romance. For the first three months, we'd all agreed, dating was casual. It was fun and, even if you weren't seeing anyone else, you didn't comment on that fact. At around three months, if the connection was going to grow into anything stronger, then you both started talking about exclusivity. Of course, some of my friends had a sweet tooth for boys in bands, and with them the whole monogamy thing rarely happened. In fact, if you were smart, you knew better than to bring it up. And that could be okay too, as long as you recognized this particular musician factor up front. But for those of us who wanted more, three months was the time to say so, and Bill and I had crossed that hurdle with ease. But then six months was time for the next step, the move into serious couplehood, and I wasn't sure I wanted to take it.

Yes, I cared about Bill. A lot. Although he was about ten years older than I, we seemed to see eye to eye most of the time. He talked to me like I was really there, and his tough-guy surface—that broken nose from high school baseball, his gruff voice—belied a gentle nature. Tall, still mostly lanky, with salt-and-pepper hair and a smile he usually ducked his head to hide, he was sexy in an understated way. As a result, not to get too intellectual about it all, our physical connection was appropriately playful and hot. And although his on-duty life as a homicide cop both thrilled and repulsed me, his off-duty life, full of books and music, good food and wine, provided for the kind of cozy Sundays that I was missing right now.

So why, when he'd told me about the wedding, did I dig my heels in and say no? He'd acknowledged the probability that the function itself, the nuptials of a cousin he barely knew, would be dull. But he'd sweetened the pot with the promise of an overnight by the sea. He'd even booked a spot, an inn somewhere between Cambridge and Connecticut in Rhode Island's unspoiled South County, where we'd get our fix of that fantastic autumnal color but also the sound and smell of breakers and sand. I'm a sucker for the seaside, as he well knew, and I've got a fondness for the clear, briney chowder particular to New England's smallest state. So his invitation had been appealing, as he'd known it would be.

Maybe that was it. Maybe it was the package nature of his invitation that had set me off; his confident assumption that I'd accept his itinerary and that I'd have no other plans of my own. I'd spent too long in my last relationship out of habit and hope, going along with whatever my ex-boyfriend suggested in the vain belief that such passive acquiescence would lead to more of what I wanted, like fidelity or commitment. It didn't, and I didn't want to make the same mistake twice. Sure, Bill was willing to see only me, but I didn't know what else was lurking around the corner. This time, I was going to be conscious of my choices and not just slump into the habit of monogamy. What I would do, I would do with my eyes open. Which meant that on a perfect October Sunday, I found myself standing on the corner, staring at the mailbox, bored to tears and desperate for the sound of another human voice.

While that was not reason enough to seek out a man, it was a damned fine incentive to reach out to a friend. After depositing my scant envelopes—each check going down the slot making me wince a bit—I turned up the corner and made my way to the Helmhold House, properly the Lillian Helmhold Home for Wayward Felines, a small cat shelter that since last spring had been staffed by my buddy Violet. Whether it was the half dozen blocks of fresh air or the prospect of companionship, I felt like a new woman as I followed the slate path around back, to the glassed-in porch where three large tabbies lay sunning themselves.

"Yo, Violet! Are you in?" I rapped on the door and opened it, careful to block one of the feline inhabitants who sought to sneak out to the yard. "It's me!"

She recognized my voice. "Hey, me!" I heard her call from the cavernous interior of the ornate, three-level Victorian. "I'm up here." Since Violet had taken over as resident caretaker, the decaying grande dame had shaped up, with new paint outlining its shutters and detailwork outside while inside the former occupant's mountains of old newspapers and magazines had been carted away, making room for cat beds and some decent second-hand furniture. Violet's girlfriend, a buff caramel-skinned carpenter named Caroline, had even added a bunch of carpeted perches up near the high ceilings, where the current crop of cats could retreat to observe the world below.

I climbed the front staircase with its curving banister and found my friend seated at a heavy oak desk in her living quarters. With a huge book open in front of her and the sunlight streaming in to illuminate the pages, she looked almost right for the period of the house. Except, that is, for the bright namesake color of her hair and the spotted cat draped around her shoulders, suckling on the ear that didn't have multiple piercings.

"What's up? Ow, Sibley!" My friend unwrapped the cow-spotted cat and lowered him to the floor, disturbing the dust that had captured the light. Her face turned up to me looked tired and pale against her habitual black baby-tee, her eyes circled with a darker purple than her short, spiked 'do.

"I wasn't sure you'd be in." I sank into an enormous velvet armchair and watched more dust and cat hair float into the sunbeams. "I was hoping I might be able to drag you out for coffee before you went off to practice." Violet's band, the Violet Haze Experience, with its wild blend of "riot-grrrl" punk and screaming metal guitar, was one of my favorites on the circuit and not just for the sake of friendship. I looked at her unusually sallow face. "Or a walk by the river."

"No walk and no practice today." She placed her hands flat on the text in front of her. "Midterms."

I knew that this job had made it possible for Violet to go back to school, but right now that didn't look much like a benefit. "You've been studying all weekend?"

"That and taking care of the cats. Someone dropped off three kittens sometime late Friday. Left them in a fancy carrier right by the door. Cute little furballs but definitely sick as all get out."

"Not distemper?" I held my breath. There was a vaccine for adult cats, but in kittens too young for the shot the disease was a death sentence. In a shelter like this, it could spread like wildfire.

"No, upper respiratory infections. Really just bad colds. But they needed intravenous fluids and antibiotics, and I stayed up to keep an eye on them." She rubbed those eyes now and yawned. "Strange, really. They're adorable tykes. Fat and fluffy and almost pure white with maybe a little brown on their paws. The carrier they were left in was one of those pricey ones, too, lined with fake fleece. So someone had money, and the kittens were totally treatable. All someone had to do was take them to a vet. Most of that upper respiratory stuff is stress related, and these looked too clean and well fed to be strays or even shelter kittens."

"Maybe they were someone's vanity pets?" It was all I could think of. "They were cute at first, or they matched the furniture, but once they got sick they just weren't worth the hassle." It was an awful thought, but I'd heard of worse.

"But why drop them here? I mean, we're only known around the neighborhood, and usually the folks who bring cats to us have a story about their landlord or a litter they found. We don't usually get kittens just left on the doorstep, not sick ones. Why not take them to the city shelter? They've got a vet hospital right on the premises."

She was just musing, and I didn't have an answer. Besides, as much as I loved kittens, what I needed today was human companionship.

"Bast knows! So, you're set on studying?" I leaned over to check out the title of the tome in front of her: *Organic Chemistry*. Violet wanted to be a vet, which basically meant following a pre-med curriculum. Today, however, I had no sympathy. "It's gorgeous out. Can't I tempt you into a little R&R?"

She sighed and bit her lip. "Well, I do have some errands that have got to get done. Prep for the Halloween open house and all. What do you say to a drive up to New Hampshire?"

Which is how, twenty minutes later, I found myself retrieving first my old Toyota and then Violet for a shopping expedition to the land of huge malls and no sales tax. As we cruised north, through the crazy quilt of hues that lined the highway, my equally colorful friend seemed to relax.

"Thanks, Theda. I really needed to get out of the house. And we really need the supplies."

"No problem." I resisted honking at a BMW with New York plates that had swerved in front of me. Interstate 93 wasn't a major foliage route—too many people driving too fast to enjoy the technicolor drama of the scenery, the red maples and gold-leafed birches, their white trunks slashed with black. But the six-lane highway was one of the main thoroughfares to and from New Hampshire, and to the many smaller New England byways that let the leaf peepers meander. "Have you been doing this run regularly?"

"Whenever I can," said Violet. "But Caro's working today, and Debbie needs the band van for her florist job." We were losing my favorite college station on the radio, so Violet reached in the back for the bag of CDs and began rummaging around. "When you're buying twenty-five pound sacks of food and litter, you'd be surprised at the difference no sales tax makes. And if I have it delivered, that eats into the savings. So…"

"Live free or die," I quoted the New Hampshire motto. "Tax free, that is."

"Amen," she replied, pushing in a disc. A moment later a nasal voice sailed out of the speakers, accompanied by the scratching of a fiddle that played more notes blue than straight.

"Canray Fontenot?" I arched an eyebrow at my companion, who grinned a great broad grin back at me.

"Yeah, ever since you turned me on to this Cajun stuff, I've craved it." Violet put her black high-tops up on the dashboard. When you're under five-four, you can do that, even in a Toyota. "It's rad."

"That's a word for it." I loved the old Creole tunes as much as rock 'n' roll. Maybe there was a connection, if Violet felt it too. Something in the raw delivery, in the willingness to stretch tonality to serve emotion.

"Hey, are you going to see Tess tonight? She's doing the solo acoustic thing at Amphibian." Our friend Tess, a superb song-writer in her own right, had established herself as a studio bassist in New York. But she'd come back to Boston a few months ago, citing a desire to work on her own tunes exclusively.

"You kidding? This is my outing for the day." She turned to look out at a stand of maples, their brilliant red a shocking background to her own purple hair. "That chemistry exam is at ten tomorrow." She turned back at me and grimaced. I regretted reminding her of it.

"What do you think of Tess moving back?" I wanted to distract Violet, but the question intrigued me, too. "I mean, she was making a living on her music and now she's got a day job." Tess' university gig, number crunching in a bio lab, paid well and was easy lifting for a woman of her computer expertise, I knew. But it still seemed an unusual choice.

"I don't know." Violet sounded more thoughtful than usual. "I mean, I'd give anything to be able to live on my music. If I could do that, and also take care of the cats, I'd consider myself a success. But, you know, part of why I went back to school is 'cause I don't think I ever will make it. Make enough, that is. I mean, will I end up being a vet who rocks out nights and weekends? Will that be enough?"

"That's a tough one, Vi." Traffic thickened, and we sped on in silence. The trees grew more bare as the border approached, and a high sad voice sang to us in French about hard times and the will to carry on.

◇◇◇

We were on a second disc, a somewhat jollier compilation of bouncy zydeco tunes, when we crossed into New Hampshire. We didn't need the sign—the one declaring "The Granite State Welcomes You"—to announce our impending arrival. All we'd had to do was watch for the malls, huge sprawling complexes that replaced the colorful country within yards of the state line. They weren't hard to miss, extending, with one megacomplex running into another, nearly the length of the border.

"Pull in up here." Violet motioned and I took my place in one of three turn lanes behind another car with Massachusetts plates. A green arrow motioned us into a spacious, well-marked parking lot, the entire complex designed to make going into one of the bright, factory-sized chain stores as pleasant as possible. "Pet Sets, there it is." She pointed to a building the size of an airplane hanger, with a cartoon puppy and kitten outlined on a red-and-yellow sign the size of a movie screen.

"Is this the latest manifestation of the military industrial complex?" I asked, sliding into a space.

"They may be the devil, but they're cheap," Violet responded, striding to the lined-up shopping carts that all carried the same cutesy logo.

We each pulled a cart free and, once inside, I could see why we'd come. No way our local independent pet supply place could compete with these prices. Stacked high on industrial metal shelving were sacks and cartons of every brand of feed, litter, and animal necessity I could imagine. The high impulse area, right up front, was glowing from its arrangement of bright chew toys and catnip mice. I found myself lingering by the greeting cards. "Sorry you're feeling Purrr-ly," read one, with a sweet-faced calico wearing an unlikely computer-generated frown.

"Theda!" Violet's voice roused me from my commercial daze. Following her around the store, I realized how well suited she was to the directorship of the little shelter. Going straight for the basics, and maneuvering around the few other midday shoppers, she soon had both our carts full up with unscented litter and the healthiest of the dry foods. When I reached for a catnip mouse, she raised an eyebrow.

"It's for Musetta," I said, and she relented, grabbing a bulk pack of sixteen smaller mice and throwing them on top of her load.

"These will be fun for the open house." Violet was doing her best to turn Halloween, which could be a dangerous holiday for cats, into something feline friendly. "Give the kids a chance to interact with the inmates." I noticed her eying a cat tree, with platforms at two, four, and six feet high.

"I don't think we can fit any more in the car." She fingered the carpeted platforms. The plush was soft and green on the level areas, rougher and brown on the verticals to mimic a tree. "Besides, isn't that something Caroline could make up for you?"

"Yeah, you're right." With a sigh, Violet turned her cart away and we headed up to the checkout. "Rapture of the cheap."

We rounded the aisle and pushed our carts toward the line of waiting registers just in time to walk into a cat fight.

"We most certainly do not! I can't imagine where you heard that." A well made-up brunette, her shoulder-length sable hair sleek and gleaming, was towering over a pudgy blonde matron in a baby blue track suit. Hands on hips, the black-haired woman glowered down at her, her lined lips pursed in a scowl over the pale blue, blond, and pink dumpling. Were it not for her red Pet Sets jacket, the taller woman would have seemed to be the customer, tongue lashing an errant clerk. "What do you think we are?"

She was not expecting an answer, but the dumpling had some spunk. "But this is a pet store. That means you sell pets." An unhealthy-looking blush began creeping up from her blue-and-white ribbed neckline. "I'd always heard that you had everything here. At good prices, too." Her eyes bulged as the Pet Set manager leaned in for the kill.

"We do have adoption days," burst in one of the checkout girls, a chubby teen, earning a glare from her boss. "First Saturday of every month the local shelter brings its cats; third Saturdays they bring dogs. That's how I got my Bootsie." Oblivious to her boss' displeasure, her round face lit up as she pointed to a photo of a reclining marmalade cat with white feet that she had taped onto the register in front of her. "She's the best cat ever."

"No, my granddaughter wants one of those special cats." The blue-suited customer seemed to be recovering. At least, she no longer looked on the edge of a coronary. "What do you call them? Maine coons?"

"You should talk to a reputable breeder," Violet answered before the manager, whose nametag said Denise, could start in again. "If you're really sure you want a pedigree cat, that is. There are a lot of great cats out there in shelters, including many that look and act like some of the showy breeds." Violet had a true punk attitude toward pedigree pets in general. DIY—do it yourself—was always better than storebought to her.

"Oh, I did that. I called some of those cat magazine ads," said the older woman, her round cheeks returning to something like a natural color. "Did you know they wanted more than five hundred dollars? And both the breeders I called wanted to know if I was going to let the cat out, if I was going to have it fixed. What I was going to feed it. All sorts of questions, they had. It was like *they* were auditioning *me*. And all for a kitten!"

"They should," started Violet, but the woman wasn't having any of it.

"It's just a cat, for Christ's sake." With a stomp of her powder-blue sneaker, she turned and stalked off past the line of registers to the exit.

"People like that shouldn't be allowed to have pets," said Violet, grabbing one of the heavy food sacks and hefting it onto the counter. I hoisted the next one as the checkout girl began ringing up the sale.

"Maybe having a pet would make her nicer," the girl said shyly, pausing to push muddy brown bangs from her eyes. "Besides, we get all types here. And, well, she didn't want the kitten for herself. Maybe her granddaughter would be good with it? A lot of people have been coming in lately, asking for the special breeds."

"Sandy, let's finish the checkout, please. Don't forget to enter the bulk discount." Denise, the tall beauty, hovered over the mousy girl like a hawk. "I'm sorry, ladies." She was addressing me and Violet, who raised an eyebrow as she grabbed another bag from the cart.

"Some people don't realize that pet *supply* stores don't *sell* pets," the manager continued. "It's considered unethical and some say it may soon be illegal, without background checks or proof of breeding or health care. I just don't want my store associated with any such practices, no matter how misguided the thought."

That pretty much closed the topic, and Bootsie's young care-taker rang up the rest of our order in silence, helping us load the big bags back into our carts when she was done.

"That was something, huh? I thought the manager was going to lose it." I wanted Violet's take on it.

"Yeah, but she's got a point," said Violet. "She's got her store's reputation to think about. If you're looking for a particular breed and you don't buy from a reputable breeder, odds are you're buying from a kitten mill, and those are pretty horrible. They keep cats in tiny cages and breed them as often as they can. The ASPCA did an exposé on one that they were able to close down, and the photos were disgusting. It looked like the cages hadn't ever been cleaned and the animals they rescued were just in miserable shape. Eye infections, bad teeth, fleas, and worse. A couple of the cats were starving, too, the older ones. The owners don't care. They just keep breeding those cats until they stop producing, then they kill them. It's like the worst type of farming, only the government has a hard time cracking down on it. Kitten mills are cheap to run, once you've got a few good cats, and because they don't spend anything on upkeep, they're like pure profit. Half the time the authorities shut one down they just start up again someplace else."

We'd arrived at my car, and I opened the trunk. "I figure it's got to be a sore spot for a 'pet store' manager. I mean, look at this." Violet was standing on the other side of the cart, pointing out a handmade poster taped to a light post. "Maine Coon and Ragdoll Kittens. Bargain Prices! Call Now!" The phone number had the local area code, but before I could read any more, Violet tore the flier off the post, crumpled it, and threw it to the ground. Feeling a little more scrupulous about littering, of the paper sort, I tossed the ripped flier into the trunk, and we finished loading the bags of litter and food in silence.

Chapter Three

The call jolted me from a deep sleep the next morning, although I should have been up and out already. I'd gotten in at a reasonable hour, but somehow, with Bill away and the change of seasons, I'd found myself tossing and turning until near dawn.

"Huh?" I said, grabbing the receiver. My discipline had declined with my fortunes, and I hadn't been up early to run in a week. The clock on my night table said ten.

"Theda Krakow? This is Lannie Kurtz. From *City Magazine?*" I agreed and sat up.

"You sent me a package?" I took a surreptitious sip of water from my bedside glass and quietly tried to clear my throat. As much as I ridiculed the badly named *City*—the mag's ad-heavy pages catered to suburbanites—if they were looking at my clippings this could mean money. I didn't want to sound like I'd just woken up, even if I had. "Some of your features for the *Mail?*"

"Yes, I did." Boy, did I sound perky.

"Well, we have something here that could be just perfect for you. An assignment?" That was my hope, too.

"I have some time in my schedule now." I started searching around on my night table for a pen or pencil and some paper. "What did you have in mind?"

"Well, do you remember our 'Women of the Millennium' feature? It ran in January 2000? We were thinking it would be fun to do an update on some of these ladies. You know, see what they're up to? What would you think of that?"

I didn't really want to tell her. "Women of the Anything" stories always get me riled up, suggestive as they are of cuteness and the ghettoization of professionals who happen to be female. More than one editor had told me I was oversensitive. But really, when was the last time you saw a "Men in the Kitchen" feature about male restaurant chefs, or "Boys in White" about one gender of doctors? I didn't care if we were still the minority in many fields, the treatment was degrading.

"Who are the women you're considering?" Then, swallowing my pride, "And what are the specs?"

"Well, we have quite a few gals to choose from. You and I could select four or five together. We were thinking three thousand words? This will be a big spread, with photos. But we're going to need it soon, by month's end?" That was two weeks away. I sighed and immediately wished I hadn't, hoping she couldn't hear me. Editors know that, barring nuclear disaster, their magazines will keep coming out, every month, with stunning regularity. Why can't they plan a little better? This wasn't breaking news. But still…

"And the fee?"

"Well, since we're pushing you a little on the deadline, I argued that we could start you at our higher rate. That would be fifty cents a word, so fifteen hundred dollars?"

Her math was on, but I knew she was lying. Although I wasn't one of them, I'd been around long enough to have heard that for *City*'s regular writers and the occasional big-name author who deigned to pen an essay, the monthly regularly shelled out a dollar a word and sometimes more. But as I opened my mouth to argue, old saws about gift horses and choosy beggars stopped me.

"That's great," I said instead, trying to muster some life into my voice. "Now let's chat about the women."

Twenty minutes later, I had an assignment I could live with. From the ten millennial names, we'd chosen four to profile; the other six would get a photo and blurb, probably to be written by some poor intern for free. Of my lucky four, one was Monica Borgia, a Web whiz who had launched an e-business

in '99, gone bankrupt in '03, and last anyone knew was starting over from scratch. The second, Lynn Ngaio, had a design
studio doing high-end fashion. Word was, she was still around
and still selling, her distinctive script-signature label showing
up on velvets and lace in Newbury Street's swankier boutiques.
Rose Keller, the third subject, was someone I'd pushed for, when
I heard her name on the list. Rose was an acquaintance, a sweet
older woman who bred and raised show cats, Turkish Angoras,
and had recently qualified to be a cat-show judge. I'd had her
in my cat-show pitch for Tim, but that wasn't going to happen
now. Because I knew her, I toyed with declining to write about
her—conflict of interest and all that. But this was *City*; they ran big
splashy stories on major advertisers! Besides, I figured the profile
might as well be written by someone with some knowledge of the
field, and, yeah, I did want to write about cats. That left just one
profile subject, someone in the performing arts for balance. Our
mutual choice was not only a natural, but sheer pleasure for me.
Jan Coolidge—a.k.a. "Cool"—was almost a household name, at
least among households that tuned in to the blues.

Cool had been a fixture in my life all through the '90s, when
she'd played in rock bands in the nighttime hangs all around
Boston and Cambridge. As different as day and night, she
and Tess had been queens of the scene for a while. Cool was
big, brash, always the last one buying, compared to Tess' quiet
elegance. That was when I was first writing about clubland and
before Tess took off for New York City and studio work. It took
a few years more to discover Cool's true talent, her affinity for
the blues, specifically the way her rich, smoky voice could make
even the oldest songs sound fresh. But once she switched styles,
giving up her loud rock for the rootsier music, it all seemed so
natural—that voice, and the timing, just a hair behind the beat,
that added so much nuance. She even looked the part, a "blues
mama" all hip and bust and wild, curly hair. Since then, Cool
had left New England also, although her particular muse took
her out west to LA and a string of Grammy awards. The critics
pegged her as somewhere between Billie Holiday and Bonnie

Raitt, a description that had drawn on Cool's flaming curls—a brighter red than mine—as well as her throaty phrasings. But the comparisons weren't that far off: Cool had a gift, the sound of an earlier age. A timeless voice, and the fans knew it.

Still, her appetites sometimes got her in trouble, and the temptations of fame didn't help. Everyone here had read of her bouts in rehab, seen the coverage of the no-show concerts and recording sessions. But word was that she'd pulled through. She was clean. No more booze, no more diet pills. Besides, we'd also all heard that at heart she was still the same-old earthy Cool, someone you could count on for a deep belly laugh or a raunchy joke, if not for closing the bar any more. So her troubles merely lent some street credence to the hard-luck lyrics she sang. I'd been told that she was back in town, and Lannie confirmed it. Seeing Cool again would be a joy.

In fact, if I could get over my attitude about the magazine, this was going to be fun. Good money, too, despite my griping. The only drawback was the photographer Lannie assigned me. Because of the tight deadline—and the necessity for big pictures in a feature of this type—I was supposed to coordinate with Sunny Letourneau. Sunny had been the photographer for the original feature story, the quizzical Lannie had told me. And though I doubted she'd be the "font of information" the *City* editor had promised, I couldn't find a good reason to object. I could hardly explain it was because she was annoying. But she was—all talk all the time, with an anxious edge that got on my nerves. Worse, she could get embarrassing, particularly in professional situations. Too often, I'd seen her on assignment and instead of simply shooting, she'd take up everyone's time making desperate pitches of half-baked ideas. Or she'd start cadging drinks, making lame jokes about how taking photos was thirsty work. I tried to be charitable. Maybe she just didn't know how to conduct herself, when it was cool to push your own projects or play, and when to just do the job. Maybe, she was, just like me, flat broke. But I didn't like her, and I sure didn't want to be paired—or compared—with her.

◇◇◇

I'd run into Sunny the night before, when I'd gone to hear Tess play. Violet stuck with her resolve to study, but there was no reason for me to stay home and ten o'clock found me in the tiny, downtown room called Amphibian. Situated underneath a boisterous bar and grill, the self-consciously Irish Stone of Killeen, Amphibian drew a somewhat less inebriated crowd. Basically a refurbished basement, it had one room and a couple of dozen rickety chairs. A threadbare rug defined the "performance" area, a space just big enough for readings and music of the quieter sort. There, in front of the day-glo salamander painted on the black back wall, Tess had tried out some new material and a new instrument, a 12-string guitar that rested easily on her knee.

The setting had to be a lot lower profile than what she'd been used to in her New York City days, but she'd pulled her glossy black mane into a simple ponytail and I could see her smiling as her long fingers danced on the strings. The music—part of a song cycle, she said—was far from finished. But what she had created with her clear alto and the acoustic guitar was a lyrical and darkly pretty whole, a folk-style musical full of sadness and loss. There were echoes of reggae rhythms in her strumming, but everything was simple somehow, as if she'd pared each chord down to its essentials. Her forty minutes passed like five, and when it was time to vacate—a young poet was already waiting, pages in hand, for her turn at the carpet's edge—the small crowd was hushed, listening so intently there was a pause before the applause. Bowing her head graciously, Tess ducked off the little stage and sat by me. A waitress brought her a beer and, while the next act recited abstract verses that seemed to deal with love, we'd caught up. Or tried to, until Sunny came by.

"So, this type of gig"—I motioned around the small subterranean space—"is okay by you?" In New York, Tess had been a big deal, earning serious money putting down bass lines for many of the best bands that came to the city to record. If she'd wanted to step out in front of a band, she might have been famous, too, maybe as successful as Cool. She obviously still had connections: It was Tess who'd told me that Cool was back in town, living in a suite at the Ritz, and I couldn't help making the comparison.

"Yeah, I like it." Tess took a long draft, managing to look elegant even as she wiped the foam from her mouth. She shrugged. "I mean, sure, it takes some getting used to. I keep waiting for the sound engineer to yell 'cut.' And for the checks to come in." We both laughed. "But that's why it's good to have the day job, you know? I don't need to fill the room, and I can play what I want to—and only what I want to."

"I can see why you're into it, I guess." I tried to imagine the tedium of studio work, with its endless repetitions until someone hidden in a booth said you'd gotten it right. The money alone might have kept me going, but there was no point saying that now. "At any rate, your new stuff is really great. Mournful somehow. I don't know, a couple of pieces sounded like they were real folk songs—hundreds of years old or something. Like they're part of life already."

"Thanks," she said, rolling the bottle between her slim hands. "But you know, those tunes aren't new, most of them. I've been working on them for years. I just never got a chance to play this stuff with anyone in New York. It didn't 'rock' enough for them."

I wanted to ask her about the New York days and the wisdom of moving back. Wasn't the studio work at least a better day job than what she was doing now? But just then Sunny appeared, wearing the multi-pocketed vest that identified her as a photographer and guaranteed her free admission. Without asking, she flopped into a chair and pulled it up to our table.

"Theda! Tess! Well, isn't this arts central." We greeted her in return and Tess, more polite than I—and taller—signaled to the waitress to come back over.

"Hi, Sunny! What's your pleasure?"

"Sam Adams," said Sunny, turning her red face back to us. I thought she usually stuck with the cheaper Bud on tap, but never mind. "Now, Tess, you've got something there."

"That's just what I was telling her." I'd always found Sunny a little overeager, but hearing her praise my friend softened me up.

"You're going to do an album, right?" Tess started to open her mouth, but Sunny didn't pause. I could almost see the connections clicking in Sunny's head. She knew who Tess had worked with, too. "I'd love to do the cover. Love to. I could do some new publicity shots for you, too. Make you look like the new Michelle Shocked or Gillian Welch or something. Will you call me?"

Tess smiled and nodded, but Sunny had already turned her pixie-ish face toward me. "You still writing for the *Mail*, Theda? I haven't seen your byline recently."

"Well, I don't know really." What I didn't know was how much I wanted to get into with Sunny. "I've had sort of a falling out with my editor there." The poet was reading again by then, but Sunny wasn't listening to either of us.

"Who is your editor, Tim Smathers? I know him. I mean, I've met him. Do you think I could use your name with him?" Wouldn't do me any harm, I figured, so I just nodded and smiled and turned away from the table to focus on the stage. Sunny stayed a few minutes longer, sipping the beer Tess had paid for, and then moved on. When the poet finished her bit, Tess said goodnight, too.

"I'm a member of the working class, my girl." She stooped to hug me and I kissed her warm cheek. "I've got to get up in the morning."

"Well, it was great to see you. And great to hear what you've been working on all this time as well."

"Thanks, doll." She beamed as if I'd handed her a million bucks, and I sat back to mull over the meaning of success.

◇◇◇

That was the topic on my mind the next morning, once I'd rung off with Lannie. If I was going to pursue it, I had to get to work. Pulling on some sweats and grabbing a proper pad, I figured I'd make some phone calls and then go for a belated run. With assignments like these, getting in touch with the subjects was three-quarters of the job. If I could come up with a few good general questions, something that touched on the struggle, making it, and what that meant, the piece would write itself.

Lannie had given me numbers for Monica, the web whiz, and for the designer's South End studio and I left messages at both, explaining the assignment and asking them to call me back as soon as was convenient. Cool was easier. I called the Ritz and asked for Ronnie, her personal manager. I figured a classy hotel might deny that a celebrity of her stature was staying there. But Ronnie was a civilian rather than a household name and, sure enough, they put me through.

"Hey darling, how're you doing?" Twenty years in New York, New England, and California hadn't robbed Ronnie of his Southern twang or that Carolina languor. I suspected he maintained both for their professional advantage. Despite his apparently lazy ways, Ronnie could be a tough negotiator.

"Fine, Ronnie. And by you?" We shot the breeze for a few minutes, but through the charm I could hear an unusual impatience.

"I'm calling for *City Magazine*," I explained, figuring it was time to get to the point. "They want to include Cool in a round-up story, a follow-up to that 'Women of the Millennium' feature she was in a few years ago."

"And they called you in to do it? *They* asked *you?*" I didn't think Ronnie meant that question as a slight, but it caused me to sit up. Did he think I'd pitched the story claiming special access? That I'd been trying to capitalize on our old acquaintance?

"Yeah, Ronnie, they did." I heard the edge creeping into my voice. "They called me this morning to see if I could write the whole feature. Profile four different women actually." Cool was special, but c'mon…

"So it's nothing about her in particular, right?"

"What do you mean, Ronnie?" This was mystifying. "I mean, she's still a big deal here in her old hometown. And she was one of the original subjects. Is there going to be a problem?"

"I'm sorry, darling." He relented. "Didn't mean to sound so sharp. We've had some, well…the move has been hard on everybody."

I waited, silent. Ronnie had pretty much used up the friend factor, and he hadn't answered my question.

"I'll talk to Cool and get back to you just as soon as I can," he said, finally. A heaviness had crept into his voice, almost replacing the charming drawl. "That's the best I can do."

"Fine," I replied, although he hadn't asked for my consent. I gave him my number, since it didn't sound like Cool would have it anymore, and hung up.

The whole interaction left such a taste in my mouth that I was tempted to leave off work for the rest of the morning. Go running. Greet the day. I unlocked my back window, lifting it open for what I hoped wasn't the last time of the season. Musetta jumped up on the sill to enjoy the view over our fire escape, and purred as I stroked her. What a bird watching team we made! But some residual twinge of discipline kicked in and I reached for my address book, looking for the Rose Blossom Cattery and the gentle round woman I'd recently come to know.

After about a dozen rings, I'd given up on a human and was waiting for the machine when I heard the clatter of a receiver being picked up. "Hey, Rose," I called out, thinking she'd just rushed in from cleaning the cages or maybe grooming one of her long-haired beauties. But all I heard was panting, a desperate panicked sound that had made me fear she was ill. I called out to her: "Rose? Are you all right?"

"Theda? Theda Krakow?" Rose nearly barked, her voice tighter and loud with something—anger, fear—that I couldn't place. "Theodosia Krakow?" Not many people knew my full name, the same as the silent film vamp—incidentally, another nice Jewish girl—but Rose had a memory like a Rolodex, which was a great asset in the breeding and show game. "How do I know that's really you?"

"Because you recognized my voice, Rosie." I hoped using her pet name might calm her down. "Because Musetta will vouch for me, if you want."

I heard her sigh.

"Rosie, it is me. It is Theda." I prompted again, wondering if I should call a doctor. Or really put my cat on the line.

"Oh god, thank god. Oh, I'm sorry." Another big sigh. This wasn't like the Rose I'd come to know. I'd met her over the summer, when the older woman had been the voice of sanity at one of the region's biggest and most frenzied cat shows. Since then, she'd taught me something about the competitive circuit, a crazy world that she regarded with gentle affection and humor. She wasn't chuckling now.

"What is it, Rose. What's happening?" I realized I was standing, holding the phone in a clenched hand. I made myself sit.

"I'm just so glad it's you, dear. I've been so scared."

"Scared?"

"The catnappers, Theda. The cattery thieves. They've called me." I could hear the panic creeping back into her voice, the tone rising as if she was forgetting to breathe. "I'm going to be next and there's nothing I can do. Unless I pay them, that is. They're going to call me back and tell me how to pay them. They want twenty thousand dollars. Twenty thousand! And if I call the cops, if I tell them anything, they won't just rob me." Her voice dropped down to a whisper. "They're going to kill my cats!"

Chapter Four

"I'm coming over." Rose lived right up Massachusetts Avenue, in Watertown. I could be there in fifteen minutes.

"No you're not. You can't!" Her voice was rising again into hysteria. "They said if I called anyone they'd know! They'd know!"

"But you didn't call me. I called you." I waited a moment for the logic to sink in. "I called you for an entirely different reason. I want to interview you for a story. Really, I do. And now I just want to come over to do a little pre-interview chat with my friend. Perfectly innocent." I could tell from the labored breathing I heard over the line that it wasn't working. "Rose? Rosie? Remember, it's just me. I don't look like a cop. Do I? And wouldn't it be good to talk this over?"

"You're right, Theda. But you can't rush over, not right away. They just called, you see? It would look suspicious. Give me an hour. No, two. And then be casual about it, won't you darling?"

"I'll do my best." I looked at the clock; it wasn't even noon. "So I'll come by at around one?"

I heard her sigh again. I knew I was pressing her, but couldn't see how facing this alone would be any better. And she needed a friend—a lot about this just didn't make any sense. "Rosie?"

"Make it two." I heard her voice fall, as if bowing to the inevitable. "And, Theda? Thanks."

There was no way I could go back to work after that, so I steeled myself for that belated run. Lacing up my sneakers, I reached for a Clash compilation disc I'd burned for Bill, weeks before. Somehow he kept leaving it at my place, but for once I was grateful. The great British punk pioneers—the "only band that mattered"—had gotten me through a lot of hard times in high school. Their raw energy, politics propelled by guitar-laced passion, was just what I needed to clear my head now.

Stretching out in silence on the stairs inside my apartment, I pressed the play button as I pushed open the door. Crash! The cymbals kicked in as I hit the pavement, crossing ahead of a black Honda. Despite the slight reggae lilt in the rhythm, the underlying beat was a straight four-four, the sound of dancing or fighting in the streets. I thought of that fighting spirit as the furious bass line got me up to speed, and I was already turning the corner as Joe Strummer's strangled vocals cried out to me, distracting me from Rose's call, from Ronnie's strange reticence, from my own financial mess, from Bill. Forty minutes later, when I walked the last two blocks home to cool off, I felt like I'd sweated out the cobwebs. Or most of them: Was that the same car, driving around the corner, and had it been behind me as I'd loped down Mass. Ave? Stretching a bit longer than usual, I lied to myself, saying I wanted to hear the denouement of one more song. Must have been a student, I figured. Or a lost parent looking for the college. Rose's paranoia was contagious, but what was the point of running if not to work out all those negative feelings? I took one more turn around the block at a slow jog and felt my equilibrium returning. The exercise had left me invigorated, ready to take on what I could. Rose was going to get my help, whether she wanted it or not.

◇◇◇

The phone was ringing when I let myself back in, but as I bolted toward the phone a small black linebacker threw herself at my ankles. A quick leap saved me from punting my pet and left me panting. Watching her bounce down the hall, I tried to regain my equilibrium and decided the machine could pick up the call.

"Theda? Are you there?" It was Cool, her deep voice bubbling up from under, and there were other voices, talking behind her. She wasn't alone. "She's not there," I heard her say, to be answered by a murmur in the background.

"Wait!" I lunged for the phone again. Musetta, at the hallway's end, just watched. "I've got it. I'm just back. Cool, are you still there?" All was silent. I thought I'd missed her and grimaced. Musetta began to wash one already spotless foot.

"Yeah, yeah, Theda. I'm here." I tried to regulate my breathing as I pulled up a chair. Panting is unattractive in humans. "Returning your call. Ronnie said you called 'cause you sold a story on me or something?"

No wonder the reception had been frosty. Years of fame had taught her to steer clear of so-called friends who wanted to piggyback on her renown. "Sort of." I figured truth was the best route. "Only, I didn't pitch it. That magazine *City* wants me to profile you as a follow-up to the one they did on you back in 2000. The one they called 'chicks of the century,' or something like that? And here you are, still a big star." I forced a chuckle as my breath returned. Cool didn't join in. "But I would've been calling anyway. I just found out that you were back in town!"

"Yeah, well, I've been laying low this time out. Real low." Cool's voice always had a lazy feel, but this time she slurred the words together into a fatigued growl.

"Cool, are you okay?"

"Of course. Why are you asking?" The edge was back in her voice with a snap, and I wondered if I'd imagined that tired drawl. "What are you getting at?"

"Nothing, nothing." I felt like I couldn't say anything right to my old buddy. Had LA changed Cool that much? Was it just my mood: the hangover from the weekend, or my earlier conversation with Rose? "I'm sorry, I thought you sounded tired, or something."

"Tired, huh? Well, I've got a lot on my mind these days."

"Anything you want to talk about?" She snorted. I tried to rewind. "So how long have you been back? What are you up to?"

"You don't know?" There was silence for a moment. "No, I guess you don't. A couple of weeks. Two, I guess. And, well,

I don't really know what I'm up to. Trying to take it easy, you
know?"

"Yeah." I guess I hadn't imagined the stress in her voice. I hated
to ask what came next. "So, could we get together? I mean, I really
would like to interview you for this article. But if you don't want
to, that's okay, too. I'll make some excuse to the editor. I'd just
like to see you."

"No, no, it'll be fine." She exhaled with a force that implied
the opposite, but then continued. "Look, why don't you come by,
I don't know, Thursday? How does Thursday lunch sound?"

At any other time, it would've sounded fine. Right now, I was
hoping she'd make it till then. I reached for a pad.

"Great. How about one?"

"It's good. Oh, and Theda?"

"Yeah?"

"Ask for Ronnie. Nobody's supposed to know I'm in town.
Fat lot of good that's done."

She rang off before I could follow up on that particular bit of
crypticism, and I realized that my wet shirt had dried onto my
skin. Musetta would not approve. Time for a shower and visit
to Rose. At least her problems had a clear-cut cause.

◇◇◇

I was crossing the quiet tree-lined street to Rose's house when I
saw her. Peeking out from behind a holly bush, her unnaturally
auburn bob could have been an unusually large berry against
the dark spiney leaves. She was gesturing, frantic. "Theda!" Her
stage whisper reached me at the sidewalk. "Theda! This way!"
She motioned me over to the side of the low-slung white ranch
house, her eyes darting over my shoulder to the vacant lane I'd
just crossed. "Did anyone follow you?" I thought again of that
car, the black Honda from earlier. Only one of the most common
cars on the road. Her fear must be getting to me. I shook my
head. "Come in, then. Come in." She took my arm and walked
me toward the back door. "I didn't want anyone to see you."

"But shouldn't we be acting as if this is just a normal visit?" I leaned over her to be better heard. "And why are we whispering, anyway?"

"I told you! They're watching me."

And they wouldn't see us sneaking around the house in broad daylight? It seemed a question better left unanswered, and instead I followed my friend in through the back.

"New wig?" After a bout with breast cancer several years ago, before we'd met, her hair had changed. It grew back, Rose had told me, but was "never right." Now she kept an everchanging roster of hairpieces busy, almost as if they were additional pets. I was trying not to stare at the purplish red of today's pick.

"It's Malaysian. Do you like it?" Her voice returned to normal as she double bolted the door behind us, and I was thankful that any need for me to respond was cut off by the loud, insistent mews of four adolescent cats who came barreling into the room.

"Pussums! Pussums! Calm down." Slim, silky kitties weaved figure-eights around our legs, making forward progress difficult. "Pussums!"

Many breeders advertise that they raise their cats "underfoot." The theory is that if the cats are constantly around people they become used to us, our noises and our movements. That not only makes them better suited to the lights and attention of the show ring, it gives the non-show quality animals better chances at good homes. Well socialized cats make better pets and, in all fairness, most breeders do try to spend a lot of time with all their charges, even taking them out on errands so they can become accustomed to fuss and sounds. In Rose's case, however, the term was literal and the people in her house found themselves accommodating the cats. As we shuffled with our escorts into the front room that served as her main sitting room and cat den, we were besieged by several more of the petite, long-haired Angoras.

"Pussums! Here." That one was directed toward me, as Rose scooped up a delicate white cat with one hand and pushed her into my arms. The plume of a tail brushed my face. "Let's go sit down." A rumbling silver tabby twining around her ankles, she directed me to one of two cat-friendly overstuffed sofas that faced a wall of cages, where those animals in isolation could still keep some company.

"How are we doing here?" I settled into the soft, floral chintz, so slick it's almost a claw-resistant fabric, the white cat already starting to knead my lap. Rose made the rounds. Two females slept in the cages, one very pregnant, and Rose reached in to stroke her fine arrow-shaped head. "Sixty days, just a week more to go," she told me, reaching around the supine puss to check her litter box and water dish. For Rose, the felines came first, but I was a little surprised when she settled onto the other, somewhat tattered sofa and asked, "Now, where were we?"

"Well, we were hiding out because somebody was watching your house and had threatened you."

"Oh, my. Yes." She looked down and the silver tabby jumped into her lap. I could hear him purring as he started to knead; she was silent. I let her be. This had got to be difficult to talk about. Rose was only about twenty years or so older than me, but she had the makings of a timid old lady in her already. And a phone call like that was scary. Threatening on the most basic level. I watched her breathe and pet the cat until his eyes closed in bliss. Stroking the milky beauty on my own lap, I waited for my friend to gather her reserves.

"You know, dear, I think I overreacted."

I must have jerked upright in my shock, because the white Angora hopped to the floor.

"Wait a minute, Rose." The change in her behavior didn't make sense. "Could we back up a bit, here?"

"Well, you know, Halloween is in less than two weeks. I have cats, and, well, I'm thinking that it wasn't anything. Some of the neighborhood kids doing a prank call." She was looking down at the cat she was petting. I wanted to see her eyes.

"Rose? Are you serious? That call sounded pretty scary to me." I had no way of knowing if it was real or not. And, well, single ladies with cats were subject to a higher degree of neighborhood pranks than other homeowners were. But still.

"If you really think it was a prank, why all the secrecy about me coming over? Why were you hiding in the bushes?"

"Oh, I'll admit it got to me." She looked up now, her dark eyes wrinkling into a smile. "How silly of me." She waved the fear away. "But waiting for you out there behind the holly, I began thinking. This is so much fuss. Why would they come after me of all people? I don't have a lot of money. I'm what you'd call pretty small potatoes in the show biz. Though I do love my pussums, yes I do!" She held the supine silver tabby up to her face and kissed its sleek forehead. The cat, clearly used to such treatment and unfazed by her wig, hung bonelessly until she put him down, at which point he readjusted his position in her ample lap and started washing his face. "And I decided, it's got to be a prank. It's just too silly, and I'm sorry I ever brought it up. So you're not to worry about it anymore, because you'll just embarrass me. Now tell me, dear, about this article of yours. What do you want me to say?"

"But, Rose, even making a call like that is a bad thing, maybe even a crime. I'd be happy to look into it." I wasn't sure how, but it seemed wrong to let it drop.

"Nonsense, dear." The hand stroking the silver tabby looked as calm as the cat, and her smile seemed real. "Now let's talk about your article."

"You're sure?"

She gave her most definitive judge's nod. "I am."

"Well, if you're positive…." I let the sentence hang between us. But she just smiled and nodded once again.

"Yes, dear. Now tell me about this story."

There wasn't any way to get her back to talking about the threat after that, and who was I to say she was wrong in dismissing it? So I took out my pad and we spent the next hour discussing her new role in the ring, as she taught me what judges are trained to look for and how they score the contestants. Rose was a good teacher. Giving frequent illustrations using the animals at hand, she began to show me the science in what I'd considered a minor sport. The length of a tail, the ratio of a leg to a torso, all became more obvious as she had me lift first one feline and then another. All were lighter than Musetta, but despite their relative lack of substance, I found myself beginning to appreciate their slim elegance and silky coats. More important, I began to recognize the distinctions in fur and body configuration for which these graceful and ancient cats had been bred.

"I'd love to see you in action." I placed one docile subject back on the floor so I could write up what Rose had just shown me. I wasn't lying: while explaining the fine points of feline conformation, the petite older woman seemed to grow. Calmer, more in charge, my round little friend lost that tension that had her balled up tight earlier, making her seem smaller and older. Even her hair seemed more natural, more relaxed as she stepped into the role of Madame Judge.

"Come by this weekend. I'll be judging the premiers around three." She handed me two passes to the Fine 'n' Fancy cat show, which I gathered was happening in a downtown hotel ballroom. Wondering what the regular hotel guests would make of that, I tucked the tickets into my pockets.

"Thanks, I'll try to work some of it into my piece. So, tell me, do you ever get bit?" Despite all I was learning about form and fur that, I figured, would be my editor's first question.

"It happens, but temperament plays a role in the judging, too." Rose was all business again, the lecturer to a willing audience. "Most show cats are handled literally from the day they are born." She reached for another cat to make her point, hefting the young female into the air by her middle. "It makes them docile and used to being picked up. A badly socialized cat is not going to have a successful career in the ring. Nor, may I add, will it make a happy pet. No, when I do get bit, I take a long, hard look at the owner. There's something not right when that happens, and it sure isn't the kitty's fault. Is it, my sweet little Pussums? Not right at all." She held the young cat to her face and I realized, scribbling furiously, that she was no longer talking to me.

Chapter Five

Despite my pad full of notes, I wasn't satisfied when I left Rose's. The way she had dismissed the threat made sense: a prank call certainly seemed more likely than extortion, a demand for "protection money." Her business was small, the profits so marginal I couldn't understand why anyone would target her. What bothered me, however, was her fear and sudden reversal. She'd sounded honestly shaken up at first, and then her conversion back to her regular self had happened so quickly. Something was off, and I couldn't figure out how to get at it.

Even after the interview part of my visit, when we'd reverted once again to friendly chit chat, a strange distance—almost a formality—kept me from asking once more about the strange call and her reaction. Maybe it was simply that I was writing about her; being the subject of a story does tend to make people put on their company manners. Maybe she was embarrassed by her earlier panic. I didn't know how to bring the subject up again, and the differences between us, her age and what seemed sometimes like frailty, as well as the brevity of our friendship made me hesitant to push. She was a tiny woman, alone, and it could be that she needed her dignity more than my support.

Still, I was uneasy and as I pulled into a space right by my building, I made a promise. I'd call Rose in a day or two, and see her at the cat show. If my friend seemed "off" in any way, if she had any second thoughts then—or if she'd gotten any other calls like that first one—I'd call Bill. He worked homicide, but he'd know someone who would be gentle with my skittish friend.

Making a mental note to follow up, I put the thought aside and opened my apartment door to find a blinking "4" on the answering machine. Since losing my cell phone, I'd realized how unneccesary that constant companion had been. And how expensive. So I'd decided not to replace it, and canceled voice mail as well, resurrecting this old machine with great results. When you're single, there's nothing like seeing proof of life in the form of a blinking message light. Now if only all the messages weren't from telemarketers, I'd be in luck.

"Hey, Theda. I've got some good news. Call me!" The distinctive lilt of my old friend Bunny promised that the news would be good, and I smiled. I'd gotten out of the habit of calling Bunny since she and Cal had moved in together. But despite their cocooning, or maybe because of it, they were great pals for a single gal. Weekends in particular were cozy in the small Allston apartment they'd made into their love nest. Bunny tended to cook huge stews and casseroles, and Cal always let us girls choose the movies to rent.

"Theda, this is Rick." The next call, from my ex-boyfriend, made me drop my keys and pull up a chair. I hit Repeat to make sure I'd heard who it was correctly. I had. His voice sounded just as I remembered. Easy, clear, a warm burr roughing up his words. And not at all like he was calling long distance, even though we'd more or less broken up when he'd decided to accept a job in Arizona. He hadn't asked me to come along, and I'd not pushed the matter. And if neither of us had actually called it quits, we'd not made any plans to visit either. With him out of state, the issue had been out of mind as well. "I'm back in town, at least for a while, and I'd love to see you again. I've been thinking and, well…Call me? I'm staying with Phil." He concluded with a number as I lunged for a pen to write it down.

"Hey, sweetie. I'm home!" My heart leapt at the next voice, but then subsided into guilt. Bill. I'd not called him to leave a "welcome back" message like I'd planned. "How's the big city treating you? The wedding was a blast—there's a story about my aunt I've got to tell you—but it wasn't as much fun as it could've been. Anyway, let me know what you're up to."

I sighed. What was wrong with me? Why was I fighting the pull? If I could convince myself that this was just some thirty-something commitment issue, I'd throw myself into the relationship, work through my fears no matter what the cost. But what if my impulse to call him back was just habit? What if all the easy times we had together were just my way of sinking into a slump? I'd wasted two years with Rick, unable to end it even when it had become clear that he wouldn't—or couldn't—meet me halfway. I was thirty-three already, and didn't want to spin my wheels for another couple of years in a situation that wasn't right. Why couldn't I have what Bunny and Cal did, an apparently effortless intimacy? And now that Rick was back in town....

The last message, at least, was simple. "Hey Theda, did I leave the Pet Set receipts in your car?" Violet, sounding distracted as usual. "I can't find them. I called the store a couple of times and left messages, but nobody there seems to know anything."

I should call Bill, I knew. I wanted to see him, too. But the call from Rick—and more importantly, my own reaction to his voice—made me hesitate. I had to be clear in my own mind before I continued down that path, if only out of fairness to him. I could call Bunny. *Should* call her. I hadn't spoken to her in over a week, which was rare for us but not entirely my fault.

A researcher extraordinaire, with the power to pull any compendium of facts out of cyberspace, Bunny worked in the *Mail*'s library. Back when I'd been a staffer on the paper's copy desk, I used to drop by her cubicle almost daily to touch base, always taking a moment to admire the latest photos of her three cats. Even when I'd quit that steady job to freelance, before my run-in with Tim, I was in the newsroom often enough to swing by. It was an easy way to be social, and the proximity had helped our intimacy grow from the casual club friendliness we'd started with over beers and bands.

First there had been the pleasure of discovery, of recognizing a sister denizen of the night world in the daytime at a straight job. Then we'd found we could talk. Really talk. We'd solved the problems of the world over iced coffee on the newspaper's roof deck, and I'd served as a sounding board as my plump friend worked through the knots of her relationship with Cal. We'd moved from the deck to an out-of-office friendship, long cozy nights, when we'd rent a movie, make popcorn, and kill a bottle or two of wine in her old studio on the Fenway.

She'd been a little darker humored then, her Catholic background making her cynical about any kind of establishment. I'd often wondered if that early schooling, back home in Pittsburgh, had also secretly made her crave some structure: the Wiccan circle she'd since joined was certainly more women-centered, and I liked the earth-friendly teachings, but with its meetings, dues, and pot lucks, it was just another synagogue sisterhood to me. Still, since moving in with Cal, my friend had mellowed. She'd let her short-cropped brush cut grow out, more out of laziness than style, she'd said. And her bouncy roundness had gotten more zaftig, making her look more like the housewife her mother had been.

Maybe that's what was holding me back. As comfortable as Bunny was, I also knew that these days she leaned toward domesticity. She was genuinely fond of Bill. More to the point, she liked being part of a couple now that she'd found someone worth the effort, and she'd gotten into making their tiny flat into a home. If I talked to her about my confusion, she'd most likely advise working things through with my earnest beau. She'd certainly roll her eyes if I mentioned that Rick might be back in the picture. I could hear her voice now, as I'd heard it during countless of those wine-buzzed late nights: "He can't help it, Theda. He is what he is. But what he is won't ever be what you want."

I remembered stretching out on her futon sofa, my head spinning, and letting my eyes close, knowing that the city dawn would wake me in time to go home and shower before work. As if unbidden, I heard one of her other great bits of wisdom:

"You get the advice you ask for, Theda." She was right. And I didn't want to be told to write Rick off. Not yet. So I couldn't call Bunny. Didn't want to call Bill, either, not just yet. I knew I was copping out, but especially when thoughts grow confused there's something satisfying about direct action. Leaving the messages on the machine where I could listen again to them later, I went back out to where my Toyota was parked and began to search for Violet's receipts.

Twenty minutes later, I was sneezing like crazy and my Renew Orleans T-shirt was gray with dust. But I'd filled an old bookstore plastic bag from behind the passenger seat with a good portion of the other junk that had made its way into my car: band fliers, shredded fanzines, and a couple of clippings so yellowed I couldn't see the sense in saving them. No receipts had surfaced from the dust and debris, at least not the one Violet was looking for, though I did find two parking lot stubs that I could deduct on my taxes, provided I didn't lose them again.

Moving on to the trunk, I thought about taking my beach chair into the apartment, finally, and decided to leave it for the winter. What the hell, I had room for it here. Then a balled-up piece of paper caught my eye. Too large for a receipt, but I flattened it out anyway and saw that it was the ad for Ragdoll kittens that Violet had torn down outside the pet store. "Bargain Prices!" indeed. I thought about what Violet had said about kitten mills, about cats kept in cages that were never cleaned, so different from Rose's spotless, comfortable breeding dens. I wondered what kind of kittens spent their first weeks in conditions like that.

Should I report this seller? The number was still legible underneath an adorable photo of a round, well-furred cat. Or was this just some pet owner who was trying to start a business? Besides, what were the odds these really were Ragdolls? The breed was one of the newer ones to be recognized, and the real cats—known for their heavy bodies, thick fur, and unflappable manner—were nowhere near as common as, say, Siamese or Persians. More likely the kittens for sale were just fat, floppy mixed breeds that someone was trying to place. After all, most of the cats advertised as

"Maine coons" were just big longhair tabbies, the public having latched onto the breed's name, and its famous easy temperament, as a useful descriptive label. Still, I shoved the flyer into my pocket. I could ask Rose about it next time we talked. She'd know if I should report the sellers. Besides, I attracted paper like a stray did fleas. One more piece wouldn't make much of a difference.

"Violet? I couldn't find the receipt. I'm sorry."

"That's okay. I'll call them again." She'd picked up the phone when I called, but was clearly distracted. Between her job and her classwork, she often was these days, and I found myself missing the old care-free Violet, the strong-willed musician who always made time for a chat.

She'd spent a large amount of money, however, so I tried to sympathize. The Helmhold House was privately funded, and Violet had gotten the shelter nonprofit status. But there were limits to her budget—and lots of cats to help. Didn't the store have copies of all their transactions? Especially an order that ran into the hundreds, I suggested, they should be able to track down. The problem, Violet replied, wasn't in finding the actual records. She never seemed able to reach anybody in charge.

"I've been leaving messages asking for the manager since we unloaded everything yesterday and I saw that the receipt wasn't there." I could hear her pacing. "Another reason why chain stores should be nuked."

I sighed, bit my lip, and then offered. "If you want to drive back up there, Violet, I'd be happy to make the run." I had lunch planned with Cool on Thursday, and two other interviews to set up. But Violet had been there for me before.

"Really?" From the rising tone in her voice, I could hear how desperate she was. "Oh, that would be grand. But wait, let me try to call them one more time. I'll put on my best dominatrix voice, see if that works. I mean, driving an hour for a receipt? That's ridiculous."

"Hey, it's the only way to get to spend time with you." I meant it as a joke, but as soon as the words were out of my mouth I regretted them. Violet had a job with the shelter, which often stretched into the nights. She had classes, and—unlike me—she had a real relationship, one that she was committed to making work. Caroline was great, a real friendly jock-type, and she'd always been inviting to me. But being with a couple, gay or straight, was still different from hanging out with just your friend. That I didn't have such a commitment of my own was at least partly my fault, and I hadn't meant to throw her relationship back in her face. "I'm sorry," I stammered out. "I didn't mean that the way it sounded. Things are just weird now, with Bill. You know?"

"No, I don't know, cause you never tell me anything anymore." We were both silent, both feeling peeved and both, I suspected, a little guilty, too. "Look," Violet finally broke the quiet. "Why don't you come over tonight? I'll tell Caro to go off to that reading series she's always so keen on. I could do with one night away from my own books, too. We'll have some dinner, maybe go hear some music. I haven't been out clubbing in ages. What do you say?"

"I say, great. And thanks, Violet."

"Say no more."

◇◇◇

Bill's voice mail, rather to my relief, didn't say anything when I told it that I missed him too, but that I was spending the evening with Violet, so I wasn't quite sure why I felt so guilty. But a long, hot shower and a good half hour of foil-ball play with Musetta exorcised some of those feelings. And after my rotund little cat had retired for a well-deserved nap, I started attacking that pile of bills: *City* would pay on acceptance so, at least for a while, I could be looser with the purse strings.

Still, I told Violet she could pick up the first round when we went out that night. Nobody we knew was playing at Amphibian, but our fallback, the Casbah, was as loud as ever. As we made our way through the crowd in the club's front room combination bar-restaurant, I felt myself warmed by the boisterous roar.

"Krakow, Violet, yo! C'mon over here." A booming male voice hailed us from the bar. "Hey, sweetie." Fully aware of her preferences, Ralph, the large male owner of the voice, planted a big wet kiss on Violet's cheek. Me, he smiled at. I'm quite a bit bigger than my friend. In return, I didn't pull his skinny little rat-like ponytail. "What ill wind blew you in?" The jovial roll of his voice let us know he had a few beers' head start.

"Just looking for trouble," I replied. I didn't need to see Violet's expression to know not to let our inebriated colleague invite himself to join us. I'd experienced enough of Ralph's attention when I was writing for the *Mail*. He was their staff music critic, which meant he ran a drink tab at every club in town. And despite the slight blackmail involved in getting him to pay up—what bar owner would risk alienating him?—he wasn't a bad guy. Just messy, especially when tipsy, and so sure he was the goddess' gift to every female under forty that he'd become something of a parody of himself.

"Love to have two beautiful ladies join me!" With only one barstool empty beside him, he patted his knee. We both backed away. Luckily Risa, the bartender, had sussed out the situation.

"Theda? Violet?" She pointed to a table in the corner, a tight two-top that was just getting wiped down, and we slipped away as she drew another draft—and Ralph's attention.

"So how did the exam go?"

"It went. I'll hear next week, so I'm trying not to think about it." Violet was suppressing a smile, so I pushed.

"It went?"

"Okay, I think I aced it." A broad grin lifted her round face into dimples, making her look more pixie than punk. "But let's not jinx anything. I mean, it's just midterms."

"Yeah, I expect the same on the finals, too."

"So does Caro. She's promised me a real blow-out at the Capital Grille if I do better than a B."

I felt a twinge of jealousy. Of course, Violet would celebrate with her partner. Why not at the ritziest steak house in town? "So you're eating meat again?" The words had more edge than I'd intended.

"Yeah, Caro's a bad influence, I know." Violet didn't seem to have noticed. "But only once or twice a year. Maybe once a semester if I can keep the grades up. So, what's up with you and Bill?"

I spilled it all: my ambivalence, the desire not to repeat the Rick experience, and my fear that maybe I was becoming as distant and cool to Bill as Rick had been to me by the time he left town. By the time I finally got around to telling her about the phone message from my ex, she and I were finishing up our mixed plates: falafel and hummus for her, the Casbah's garlicky lamb and a feta-studded salad for me.

"You didn't call him back, did you?" We were both licking our fingers, and I could taste the garlic in my breath. Heaven.

"Not yet."

"Good. He doesn't sound like he's worth the trouble." Violet pushed her plate away and grabbed a napkin, which she started shredding. "And I think you're right to get your own head clear first." Her eyes darted from the paper pile in front of her to the condiments. One hand began drumming on the tabletop. "God, I can't believe I'm still looking for an ashtray. I can't believe there's no smoking here now!"

"Since when do you smoke?" I'd welcomed the citywide ban that made even clubs and bars more breathable, but I also didn't mind changing the subject.

"Organic chemistry."

"Meat, beer, tobacco…so much for the 'edge.'" When I'd met Violet, she'd only recently abandoned the hardcore straight-edge punk lifestyle of no stimulants and meatless, dairy-free vegan food. "What happened?"

"It was working in the coffee house," she smiled back now, a tight sly smile. "You kept telling me how fine that caffeine hit was, and it only took a little push."

"Well, I never said anything about tobacco." I stared at her for a moment, resisting the guilt. It's true that when we met, she was responsible for feeding my caffeine habit—I was a regular at the Mug Shot, when she'd been behind the counter. But she knew how I felt about smoking, even if I had helped edge her from her hardcore purity. She stared back. "Okay, okay. I can't stand to see you jonesing," I said finally, and her tight smile opened up. We got Risa's attention and paid the bill. Two steps out the door and Violet was lighting up.

"Don't tell Caro, will you?" she asked between puffs. The shelter was only a few blocks away, but she was walking slowly, dragging out the time as she sucked in the smoke.

"She doesn't know?"

"I don't think so, though who knows? I've been chewing Tic-Tacs like they're going out of style and, until the ban, I could always say I was just smoky from all the other nic fiends in the clubs. Second-hand smoke and all that. But I've been really careful about not smoking in the house. Besides, it's not good for the cats."

I bit my tongue to keep the obvious lecture from rolling out and walked beside her in silence, thinking evil thoughts about each of my friend's deep desperate drags. By the time we reached the shelter, Violet had power-smoked almost an entire extra-long. The porch light illuminated three cats in the window, two on the lookout, one deep in her dreams, and cast a glow onto the sidewalk, but Violet stood to the side, savoring the last of her butt. I stood with her, thinking I should enjoy the clear autumn sky. Soon, it would be too frosty to stand out here taking in the smell of the leaves, the faint woodsmoke. Above the university's towers, I could almost make out the Big Dipper, October giving us one of those rare nights when you can actually see stars in the city. But beer will out.

"Hey, Violet, I've got to pee."

"Enjoy." She handed me her key ring. "I'll be along in a minute."

I didn't like seeing how hungrily she drew on the glowing ember, but I had more pressing needs. Crossing behind the house to the back door we always used, I fumbled for the right key. I almost didn't notice that further along the enclosed porch, one of the shading yews was trembling, as if something was shaking it.

"Hey, Violet, do you have a raccoon problem?" She couldn't have been silly enough to leave the cat's food out. Maybe I could shoo it away. I stepped toward the hedge-like plantings and started to separate the branches when something pulled me back. Had I caught my jacket on a branch? Then I was looking at the sky, but all was black.

◇◇◇

"The kittens are gone!" Violet's voice seemed to come from miles away, but the panic in it made me sit up, a move I instantly regretted. Dizziness and pain spread from my head down to my stomach. A spasm caught me. I threw up on the lawn, and sat there, too weak to even move away. "Theda, Theda, where are you? The kittens are gone!"

"Here," I said weakly, my own voice hurting my head, and in a moment the back porchlight was on, it's white flood piercing my eyes as it illuminated Violet. Backlit, her hair looked positively luminescent, but her face, pale with worry, was what I looked up into, blinking weakly.

"You okay? What happened? I thought you'd gone in to use the bathroom. The door was open. Eww!" She sidestepped my vomit. "Are you sick?"

"Something, someone jumped me. I'm not sure." Still sitting, I rested my head on my folded arms and tried to breathe evenly, hoping the dizziness would pass and knowing that I was going to have to get up soon. At least I hadn't wet my pants. "I think you should call the cops."

"I'm calling Bill," said my friend. Shaky as I was, I had to smile.

When I first started seeing Bill, my atypical beau was something of a hero. He worked in homicide, as a detective here in the city, and in his thoughtful, careful way he'd helped solve the murder of a neighborhood woman, the founder of the shelter where Violet now worked. That case—and the fact that he seemed to consider the victim as a person—won him a lot of slack among my friends. But the idea of the police is not one that is usually welcome in our circle. We're more the type to automatically hit the brakes or look for the bong when someone says "cop." Not that we're lawbreakers, per se, but we're anti-establishment on principle and habits left over from college die hard. Violet had reasons: back when she was straight edge, not even indulging in coffee, she'd been picked up for a band mate's stash. She didn't like to talk about her night in the lockup, but I knew it was a sign of something good when she warmed up to my soft-spoken, but still sometimes macho beau. Of course, as she said, he wasn't "cops." He was Bill.

"Violet, Bill's homicide. I'm not dead." Reason seeped back in behind the pain.

"Bill is going to want to know that someone bashed you over the head."

"Huh?"

"You're bleeding, honey. Here, can you stand?" She put one wiry arm around me and practically lifted me from the ground. "Come inside. I want to get some ice on that and then I'm getting your boy on the phone."

◇◇◇

The rest of the evening passed in a blur, though I remember the lights were way too bright at the emergency room, the doctors much too loud, and the lines around Bill's blue-grey eyes looked more deeply ingrained than I remembered. He met us at the hospital, after telling Violet to call an ambulance for me, and after a couple of hours he was able to sign me out and take me home, with the caveat that he was going to have to wake me up every few hours, presumably to see if I was still alive. The prospect didn't seem to bode well for a romantic reunion, but I didn't mind being coddled a bit. I held the artificial cold pack to my head and let him support me to his car and then to my apartment. The rough warmth of his sweater as he helped me up the stairs almost had me in tears, and I confess I leaned on him more than was physically necessary as he took my keys to open the door. He knew just how to hold me, and that a nuzzle on the ear could be reassuring as well as sexy.

As comforting as it was to have him take momentary control, though, there remained something that wasn't right. Maybe it was the sour taste that lingered in my mouth, even after all the hospital mouthwash. Maybe I felt too much was unresolved between us. Maybe I just don't like being vulnerable, but it wasn't until he'd opened the two locks on my apartment door and I felt a warm, soft pressure against my shin that I lost it.

"Kitty!" I murmured, dropping the cold pack to scoop up my purring pet. "Oh, kitty." I burrowed my face in her long, thick fur and felt the pinpricks of her front claws kneading my shoulder. We stood there for a few moments, and in the warm weight of her I felt my reserve dissolve. "Oh, kitty." My eyes welled up, the pain and confusion of the last few hours hit me and I stumbled to the sofa. Musetta clung to me like she needed comforting, too, and I curled myself around her, rocking and nuzzling my pet's silky, vibrating back.

"Um, I'm going to put this back in the freezer, okay?" I looked up to where Bill was standing, holding the abandoned cold pack, and nodded.

"I almost feel I should leave you two alone." He smiled awkwardly, and then bent down to hide it, reaching to pick a magazine from the mess on my floor. "But the doctors said that you should be woken up every four hours, and I'm not sure Musetta can be trusted to tell time." Almost too tall for my tiny kitchenette, he stood there like a supplicant, twisting the latest issue of *Mojo* in his hands. I was so comfortable on the sofa, with my purring cat in my arms. But I reached one arm up to him and took his hand, and he settled in behind me, wrapping his arms around me and the cat. "I was so afraid when I got the call," he murmured into the damp, tangled mess of my hair, his bristly stubble just making itself felt. "I didn't know what had happened."

"I'm okay, Bill." I pulled his arms closer around me, so I could bury my face in the thick wool of his sweater. He smelled warm and slightly spicy, of soap rather than any perfume, and I felt myself relax. "It was just a bump on the head, and a fright." I was mumbling now. "I'm tough."

"Maybe too tough." I stiffened, and I could tell he felt me straighten out. His voice rose. "I mean, what the hell were you thinking of, Theda? Interrupting an attempted burglary?"

"I didn't know it was someone breaking in. You read the report." I'd been over this at least twice with the uniform cops. At Bill's urging, Violet had finally called 911. "I thought it was a raccoon or something. Some animal." I could hear the peevishness creeping into my voice, but I was tired and hurting and didn't want a lecture. "And what do you mean '*attempted* burglary'?"

"Nothing was stolen, sweetheart. The big window on the porch was forced open and it looks like someone had been inside, but nothing had been taken." Violet didn't have much cash in the house, but when she'd gotten the job she had splurged on an amazing sound system. It relaxed the cats, she claimed.

"What about the kittens?" I remembered Violet's cry, dimly recalled that the new arrivals, the white ones, had gone missing.

"They might have gotten out on their own, through the open window." I tried to visualize where Violet would have stashed them—new cats were always kept in isolation—but my head hurt too much. "Besides, they're lost or strays. Why would someone want to steal stray kittens? They've got no monetary value."

"Violet values them." My headache was suddenly worse.

"I know, honey. I'm sure she'll find them by morning, too." I didn't answer. My head pounded, the pain spiking down through my left eye. I wanted to pretend Bill wasn't there. Just me and Musetta, curled and warm and comfy on the couch.

"Come on, sweetie, let's get you to bed." I don't know how he got me into my old flannels or all tucked up, but I do recall him putting Musetta back down next to me. Normally adverse to being placed anywhere, this time she circled a bit and then settled down against my belly, letting me curl around her. I felt Bill slide in soon after, molding his tall, lean body against my back. He's conscientious enough so I believe that he set the alarm to wake me, checking for signs of concussion, but I had no memory of anything until mid-morning the next day when I woke alone and ache-y, the towel-wrapped cold pack on the pillow beside me.

Chapter Six

Bill had left a note, promising to call in—and threatening to leave work if I didn't answer—but closed with his assurance that I seemed to be sleeping quite normally. He signed it "love," which I took as a tribute more to my vulnerable condition than to our actual relationship. It also served to soften his postscript, which suggested that perhaps I might take it easy for a day or two. An innocent suggestion, and probably a good one, but Bill, whether because he's a cop or almost a decade older than me, tended to act as if he knew best. I could hear the pressure in his voice as I read his carefully worded note. It was an order, no matter how he couched it. That was his habit: one of his less endearing ones, even when he was right. My fist tightened around the slip of paper: One of my particular weaknesses was my tendency automatically to do the opposite of what anyone in authority suggested. I was a pusher, a questioner, which made my personality perfect for journalism and, at least until recently, for freelancing. Of course, it also made me broke. That thought, and the throbbing it produced in my temples, argued the wisdom of his words. So I smoothed out the paper that had crumpled in my hand, set it aside, and put on the water for a mint tea.

Even after a pot of tea liberally laced with honey and a good long soak in the tub, I couldn't seem to get moving. The glowing screen of my computer aggravated the throbbing behind my eyes, and I wasn't in the mood to finish paying bills. I thought about returning those phone calls from Bunny and, even more, from Rick. But the same issues that had stopped me from calling them back yesterday only loomed larger today, magnified by a headache that two extra-strength Advil had barely dulled. Once Bill checked in—I allowed myself full grumpiness, knowing he'd give me slack—I thought about going for a walk, but just then it started to rain.

I looked around my apartment, which seemed more of a mess than usual now that I was cooped up in it, and decided at the least I could do something about that. I managed to neaten up a towering newspaper pile that the cat had toppled, and slammed the back window before it could let in more of the chilly drizzle. Then I opened my one big closet to expose the disorder of shoes and god knows what else that lay within. Which is how I found myself curled up under my comforter on the couch watching some stupid entertainment news show when Violet called. I let the machine answer.

"Theda, are you okay? Bill called to tell me the hospital let you go." The TV and I were just getting to the juicy bits about Orlando Bloom's sex life, so I wasn't going to pick up. I heard Violet rambling on sympathetically, which I enjoyed, but then her tone changed. "I still haven't found the kittens, Theda. I'm worried."

"Hey, I'm here!" I reached over and grabbed the receiver.

"Oh, I thought maybe you were napping."

"Just watching E! and screening my calls," I confessed. "I didn't realize it was you." What was one lie? She started in by asking about my health, so I quickly moved her up to the problem at hand. "What's up with the kittens, the new ones?"

"I can't find them."

"They couldn't have gotten out?"

"No, no way. They were still in isolation, in the upstairs kitten room." I'd forgotten that new arrivals, especially sickly ones, were always put in the small, safe room on the second floor. With just one small window, it was easy to keep warm. That window hadn't been forced, and although the room door didn't lock, it did close quickly and latch automatically to keep sick kitties from straying out.

"What, there were three kittens?" My head still felt fuzzy.

"Yeah, three came in together, sick as—well—dogs. But the bigger two were already doing better. They're the ones missing, the ones I was keeping in the kitten room. I was going to let them join the rest today. The littlest one still had some congestion. I was keeping her in my bathroom, with the humidifier on. She was hiding behind the toilet when I looked in, but she was there, all right. It's her older sisters I don't know about."

"And you checked around the baseboards, right?" I tried to visualize the kitten room, to picture if anything in that one small enclosure could hide two healthy furballs.

"Theda…" Not only had I sounded condescending, I was casting aspersions on the excellent renovations Caroline had done. There wouldn't be any loose boards or stray holes in one of her walls that a kitten could get lost in.

"Sorry. I just can't see why anyone would steal kittens from a shelter. I mean, you'd be putting them up for adoption soon anyway, right?"

"Right. But you know, I don't let just anyone take a cat. We have a lot of things we check first. So it has got to be someone who wouldn't qualify, and that worries me, especially so close to Halloween."

"Feline felony," I muttered to myself. "The case of the kidnapped kittens." Violet was in no mood for a chuckle, and I did understand her concern, but I was just musing. Something she'd said rang a bell, and I couldn't put my finger on it. Why would someone steal two kittens?

Just then my call waiting beeped, and the trace of an idea was gone. "Violet, can you hold for a minute? That's my other line."

It was Bill, checking in. I told him I was fine, and when I added that I was watching TV on the couch while talking to Violet, I think he believed me. I promised to touch base again later, and rang off. Violet and I hung up soon after; she was distracted, and talking had aggravated my head. I made myself some scrambled eggs, adding an extra one for Musetta, and sprinkling some aged Parmegiano-Reggiano that I'd splurged on so I could call it lunch. Back on the sofa, I found an old movie that hadn't been colorized and settled in, pushing my kitty's eggs to her side of the plate. Naturally cautious, she first sniffed mine, which I'd also doused with Tabasco, and backed away as if slapped.

"I know, kitty. I'm weird and nobody understands me. But you still love me, don't you?" In response she washed her front paws and face, and promptly fell asleep.

◇◇◇

By the next morning I felt almost like myself again, albeit an older, stiffer version. The rain had given way to a dense, billowy overcast, but I didn't think I could face a run. So after swallowing some aspirin I steeled myself to make some calls. Knowing I should get in touch with Bunny, and wondering still what to say to Rick, I looked through my pad for the notes I'd taken on the *City* story. Work can be easier than life, I thought, as I dialed Lynn Ngaio's number.

"Ngaio Design," said a cultivated and accent-less voice, leading me to make a note about the pronunciation, a sort of cat-like take on "now." "If you'd like directions to our showroom, please press 1. For our hours, please press 2. If you are calling to place an order, please contact our distributor directly."

I waited through the rest of the message and left my own. At least someone was doing well. I had better luck reaching Monica Borgia, the one-time web whiz whose business had crumbled.

"Theda Krakow, I've read your stuff!" Monica sounded surprisingly chipper for someone who'd made and lost more than a million dollars, if the reports I'd read could be believed. I looked at the details my editor had given me: Yes, she was young. At twenty-five, maybe the future still looked bright.

"So, I'm calling because *City* magazine wants me revisit the 'Women of the Millennium.'" I started to explain, but Monica interrupted me.

"Oh yeah, Sunny told me all about it. She's coming over to shoot tomorrow. Want to come by then?"

Sunny had beaten me to the subject? I wasn't sure why that bothered me, but I did know I didn't want to conduct an interview with a photographer—any photographer—around. How can you establish rapport when your subject is being asked to hold still, to turn, to look like she's typing something into the computer?

"I'd rather get you alone, if that's okay. This will just be easier without distractions."

"That's fine. My time's pretty much my own these days." She laughed. Clearly, bill collectors weren't hanging around her door. "How about this morning?"

"You mean, now?" I'd hoped to schedule something for later in the week. Not that I still felt shakey, not really. But I'd figured making some phone calls would be my labor for the day. Still, an interview in the hand was worth something. And, yeah, Sunny's timeliness irked me. I took a breath. "Yeah, sure."

"Great, do you know where Beacon Street crosses into Somerville?" She gave me directions to a onetime industrial building not ten minutes away, and I told her I'd head out as soon as I'd made a few more calls.

"Hey, Sunny, this is Theda." I couldn't get her pulled from the assignment, but I wanted to make it clear that this was my story.

"Hey, Theda, how're you doing?" We went through the pleasantries, and I found myself growing more annoyed. Maybe it was just that my head had started hurting again.

"I'm sort of confused, Sunny." Musetta began to rub against my ankles and I reached down to pet her, feeling my blood pressure begin to subside. When she suddenly nipped me, I blamed Sunny. "We're both on this *City* story, but shouldn't you be waiting until I do the interviews? I mean, how do you know what angle I'm going to take?"

"What angle are you talking about? Borgia's a computer pro. Ngaio"—she mispronounced it to rhyme with "Ringo"—"makes clothes."

"But it's not always that simple. I mean, I just interviewed Rose Keller and only after we talked for a while did she tell me she's judging a cat show this weekend. And that's where the good photos will be." A bummer thought pounded into my head. "You haven't already shot her in her home, have you?"

"Keller, no." Sunny sounded supremely unenthused. I thought I heard a refrigerator open in the background. "I figured I'd get around to her. She's not going anywhere. I mean, she's hardly a player, right?"

"And Monica Borgia is?"

"She's one to watch, just you wait." The more Sunny sounded like a *City* cutline, the worse my head hurt. She crunched something loudly, maybe my nerves.

"Well, Rose Keller's in the story, too. But don't call her yet, okay? I'm going to ask her about the judging on Saturday, see if we can set up something special."

"Suit yourself, Theda." I fumed as she chewed. "Hey, have you talked to your editor at the *Mail* yet?"

"Not yet." Like I was going to tell her I'd been effectively fired. "It's on my list."

We hung up and I tried Rose's number, to give her a warning if nothing else, but there was no answer. When voice mail picked up, I left a greeting, and then gathered my tape recorder and two pens that both seemed to work, and headed out of the house.

<> <> <>

Monica Borgia's office was about what I'd expected: a big, nearly empty loft space with a huge flat computer monitor, a few chairs, and hidden speakers playing the new Modest Mouse. Monica was not. Oh, she was energetic, all right, bouncing over to meet me as I came off the industrial lift. But instead of a chic young thing, I was greeted by a little butterball of a girl, short dark curls framing a cherubic face, in a bright pink sweatshirt that made no attempt at camouflage.

"Monica?" I asked the obvious.

"And associates!" She spread her arms wide and I took in the layout, which included three marmalade cats lounging on the large windowsills. "They don't really do much. But I needed to sound as established as I could to get one more loan, and

'Borgia and Associates' sounds so much better than just 'Monica Borgia,' doesn't it?"

I agreed and she began to walk me around the stripped-bare premises, all that remained of her once thriving Internet business. The music segued into Guided by Voices, and I wondered if she'd figured my age into the mix.

"We got hung up on the distribution," she was saying, telling me about the online music outlet that combined cutting-edge commentary and state-of-the-art cross-referencing with customized mix CDs. "These days, with everything being available as downloads, we might have made it. We could have offered compilations and emailed them directly to the user. But a few years ago, most folks didn't have the high-speed hookups." She motioned me over to the black leather chairs by her worktable; only the gears and levers on the side revealed they'd been ergonometrically designed for computer work. "And when push came to shove, they didn't want to wait a week for UPS when they could get overnight delivery from Amazon."

Turning to face the screen, she began to call up web pages, clicking through to show me how her plan had worked. I had to slow her down at that point, feeling like every one of the eight years I had on her put me a decade behind in technology. Pretending I just wanted to hear it in her words, I let her talk me through her old business model, and she was gracious enough to comply. As I took notes, I remembered hearing her name around town. I'd known scribes, other music lovers, who'd felt lucky to contribute "content," that is, reviews, to her site. She'd encouraged them to stretch, letting them post pithy, opinionated critiques that would guide listeners to additional—and often preferable—choices. Plus, she'd paid well.

"In some ways, it seemed like you wanted to educate listeners." I wasn't doing really well with the questions. "Does that make sense?"

"Yeah, maybe." She laughed at the idea, and I felt absolved. "Truth is, the selling was an afterthought, just kind of tacked on to make my pet project a business. I guess it was really more of a web 'zine. I got so caught up in the rush that I didn't realize that at first. Didn't realize it for a long time." Her round face grew pensive. "Sometimes it takes a crash to make you clean up your system, you know?"

I got the theory, but it was the energy to restart that astounded me. Before I could comment on her resiliency, however, Monica had jumped up, clapping and stamping her sneaker-clad feet. "Colette, no! No! No! No!"

I started up with a jolt—how long would my nerves be like this? But then I looked over and saw an orange streak as one marmalade longhair scooted off a tabletop and into a closet. "Bad girl! Bad!" She chased after the cat, clapping her hands.

"Sorry about that," she said a moment later, retrieving the chair, which had rolled in the opposite direction. My breath had slowed to almost normal. "They can do anything, but they can't be on my work space. Colette, especially, gets jealous of the time I spend there. A few months ago she vomited right into a new set-up, blew the entire monitor."

"Destroyed it?" The desktop arrangement in front of me had to include five grand of equipment easily.

"Completely. In the old days, when I was building my own machines out of old Kaypros, I could've just taken it apart and wiped it down. These new components are just too sensitive."

"And you think it was intentional on the cat's part?"

"It wasn't a hairball, and she wasn't sick. You tell me."

I couldn't argue with that, and so instead we moved on to her current project. After going bust, she explained, she had come to terms with her real motivations.

"I love music. I love talking about music. I love that online you can tell someone about something and they can instantly hear a sample. What I don't care about is selling."

What she was saying resonated with me, but I had to ask the obvious question. "So how do you feel about file sharing?" Call it the Napster litmus test. I was waiting for a statement about how art should be free, how information "wanted" to be free. But Monica wasn't that naive.

"Entire songs? I'm against it. I believe artists should get paid for their work. And I'm selfish: I want them to keep producing! But samples, especially with some good encoding? That's different. Play it once, copy twenty seconds for your friends. Write what you think for others to share. That's what I'm about now. The key," she wheeled back to the wave-shaped keyboard and started typing, "is in the code." She pecked away. "Here, try this."

"Welcome Theda," the screen read. "What do you like?" In a nod to present company, I started to type in Guided by Voices, but as soon as I'd gotten a few letters into the Ohio alt-rock band's name, the keyboard filled it out for me. "If you like Guided by Voices, have you checked out Redd Kross?" I typed in yes, then erased it and clicked on a button labelled "Tell Me More." Immediately, the screen directed me to audio and video clips of interviews, one of which started playing on a small inset window. Six print articles, with headlines and leads showing, popped up, too. One of the stories had my byline on it. I pointed it out to Monica, with a chuckle.

"Okay, so there are still a few bugs in the system." She grinned and hit a key. My review disappeared, and another popped up to replace it. That story had been written by Rick, and I turned away from the screen as if I didn't care. I had more questions anyway, and Monica and I talked for another half hour, rambling from the details of her business to the latest releases by some of our shared favorite bands. I really had more than I could use, but didn't mind. The morning had been invigorating, as if some of the younger woman's elasticity had bounced into me. When I wished her luck, I meant it, and we both said we'd keep in touch. Driving away from her building I wondered again if I'd simply become too much of a hermit recently. I should be more social, more spontaneous.

As I turned onto Mass. Ave, I thought about Rose. I could get to her place in less than five minutes probably, and make her come out for lunch with me. Sunny's flip dismissal of her still rankled, and I wanted to let my old friend know she mattered. Besides, I'd skipped breakfast and I'm not constitutionally created to go without food for long. My favorite college station was playing something abrasive and loud, so I turned up the volume and turned left for Watertown, and the Rose Blossom Cattery.

◇◇◇

"Hey Rose! It's Theda!" Nobody had answered the door, and my friend's old Saab was in the driveway, so I'd walked around back. I sidled past the big holly, looking for any sign of her. Despite Rose's strange behavior of the other day, I hadn't thought she'd be avoiding her front door. But who knew? More likely, I figured, she was raking the yard free of its red-gold blanket of leaves, or taking out the trash. That one Angora female had looked near her time, and with a litter of kittens due imminently, the conscientious Rose wouldn't be far from home, at least not for long. "Rose? Are you there?"

The side door, off the garage, was ajar and I let myself in, calling so as not to startle her. "Rose?" If something had happened to one of the cats, she'd probably have the vet come by, rather than move a pregnant feline. "Rose?"

I walked through the kitchen and into the living room. The wall of cages rocked as agitated cats paced back and forth. "Rosie? It's me!"

Then I saw it, on the ground by the sofa, rich, bright red and glossy. Quickly, I ran my mind through Rose's menagerie, trying to figure out which animal could be lying there so still. Then my brain kicked in, and I realized what I was seeing was no cat. That was Rose's wig, her new favorite. And on the other side of the couch lay my friend, her sparse, gray hair no longer covered by anything but blood.

Chapter Seven

I recoiled out of Rose's house without thinking, slamming into my own car door before I remembered that I no longer had a cell phone stashed in the glove compartment. Cursing my stupidity, the feet that kept tripping me up, I couldn't bring myself to go back and instead banged on first one door and then another before a neighbor opened up enough to understand that I had to call the police, an ambulance, emergency. Now! I was sprawled on that poor neighbor's stoop when both the police and the EMT arrived. (The neighbor had enough faith to make the call. I couldn't blame her for not letting me in.) But when I saw the covered stretcher emerge from the same opened side door that I had used it was like getting hit over the head again myself.

I could take no comfort in the knowledge I'd acted as quickly as I could once I arrived. All I could think of was that last half hour with Monica. We'd not been discussing anything of importance. I had even shut my tape recorder off by the time she pulled out her vintage vinyl.

Nor was it any help to hear that I had done the right thing, as the cop in the dark blue uniform had said, once he took my statement and pressed a lukewarm but very sweet and milky Styrofoam cup of tea into my hand. It seemed likely that Rose had interrupted a robbery, he told me, as an EMT wrapped a blanket around my shivering shoulders. If I'd arrived earlier—if I'd gone in, even to look for a phone, I might have met the same fate.

It was the mention of the phone that broke through my shock, though the sugar in the tea probably helped.

"She'd gotten a call. She'd told me." I wasn't feeling particularly coherent. "A threat." Now I had his attention. "She told me, but then she said not to tell anyone."

"Now, calm down, ma'am. Let's just start at the beginning. When did she first mention a threatening phone call?"

"Monday." Was it only Monday? Two days had passed and I hadn't thought to check up on my friend. But she'd decided finally that the call was a prank. That it had been some kind of a bad joke. Or had she just been saying that to get me to leave it alone?

"She thought it was a prank?" I'd been thinking aloud.

"Yeah, because of Halloween coming up and all." To me it was perfectly clear. The young cop sighed and looked down at his own notes.

"The deceased received a threatening phone call or calls, but she thought that the caller was making a joke?"

"She's used to that kind of thing." I had his attention now. "Especially this time of year. People get weird about cats. Weird about single women who live alone with a bunch of cats. So when they threatened to kill her cats she said…"

"Hang on a minute. The threat was to her *cats*?" His previously kind, concerned face twisted up into a grimace. I got angry.

"The cats were everything to her. She's a professional. She *was* a professional." I had to stop and breathe before continuing. "A top quality breeder and a judge. If someone wanted to get to her, they'd threaten her cats. She'd do anything to protect them."

"So, you're saying she would have died for those animals?"

I paused, caught up by the obvious next step. "Maybe she did," I said, clutching the warm Styrofoam. The blanket did nothing to stop the shivering now. "Maybe she did."

◇◇◇

To say I was a basket case would be an understatement. Somehow, once the cops let me go, I did get myself home without further incident and crawled into bed. I think I even slept a bit, Musetta snuggled under my chin, because it was dark when I woke up, and I was hungry. At least my head didn't hurt, though I did jump three feet when the doorbell rang.

"Bill?" I asked the intercom tentatively. Until I heard myself ask, I hadn't realized how much I was hoping he'd come over. I knew how fast word spreads among cops, and, even with everything outstanding between us, it would be so easy to melt into his arms.

"Bunny!" came the response. "Let me in."

Comfort of a different sort had arrived. Clutched to a shiny beaded top that only Bunny could get away with were two huge, stapled paper bags, and her usual vanilla-bean perfume was overwhelmed by a marvelous wave of garlic. The vision in purple who trundled up the stairs had stopped for Korean take-out on her way from the *Mail*. The outfit was just what she wore to work.

"Yuk kai jang, bi bim bap. Some short ribs, and those dumplings you like," she said, clearing the papers from my table and parceling out the fragrant foil dishes. "Bill called." Business-like as always, she tucked her long henna'd curls into a rubber band and began to rustle through my kitchen cabinets, emerging with soup bowls, spoons, and a couple of pairs of mismatched chopsticks. "I should have just called him days ago, when you didn't get back to me." She examined the chopsticks, settled on four that seemed clean, and pulled up a chair facing me. "But he told me what's been going on. And today, damn....He sends his love, by the way. He'll be calling you later." She fixed me with a look, but then pushed up her spangled sleeves and began scooping dumplings into my bowl so I forgave her. "Girl, why don't you call your friends when you're in trouble?"

"Oh," was all I managed. The hot meat dumpling reminded my stomach of the meals I'd missed. "Good!"

We ate in silence for a good ten minutes, my furious shoveling interrupted only when Musetta came in to request some lap space. The doorbell rang again. "Violet," Bunny announced, and sure enough our diminutive friend was soon trudging up the stairs, a vision in a vintage CBGBs shirt and black jeans, and lugging what looked like three pints of ice cream. "None of that frozen yogurt crap," she confirmed, cramming the cartons into my ice-crusted freezer and getting herself a bowl and utensils. She smelled of smoke when she hugged me, but I was in no mood to complain.

We ate in relative silence, Bunny asking after Violet's classes, Violet removing Musetta from the table when the latter began to paw at the marinated bean sprouts. "We're playing Jato's Saturday," Violet told us. Bunny and I both raised our eyes. Jato's was an expensive club, the kind of place best known for touring bands on the rise. "Scarcity breeds demand." Economics was one of Violet's fall classes. "No, it's not the money. Not *just* the money," she corrected herself. "If I kept turning down gigs I'd have a mutiny on my hands from the rest of the band. You'll both be on the list. Bunny, I'll try to get you a plus-one. Theda, I've seen Bill's face when we play. Tell him he doesn't have to come." I nodded and kept eating. The Violet Haze Experience playing out. Going to hear music. Normal life continuing.

When I finally pushed my bowl away, after seriously considering the last of the tangy barbecue, I felt I could breathe again. My belly couldn't hold any more, but my head felt better too. This was just like the old days, before I'd begun spending so much time with Bill. Who wasn't there. Back when Rose was alive.

"Oh, Bunny!" Suddenly my composure gave way and I felt the tears start to come. In a moment, her considerable bulk was leaning over my chair, hugging and patting me. Violet reached to pull the bowls out of the way and Musetta ducked for cover.

"Oh, honey." Making the appropriate sympathetic noises, she pulled my head onto her copious breast, which would have been soft were it not for the ornate decoration on her sweater and a couple of spiky crystals on a chain. I pulled away.

"No, you don't." She misunderstood my resistance. "Come on over to the sofa."

Better placed to avoid injury, I curled up over one of my own velvet sofa pillows. Both my friends flanked me with hugs, and I began to cry in earnest.

"It was so horrible," I began, between sobs. "She was lying there. Her wig…" I broke off for a while and let my friends hold me. Finally, the sobs subsided and Violet left to get a roll of toilet paper and a glass of water.

"Blow." I did, and then drank.

"One side of her forehead was just gone. Smashed in." If I closed my eyes, I could see it still: Rose's vulnerable scalp, thin gray hair matted with blood. Her eye staring open up at nothing. Empty. The skin above it caved in. The cops hadn't said anything to me about the cause of death or the nature of her injuries. They didn't have to.

"And this right after you'd been bashed in the head," said Bunny, who began patting my back as if afraid I was going to lose it again.

"But that was a break-in. I don't know, we must have stopped them."

"No we didn't," Violet reminded me. "Two kittens were taken."

"Kittens?" While I rocked back and forth, my feet tucked beneath me, Violet filled Bunny in on the shelter invasion, including the cops' unwillingness to count two missing kittens as stolen property. The remaining kitten, I was cheered to hear, was doing great, all trace of the upper respiratory infection gone.

"Could it have been a prank? Somebody's bad idea of a joke?" Bunny sounded as skeptical about the idea of cat stealing as I had.

"No, I don't think so." Violet seemed to have considered the idea. "I was thinking that, especially so close to Halloween. But these kittens weren't black or even dark-ish, like you'd expect to be grabbed for 'witch cats.'" Bunny shot her a look. "You know what I mean, Bunny. Not Wiccan, but like those cartoon Halloween witches. They were more or less white, with a little brown. Real cuties, too, all roly-poly and very friendly. The littlest one seems to miss her sisters."

"Poor lonely kitty," I chimed in. "I should have pushed. Should have insisted. But nobody had threatened her. You didn't get any calls."

"Drink some more water, honey," said Bunny, still holding me. "You're not making sense. Someone threatened a kitten?" I shook my head. "Threatened Violet? This was a break-in, most likely. Bill told me."

"No, Bunny, this was planned. Someone had been calling Rose, saying there'd be violence if she didn't pay up."

"Threatening Rose? Did you tell the cops this?"

It was too much to go into again. Even Bill hadn't believed me. I nodded and started to sniffle once more. When we'd gone through another round of back-patting, I finally got the whole story out, from the first terrified phone conversation to Rose's denial. I told them, as well, about talking to the cops. They didn't seem to understand, I said, to which Violet snorted in response. By the time I'd gotten through it, some of that great dinner must have worked into my bloodstream. I was feeling more myself again.

"So, what was your news?" I asked, wiping a still-sore nose.

"Nothing so big."

"C'mon. Is it good? You said so on your message. I could use some good news."

Half turned away from me, I could see the side of two big grins. Bunny and Violet exchanged glances. For some reason, this made me anxious. "C'mon Bunny, tell me."

My friend pivoted to take both my hands in hers, pinning me down with a smile. "We're getting handfasted. Cal and I. We're going to get a license and everything. Make our union permanent. Violet and Caro are going to do a reading. And we want you and Bill to stand up with us."

"This is so great, Bunny," said Violet, beaming at her. "Caro's already looking through lyrics. This is wonderful."

They both thought it was happiness when I started to bawl once more.

Chapter Eight

I had to talk to Bill. That was my first thought, when I woke on Thursday morning. My sinuses felt like concrete, but my conscience was worse. I'd been a wimp. I had to straighten out what was going on between us, figure out where I stood on what everyone besides me seemed to think was an express train to monogamous happiness. I'd ducked his call the night before by falling asleep on the couch, and had only a faint recollection of Bunny talking to my beau as Violet cleaned up. He was taking me to dinner tomorrow, if I felt up to it, she'd said. If not, he was getting take-out to make sure I ate. I wasn't sure I needed his nutritional nursing, especially after last night's feast. But I wouldn't cancel. Food was always good, and I owed him an explanation for how I'd been acting. More to the point, I owed it to myself to work out what was what.

I also had an appointment to interview Cool today, and considered calling her to postpone. It had been a hell of a week. But Violet had found out that Rose's funeral would be Friday, and with that damned *City* deadline approaching I realized maybe I should just get it over with. Considering my mood and her chilliness, it wasn't going to be a long catch-up lunch anyway. I only needed seven hundred and fifty words on her.

Dragging myself off the sofa, my comforter still tucked around my shoulders, I lurched toward my tiny, dark kitchenette, still shrouded in shadow. Something warm and sticky welled up between my toes and I jumped and shrieked. Fur flew by me, and—fully awake now—I looked down to see an empty ice cream carton lying by the overturned garbage can, its melted remains spreading across the floor.

"Sorry, Musetta," I yelled down the hall, and reached for a paper towel to clean up the mess. "I'm losing it," I added, as much to myself as to my now invisible cat. What had I thought I'd stepped in? Blood? I had to snap out of this.

The phone rang. I hadn't had any coffee, but my spine had to kick in sometime.

"Hello?"

"Hey there, stranger. You're a hard woman to get in touch with." The warm tones almost misled me. The last few times we'd talked, he'd been distant, gone from me long before he physically moved out of town. But I recognized the underlying voice. It was Rick.

"Hey, yourself," I replied wittily. "What brings you back to town?" Okay, so maybe I wasn't at my most scintillating, but as enticing as it had been to hear his message, the actual reality of Rick set off some alarm bells in my head. It wasn't just that he'd left town—and me. My former beau had charm, musical taste, and a wide, sexy smile that could melt away any sins. But sins there had been, at least by my accounting.

I understood why he'd left, and a lot of the problems we'd had were in keeping with the life he'd led here. Rick had been a freelancer for most of our two-something years together, depending on how you counted the off times, when we were barely speaking. We freelancers are not known for our sense of commitment, and his on-again, off-again fidelity had bothered me a lot more than I'd let on at the time.

Plus, there was the work. He'd focused on music, more than I had, talent and temperament making it too difficult for him to bend his wordsmithing skills to the kind of service features that until recently had paid my bills. That love of music was what had brought us together—the basic passion for loud, fast beats; solid hooks; and the communal underground that celebrated such joyful noise—but it also sometimes set us up as competitors.

So when a staff job—with benefits—had opened up in Arizona, it made perfect sense that he'd grab it. And I almost understood why he'd never consulted me. The problem was more that when he left for warmer climes, he also left most of my questions about us unanswered. Were we breaking up? Had we ever been more than a couple of convenience? At least now I seemed capable of asking him a direct question. Maybe I'd grown a little. Or maybe it's just that he was on the phone and I couldn't feel his dark eyes, or his hands, on me. What I did feel were claws. Musetta was stretching, her white mittens reaching up and into my leg as her round green eyes stared straight at me.

"Ow!" I detached her extended paws. She blinked once, then walked away. "Sorry, I was being used for a scratching post. So, what happened?" I asked again.

"The cat? Oh, the job thing," he replied, and I caught an echo of the laugh that always charmed me, no matter how infuriating he got. "Well, let's just say that ten years of good music and no money didn't accustom me to churning out copy for the man."

"You *quit*?" "Man" or no man, staff jobs writing about music were few and far between. His silence clued me in that maybe the move hadn't been voluntary. "Well, whatever, welcome back." I laughed a little to cover my awkwardness. In our world that was a supremely uncool question. "You think this is for good?" I waited for him to mention our relationship. If we had one.

"For now, anyway. But, hey, I really don't want to do a post mortem on the job. I want to see you. I want to catch up. The way we left things…" His voice trailed off, but I didn't care. This was as close as he'd ever come to an acknowledgement of our relationship.

"Yeah, I know." I settled onto the sofa and curled up with the receiver. The last few months faded away.

"I realize I was sort of distant, and I've been thinking a lot." My toes curled with glee. Was this the same club-cool charmer I remembered? The man who'd driven all night so we could catch Robyn Hitchcock's last set in New York, but then left me to find my own way home? "How about dinner tonight? Maybe we could meet at the Casbah?" He'd put on his bad Omar Sharif accent with the invitation, but my stomach fell. Dinner. I had plans with Bill. I would have to tell Rick about Bill. And tell Bill…what? I didn't even know where Rick and I stood.

"I may be booked." What the hell, hadn't Bunny always advised me not to be so readily available? "What about coffee at the Mug Shot? See you there at four?"

"Uh, okay." Rick's smooth delivery almost cracked, and he joked to recover. "Will I recognize you?"

"We'll see." I felt more in control than I had all morning. "Won't we?"

◇◇◇

I was decidedly more conscious of my appearance than usual as I dressed for the interview with Cool. If this had just been catching up with an old friend, I doubt I'd have looked for my good jeans or worried so much about my hair. But Cool had gone beyond our local bar stars: she was a real celebrity, a Grammy winner, and I was no longer sure if she was also my old buddy from the clubs. I stopped before getting the blowdryer out, however. The Cool I remembered could barely tame her curls. But I did take the time to read up on her official web site. Much of it was the history that I knew well. Hell, I'd been there with her, during the rock and roll years. And I'd gone along as support on those first blues gigs, when she'd broken with our town's prevailing format to try the older music at coffee houses and such. I'd even been in the audience when that first festival scout had approached her, asking if she would be interested in three dates opening for a summer shed tour. It hadn't sounded like much at first: one of those all-day affairs that brings out a couple of veteran acts that can't fill the stadiums anymore and builds a show around them, complete with a half dozen unknowns. But for Cool, it was the beginning of a magic carpet ride.

Even though she'd been booked to play the second stage at the festival, Cool didn't remain an unknown for long. It wasn't just that Minnie Wright had noticed her, bringing the younger white woman up on stage during her own closing set. It was that the crowd did, that they loved to see a girl working her guitar up on the stage, like so many of them dreamed of doing. They got how Cool's bluesy licks twined around Minnie's husky voice. And when Minnie had Cool sing a verse one night somewhere outside of Milwaukee, her own deep contralto taking over from the older woman, the audience first got quiet, and then went wild. The duet became a regular part of the show, a way to bring a new generation of fans into Minnie's act. By the time the tour ended—the original three dates had been extended into two months—Cool had a contract and an audience primed to buy her product. The move out to L.A. was natural, and in many ways she was already gone before she made the rounds of farewell parties here in Boston. Those were wild, all-night loft affairs that I never saw close.

So maybe Cool's problems were inevitable too, or at least already well launched before she left town. Even her official site remarked on how, after her Grammy-winning debut, Cool had taken time off for rehab. Once her drinking was behind her, it became almost a badge of honor, proof that she was a real blues musician, and the depth of her two follow-up releases always referred to the struggle. These had all sold well. They even got some airplay on the adult stations; Cool's mellower tracks and deep voice suggested sultry nights rather than inner torment. But that last disc had come out more than two years before, and there had been no announcement of any others pending.

I tried plugging Cool's name into a search engine, knowing that fans can be better at documenting the travails of their idols than labels may be. I didn't find any of the usual star-search gossip: no reports of label in-fighting, no bidding wars that held up recorded product. Not even any hints of star tantrums, band members leaving, or the like. No news of any kind. Nothing but silence. And the fans weren't happy: "UnCool!" began one site. "Where's 'Cool' Coolidge Gone?" read another. Clearly, we had a lot to discuss.

◇◇◇

It was Ronnie I asked for at the front desk, and Ronnie who let me in when I arrived at the grand suite for lunch.

"She'll be here in a minute, darling." He poured me coffee from a plastic room service carafe. "Her trainer stayed late today."

I sipped and looked around the suite's living room, feeling a bit out of place among the overstuffed ivory upholstered furniture and the gilded lamps. If this was "making it," I could maybe almost see why Tess had opted out. The room was comfortable, but anonymous. Fresh flowers and coffee on demand not quite making up for the bad, heavy art that aped styles of a century past. Couldn't Cool have gotten a funky loft on a short-term lease and had it decorated for her? Or at least had Ronnie bring some photos or music to liven things up? I wandered around, drinking the weak hotel coffee, my head full of questions.

When Cool walked in, several minutes later, I began to understand. My old friend had just stepped out of the shower; her red mop was hidden by a toweling turban and an oversized terrycloth robe nearly dwarfed her solid form. But despite the clean soap smell that preceded her, the usually bright, brash redhead looked anything but fresh. Dark half-moons dragged at her eyes, and the round cheeks that, post-workout, post-shower, should have been a lively pink were pale, almost yellow.

"Cool!" I rushed to embrace her, stopping short as I noticed her flinch. Instead I sat on an overstuffed couch and patted the cushion beside me. "Come, sit down. Are you ill?"

"Hey, thanks a lot, old friend." She tried to laugh as she settled onto the sofa beside me. However, the hands reached out to take a coffee cup from Ronnie were trembling. "Yeah, so okay, I had a rough night."

I sat there, leaning back on a damask pillow, not knowing really what to say. I could tell her something about rough nights, but right now it seemed better to focus on her. Behind me, Ronnie cleared his throat.

"Theda, we know you're working on an article, but there are some things we'd like to discuss first."

"Of course." Setting up the ground rules for an interview only made sense. Usually, I'm the one who lays them out, warning people not to say anything to us journalists that they don't want to read in the paper. We're human, we're working, we want you to let something slip. Plus, if it's "off the record," why even say it? I also usually warn people, at least when I like them, that telling me afterward that something is not for attribution doesn't cut it. You knew I was here to interview you, you said it, you deal with it. But Cool was a friend and clearly a friend in need. I made a point of pulling my tape recorder, pad, and pens out of my bag and placing them on the coffee table—almost out of reach. "Both of you—Cool, Ronnie—I'm not working right now. I'd like to interview you for this story, but we can talk first, totally unofficial and just between us." I turned back to my friend. "Cool, what's happening? How are you?"

She smiled, leaning back to address her manager. "I told you, Ronnie." To me, she said. "Isn't it obvious? I'm in trouble."

I nodded. "Drinking?" It would explain the dearth of new music or recordings, even the move back to Boston.

"Oh, that's the least of it." She put down her coffee and turned to face me, tucking her tiny bare feet underneath her. "Look, Theda. I'm okay, really. I'm going to be okay. But, yeah, I got myself in trouble again. I could say it was the touring, or the pressure. Or even the damned label always after me to lose a few pounds so I'd look more like those damned posters they give away."

I knew the ones she meant: I'd thought that her waistline looked a bit too concave in them, even in a belted jacket. For a while, it had seemed that the powers that be had finally accepted that Cool was never going to look like Whitney Houston, and instead had marketed her as the "blues sweetheart," a chubby version of "the girl next door" with her own earthy pizazz. But those photoshopped posters were proof that they had never quite relented. Now it sounded like they had continued to push for more conventional sex appeal from Cool herself, as well.

"But it was my choice. I did it to myself. And I am getting myself together again. One day at a time."

"Good for you, Cool. But, well…." How did I say she still looked like crap?

"But why do I still look like crap?" Either she and I were still closer than I had thought, or she was psychic. Maybe she was simply very good at reading faces. At any rate, I nodded.

"I'm just out of rehab. That's part of it. Truth was, when Ronnie took me in, they said I had blood levels that would've killed a less habituated user." The way she accented "habituated" made me think the word had been bandied about a lot. "But I survived. It's just that, well, we're older now. It's a lot easier to kick when you're in your twenties."

"Kick?"

"Nothing illegal, thank god." She reached for her coffee again. "That's the plus of fame, I guess. You get anything you want with a good doctor's scrip. No, if I was broke, I'd have been a street junkie and I'd probably be facing charges. As it is, I just had what they call multiple dependencies. Alcohol, pills, you name it."

"But you're okay now?" Her pallor still worried me. Even against the white robe, her skin had so little color.

"Basically," she grinned, and her cheeks pinked up a bit. "I mean, it may take a while for my liver to forgive me. But, yeah, I'll be okay. I think. If I keep going to meetings and working the steps."

"So, that's why you dropped out of sight?"

"You've been reading my press! Yeah, that's why. Well, not so much the rehab as the year of hell-raising before. Part of it was the label. They spent good money on keeping things quiet, and they're reminding me of it every day."

"But why?" Even the official press had been quite open about Cool's earlier battle with demon alcohol.

"Everyone loves a reformed sinner, Theda. It makes you humble, makes you real. But I'm a heritage act now. A confirmed adult-format star. A past lapse gives me credibility. Anything new makes me unreliable."

"Like it hurt Aerosmith?"

"That's rock, honey. And they're men. Not to mention that those guys made their name as the 'bad boys of Boston.' I'm the 'blues sweetheart.' Sweethearts don't pass out at parties."

I knew enough about radio—and about record labels—to believe her. Almost. There was still something going on, though. Something she wasn't sharing.

"So, I'm assuming they paid for you to go through rehab? And they know that you're here?"

"Getting away from the bad influences." She nodded.

"Then why all the secrecy now? Why don't they just announce that you've been on sabbatical? That you've been 'suffering from exhaustion' or something?"

For a moment, I thought the big sofa had swallowed my questions. Cool sat there, frozen, her pale face staring at a point somewhere beyond my left shoulder. Then she turned toward Ronnie, and I could see where one curl had escaped the toweling, dark Titian red against the white turban and her too-pale skin. The silence continued.

"Cool?" The softness of the sofa made it difficult to sit up, but I did, leaning toward her.

Ever so slightly, Ronnie nodded. Cool turned back to me, her eyes holding mine.

"This has to remain private, Theda. My professional life may depend on it."

I nodded. Found my voice, and said, "Yeah."

"I'm being blackmailed, Theda. Someone out there knows some of the horrible things I did. Things I barely remember. And they want money, Theda. A lot of it. Or the blues sweetheart is going to get broken."

◇◇◇

We were silent then. Cool refilled both our cups, lacing hers liberally with cream and sugar. Ronnie looked at me and I, digesting everything, stared back. I let my cup sit on the table, getting cold, and began to feel rather bitter myself. Slowly, everything from Cool's coldness to Ronnie's protectiveness had begun to make sense.

"You thought it was me. That I was the blackmailer." I looked at him, rather than my friend. He was the one whose Southern smoothness had kept me at bay, and the alternative was too painful to consider. "You thought that's what I wanted."

"We didn't know what to think, honey." Ronnie pulled up a chair opposite us. "Cool wanted to trust you. She did. But I had to be careful, to look out for her. That's my job." He had the grace to look abashed. "I can see now that she was right."

Cool put her hand on my arm. "We were both so freaked out, Theda, we didn't know what to do. We got two phone calls, one last weekend and another one on Tuesday, telling us to have the money ready by the weekend. I wanted to call the cops, at first. But that would blow the whole thing open, wouldn't it? That's what they said, anyway."

"What did *they* say? Exactly?"

"That I had to pay up, or else certain stories would get out. Both times, the voice was muffled, but it could have been a woman. I'm not sure. They—she, I guess—wanted two hundred and fifty thousand dollars. They're going to call me back with the details."

"What are you going to do?"

"I don't know. I may just pay up. I mean, I've got the money."

I looked at her. "Yeah, I know," she said in response. "And I know that paying wouldn't stop it. But if I could do some kind of trade. She said she had proof that I wasn't 'anyone's sweetheart,' as she put it. If I could get whatever she had…"

"What does she have, photos or something?" I envisioned a Paris Hilton-style video.

"Who knows. Theda, I was pretty far gone all of last spring. Blackouts. Waking up in all the wrong places. You name it. Three months in rehab and a few weeks hiding here, going to meetings every day, and I'm just beginning to get some of it back. Some of those nights may be gone forever."

I nodded, and thought of Bill. If only I could tell him, but Cool and Ronnie would never agree to that. Given my recent history with my cop beau, maybe that was for the best. Then I thought of Rose.

"They didn't threaten to hurt you or anything, or anyone close to you, did they?"

"No, I can damage myself enough." She laughed, and a little more color began to creep back into her cheeks. "Just my career. Why?"

I told her Rose's whole story, then, from that first frantic phone call to the horrible discovery. Somewhere in there, I also explained about the cattery break-ins, about the prized animals that had gone missing.

"Man, that business sounds even more screwed up than mine. But, that's different, isn't it? I mean, nobody said they'd hurt me, not physically. I don't even have any pets, not anymore. You have to have a home to have pets. This has just got to be some kind of sick coincidence, right?"

Chapter Nine

My head was reeling as I pulled up in front of the Mug Shot, the neighborhood coffee place where I'd agreed to meet Rick a few hours ago. Man, only that morning, I'd seen this little reunion as the high tension part of the day. Now, in light of Cool's news, meeting with a troublesome ex seemed relaxing. I pushed open the glass door on the little café, breathed in the tang of a fresh, dark grind, and thanked the goddess for such refuges.

"Hey, Theda, what'll it be?" Joanie wasn't as conversant with my caffeine needs as Violet had been, back when my friend had been a full-time barista.

"Tall skim latte, I think. I need something comforting."

"You got it," said the buzz-cut counter girl. "I'll bring it back to you. There's someone been waiting."

There, tucked behind one of the woodblock tables that filled the back of the long, narrow storefront, was Rick. His dirty blonde hair was still shaggy, sticking out like a grownup Dennis the Menace as he bent over a magazine—*Spin*, it looked like. The coffee house's sound system, now spinning some vintage funk, had covered my entrance. But as if he could sense my presence, he looked up. Our eyes met and in that moment my mouth went dry.

"Theda!" He stood, brushed his bangs from his eyes, turning to inch toward me between the closely spaced tables.

"Rick!" I croaked, weaving my way back. A chair found its way between us, and maybe that was just as well. Unsure whether to embrace or shake hands, we stood there, staring.

"Hey," he said, his grin boyish and awkward.

"Hey." I couldn't have looked much better.

"Tall skim latte." Skinnier even than Rick, Joanie weaved with ease between the tables and deposited a steaming pint glass. I handed her two bucks and, grateful for the reprieve, sat down.

"You look great, Theda."

"So do you," I lied. Truth was, Rick looked beaten. I couldn't figure out if that shaggy mop was just a shade too long, or the late nights were beginning to show in the skin around his eyes and mouth.

"Thanks for lying." He flashed a full-blown smile, but it faded quickly. "Truth is, Theda, I've made some bad mistakes."

Here it comes, I thought, feeling a flush spread up my chest. The fantasy. Would it be "I never should have left you" or "I didn't know what you meant to me"? Both had kept me tossing and turning in the first months of silence following his departure.

"Mistakes?" I prompted.

"I don't know how you do it. Write for so many different people, even when you don't give a damn what you're writing about." The flush disappeared, replaced by a cold, sick feeling I remembered all too well. "I mean, I've been so cocky, and I figured, 'Hey, they hired me. They want me.' I didn't think through the reality of what I'd have to be doing."

He paused, but I just sat there. With no choice, he continued.

"Theda, they wanted me to write, like, three stories a week. Features and those stupid puff profiles that really drive me mad. Plus a round-up column. And I had to go to departmental meetings almost every morning."

Inquiring what was wrong with such a schedule didn't seem necessary so I sipped my latte instead. Right now, I needed the warmth.

"Plus, I was supposed to be in the office all the time. I mean, I'm a rock writer. If I'm not out there every night, I lose my profile. What were they paying me for anyway?"

My sympathy was following my hopes down the drain. I wanted him to get on with it.

"So, what happened finally?"

"I had the stupidest fight with an editor. Not even the top guy, some young Asian woman they hired, obviously as an affirmative action move. She didn't even know what CMJ was." Rick had been attending CMJ—the *College Media Journal*'s New York convention—every year since I'd known him, using the week-long barrage of international media and cutting-edge bands to schmooze editors and stock up on story ideas for months to come.

"They wouldn't send you to New York?"

"They wouldn't even give me the time off. Said I hadn't earned the vacation time yet. I told her what I thought of her. I mean, she wasn't the one who had hired me."

But she was an editor, and reading between the lines, I gathered he hadn't made any allies to counter her complaints. The result, he said, was a rapid chain of events that had led to his dismissal, leaving him to make his way back to Boston, broke and defeated.

"So, now you're back." It wasn't how I wanted it, but I couldn't resist feeling smug. I dipped my face down to the latte froth to hide my smile.

"Yeah, and, Theda, if it isn't trespassing too much on your territory, I wanted to ask about the *Mail*." For the second time since I sat down, I felt vaguely ill. "I mean, I've been looking for your byline and I haven't been seeing it. Would you mind too much if I hit them up? I could really use the work."

So much for self-satisfaction. Did I want to explain about my own tiff with an editor? Were my issues that much more evolved than his, or were Rick and I truly flip sides of the same coin? I didn't want to answer him before I knew myself. "You've been looking for my byline?"

"Well, yeah," he chuckled, a little uneasily, I thought. Thank god the diversion had worked. "I mean, I thought about you a lot when I was out in Phoenix, so until I got up my nerve to call, I'd been looking around for you. For signs of life, so to speak."

"Yeah, well, I'm still here." Barely, I added to myself, placing the empty glass back on the table. He could cozy up to me all he wanted to now, I knew what he wanted.

"Well, I'm glad of that." Rick reached across the table. "I can't tell you how glad." I looked down at the bitten nails, felt the smooth guitar callouses as his two hands closed over mine. They fit, as they always had. And my fingers had a few bitemarks on them as well. Were we really that different?

"We feral animals have to stick together, Theda." He always could read my silences. "Nobody else will ever totally understand us."

◇◇◇

"You need that man back in your life like Musetta needs fleas." Bunny pulled no punches when I called her a little later, and the force in her voice tossed my head back. I'd called to finalize plans to carpool to Rose's funeral and meant to tell her about Cool, what I could anyway. But once she checked in about my physical status—headache more or less gone, no blurred vision—she honed right in on my romantic woes. "He's bad for you, Theda, and I don't care if you both have the same job problems right now. That's the only thing you've got in common. You've moved on, girl. And if I know him, he'll manage to come out all right even if he has to climb over you to do it." Bunny had never forgiven Rick for keeping any news of the Phoenix job opening from me, even as she swore she'd never let me leave town. It was the principle, she said.

"Don't worry, Bunny." I held the receiver back up to my ear. "I'm not going to get involved with him again." Well, I had told Rick about Violet's gig on Saturday. He'd never heard her band and it wasn't the kind of thing Bill would enjoy anyway. "And I certainly didn't tell him about working for *City*." He would've scoffed.

"Well, that's a blessing. How did lunch with Cool go?" Bunny let me get back on track. With a moment's thought, I decided not to tell her about the blackmail—it wasn't my secret, and once it was out, I couldn't pull it back—but I did give her some of the news, sharing everything our mutual friend had told me in the hour-long "official" interview we'd done after our real heart-to-heart. Most of what Cool had been willing to go on the record with wasn't really breaking news—her last album had been out for nearly two years—but she had given me enough to update the original *City* story. There were some new song ideas, a couple of potential collaborators, hip names who might interest younger listeners, and we'd agreed that my story would be a great way to announce Cool's return to the East Coast.

"Well, I'm glad she's out of Tinsel Town. There's no *there* there," said Bunny, speaking from all of about a week's experience with the West Coast. "I wonder what the real story is behind her silence, though. You think she's in some kind of trouble, Theda?"

Bunny had a nose for trouble. Also for gossip, and I was glad I'd held my tongue.

"She did look tired, like she needed a break." That much I could share. "But when we chatted, she was the same old Cool. Did I tell you she's got a personal trainer now?"

"That's so LA!" Back on safe ground, we rambled on for another forty minutes. Musetta came into the room and, finding me extended on the sofa, jumped onto my belly. As the subject turned to plans for Bunny's upcoming nuptials, I found my mind wandering, but by then Musetta had quit kneading and was sleeping peacefully tucked between me and the sofa back.

"So, you don't want to do it on Halloween?"

"Samhain," Bunny corrected me, using the Gaelic pronunciation, "SOW-in." "No, we've got enough going on then. Besides, that's just next Sunday, Theda. Way too soon for the big shindig I'm planning."

As Bunny returned in detail to the kind of wedding plans that only interest the primaries, I sighed, and Musetta did, too. The doorbell startled—and saved—us both.

"That must be Bill." I interrupted some account of a vegetarian caterer who could do wonders with walnuts. ("My family will freak," Bunny was saying. "But a lot of our Wiccan circle don't believe in killing anything.") Musetta hit the floor with a thump and ran to the door. "Love to Cal."

"And to Bill, too, Theda." She sighed. "I'll pick you up tomorrow at ten. Blessed be."

"Back at you, Bunny. Blessed be." We could all use the goodwill the Wiccan greeting called for. I signed off and turned to Musetta, who was already stretched out to her full length, reaching for the knob.

◇◇◇

Three hours later, I was closing it behind me again. Somehow, I had done it once again, turned an interesting situation into something worse.

The evening had begun well enough. "Hey, darling, how's your head?" Bill had greeted me with a kiss and a mixed red-and-purple bouquet, which I'd managed to place in water and out of Musetta's reach before we went in search of food. We'd been halfway to Anna's, the local pizza place, before I'd gotten him to believe that I was healed enough to share a carafe of the house red along with the large pepperoni and mushroom that had become our regular. But I had convinced him and once we'd ordered, had even managed to tune down his solicitous questions long enough to hear a little about his day. Being a homicide detective, Bill was always somewhat reluctant to talk about his job. Partly, I knew, he was often working on cases in progress and he had to be careful about what he said. Partly, I suspected, he didn't want to gross me out. But I'd seen enough of violence and crime recently to believe myself inured. Besides, if we were going to progress as a couple, he was going to have to let me in. Once our pizza arrived and we'd each torn off a slice, my campaign began in earnest.

"So, open cases?" I'd asked.

"Let me leave that at work," he sighed and wiped his free hand over his face.

"C'mon, Bill, don't shut me out." Subtlety wasn't my forte.

"Did you hear about that abandoned baby? The one they found in a pile of leaves on the Common?" I nodded. "Well, she died. Now that's my case. You sure you want to hear more?"

What could I tell him but the truth? "I do if it's what's on your mind." We'd gotten our wine by then, and maybe I'd downed a glass too quickly while the pizza cooled. "I mean, I've got to, if we're going to continue."

"So that's what this is about: Bunny and Cal's wedding."

"Handfasting." I corrected, pulling a string of cheese into my mouth. "It's a Wiccan thing. And no, not exactly."

"Theda, your friends are tying the knot, whatever you want to call it, and you want to know what's up with us. If I'm serious."

Oh, he was infuriating. "No, Bill. I'm not worried about you. You've been a rock." I meant it sarcastically, but it came out like a compliment. Damn. "I'm trying to figure out how *I* feel. What *I* want to do."

"Pre-handfasting jitters?" He was smiling now, as much as a man can while maneuvering molten cheese.

"Damn it, Bill, listen to yourself. You're treating me like a child. And, well, maybe you are too old for me. I mean, do you know what I really care about? Music. The scene, the clubs, the bands. Yeah, you'll go out with me, but it's like you're suffering through it all for my sake. But for me, that's what's important. Music unleashes something in me, and that's where I've always connected with my friends, my *best* friends." He winced. "It's not just going to see some band, hear the tunes, and go home. It's a community, my community. Until I started seeing you, it was my life!"

"Great, so you want to cruise into your forties hanging out in smoky dives."

"They're all smoke-free in the city now, Bill. And I've got quite a few years before my forties, thank you very much." I was getting off track. "But, yeah, maybe I do want to spend my time hanging in the clubs. Maybe that's what I'm really about and you're just an aberration."

"An aberration from boys in bands who can't remember your name." He paused, put his pizza down, and shot me a look. "Or devil-may-care rock critics who treat you like another cut-rate freelance assignment. Good enough when nothing better is around?"

Had Bunny told him about Rick? "What are you getting at?"

"I know about Rick." The wine and pizza in my belly threatened to revolt. "You told me all about that relationship and how he treated you." I relaxed. He'd not heard that my ex was back in town. Still, this was not the road I wanted to pursue.

"It's not that, Bill, not just that anyway." Putting my own slice back on the plate, I began to list the ways we were different: age, interests, history. Even friends: "You don't have any, and I live for mine."

"I have a few good friends, that's not fair." He pushed back from the table. "Besides, some of that's a gender thing. Women bond."

"Oh great, so now you're going to pull a sexist stereotype on me. My friends aren't some 'girl thing.' They're serious women who I share quality parts of my life with."

"And about whom you know nothing."

"What are you talking about?"

"Like your *friend*, Rose? Well, because she was such a close *friend* of yours, I asked around." He leaned closer and I could see that his eyes had grown cold. I wasn't liking his tone, but I couldn't interrupt him now. "Your friend, the upstanding breeder, may have been involved in those cattery thefts you were so up in arms about."

"No way."

"Way, Theda." His mouth was set in a tight-lipped grin, but there didn't seem to be any happiness behind it. "Not my bailiwick, but I made some inquiries. Believe it or not, I worry about you—and with all this female bonding you can be just too trusting sometimes. Seems your 'good buddy' Rose was hard up for cash, was putting out feelers for selling a lot of cats, quickly and with no fuss. In fact, the undercovers who are investigating this say they would've had her, too, if she didn't keep backing out of meets, changing her mind about sales. They think that's what got her killed. She dallied when the muscle wanted her to move."

"I don't believe it."

"Evidence, Theda."

"Of course she needed money. She was being hit up for protection. Someone was threatening her. I told you, and I told the Watertown cops." Damn, I wished I'd pushed her to go to the police back when she'd first told me. "She was probably looking to sell some of her own cats, to save the others, poor woman. No wonder she kept backing out."

"That dog won't hunt, Theda. Sorry."

"What are you talking about?"

"Don't you think the Watertown cops have any brains? They've gone through her phone records for that Monday, the day she told you she was threatened. And the weekend before and several days later. There are no incoming calls that don't have a good explanation. No strangers phoned Rose. None at all, so there were no threats. No threats, no crime. The only thing off in the whole equation was your 'friend.'"

"No." I shook my head. A mistake, especially after the wine. "No."

"Maybe, Theda. Maybe. But think about it: what if the attack outside Violet's was planned, and the break-in just cover for someone who was really trying to hurt you? Slow you down, scare you off, or worse? That was after you had talked to Rose, right?"

"Yeah, but no." I couldn't believe it. I wouldn't, and just kept shaking him off despite the growing pain in my head. "No."

The pizza had gotten cold by this time and I certainly didn't want any more wine. Somehow we made it back to civil conversation long enough to pay the bill. But when I told Bill my headache was back, he didn't offer to take care of me again. Instead, he walked me home and we parted with stiff, formal words—and no mention of seeing each other again. I walked in to a hairball and a cat who was nowhere to be seen.

Chapter Ten

Sleep eluded me, as did the cat, and I found myself eyeing dawn over a cup of coffee already gone bitter and cold. Was I being a fool? Was I really in danger? I knew I needed time to think, and the week had just been too full. But these questions echoed through my head, as did one even closer: Was pushing Bill away what I really wanted?

"Be careful what you ask for," I said aloud, to no one but myself. That was another of Bunny's favorites, and it rang true. Of course, I was too tired to be thinking clearly, now that I had the peace and relative quiet in which to mull over my life.

"Kitty?" I was feeling deserted, and would've started worrying about my chubby little companion's well being if she hadn't chosen that moment to appear, body-checking my ankle with her soft, warm bulk. "You still love me, don't you?" She was silent, but at this point that was consent enough and I hugged her to me.

"Eh," she pushed away, cool pink paw pads pressing against my face. Chastened, I went instead to open a can. The kitchen clock told me I had hours before the funeral. Dumping my coffee, I walked back to my computer and booted it up. Might as well type in my interview notes.

"You've got mail!" Finally, a friendly voice. Better still, I saw as I opened the note, a profitable one. Carrie, my editor from the bridal mag *I Do*, had finally gotten back to me, ending the months-long drought.

"T - Can you do 800 on new trends in bouquets? We have art already—so one trend must be all-white. Need by Nov. 8."

I Do had an annoying habit of telling me what conclusions to find before I'd begun my research. However, eight hundred words meant four hundred dollars. For that, I would find a florist who swore that the hot new bridal bouquets all had polka-dots. I fired off a cheery assent, and started sifting through the barrage of sales pitches and pornography offers that had filled my in box since I last logged on. Why was everyone so interested in farm animals?

Ten minutes later, I'd deleted most of it, but a few items caught my eye. One was from an old club acquaintance. A wedding announcement. Great, but the woman sending it hadn't contacted me in three years and the name of her fiancé didn't look familiar. If she was hoping for a gift, she was out of luck. More promising was another with the subject line: "Big Cats are Huge." It proved to be a short wire story, forwarded by my old college roommate in California, talking about the growing international popularity of large cat breeds. My former roommate had known James, my last cat, back when he was a hefty eighteen pounder, and I assumed this latest story was prompted by photos I'd sent her showing off Musetta's rather pear-shaped profile. The cats in this story, though, were bred to be big, from the docile Ragdolls to the newer Pixie-bobs, a hefty feline supposedly produced by crossing some poor domestic tabbies with bobcats. The attached photo, of a moon-faced Ragdoll, looked somewhat familiar, and I remembered the Newton cattery theft.

Were these cats becoming too popular for their own good? Maybe I was just cranky from lack of sleep, but it seemed a possibility. Hadn't that crime been reported as one of a series? Earlier in the week, I'd been too busy to follow up, but this morning loomed like an early winter storm. I started typing. Within minutes, the Internet and my trusty iMac had coughed up competing newspapers' write-ups of a few similar crimes: A breeder of Maine coons, also large, long-haired cats, had been hit less than a month before, as had a cattery known for its Norwegian forest cats, an athletic, densely furred animal that reminded me a bit of James. In each case, only a couple of animals had been stolen, but each time the purloined pusses had fit the pattern: big, cuddly cats.

Which made me wonder about Rose's cattery and the crime that had ended her life. Angoras have great fur: silky, long, and soft to the touch. But they're tiny, compared to those other animals. Small-boned and delicate, with a build that always reminded me of Siamese. Maybe the thieves were branching out. If, in fact, the threats Rose had received and the cattery thefts were all the work of the same criminals. Maybe we were just entering a new age, I thought as I powered down my computer. Maybe animal security was going to be the next hot profession. Once I got the flower story done, I should look into it, I thought, as I went to brew more coffee.

◇◇◇

Maybe it was the extra gig that gave me a sense of security. Maybe it was Musetta, finally purring by my side. Despite the caffeine refill, something lulled me back to sleep and I woke with a start on the sofa, under the newspaper, the phone ringing by my ear.

"Theda?" It was Violet. "Are you going to Rose's funeral?"

"Mmm." I wasn't quite awake yet. Then I saw the wall clock and bolted up. "Yeah, Bunny's picking me up in thirty minutes. Why, do you need a lift?"

"Yeah, I think I'd like to go. I was thinking, with classes and all, I'd take a pass. But I'm all set for the Econ midterm, and I wouldn't feel right missing it." Since I'd introduced them over the summer, Rose had done a lot to break down Violet's antipathy toward pedigreed cats and the people who breed them. My punk buddy still thought the industry was a waste—"bogus" was her word—since so many perfectly fine and healthy beasts had to be euthanized each year. But Rose had made her case, explaining the pedigreed animals can raise public interest. Any animal that commands a high price is seen as having value, she pointed out, as screwed up as that may be. Besides, Rose genuinely loved animals, and Violet could see that when the diminutive older woman in her crazy wigs started coming round, using her rare spare hours to help out at the shelter. Rose knew how to "pill" a cat with the best of them, and she wasn't above getting down on the floor to coax a timid kitten out to play either.

"Well, we can swing by. Bunny knows how to get there. And Violet?" I didn't want to offend my friend, but as I rooted through my own closet I figured a word to the wise couldn't hurt. "This is all happening at a conservative synagogue. Rose's sister is older and, I gather, distinctly suburban."

"No sneakers, gotcha."

"Ciao."

◇◇◇

Violet was wearing black Doc Martens when we picked her up, but she'd paired the heavy workboots with a long black dress made of sweatshirt material. Despite some fevered brushing before Bunny had arrived, I seemed to have more cat hair on me than either of my friends. Somehow, Musetta's white belly fur, rather than the black hair that covered the majority of her round form, had found its way onto my one good navy suit. Next to my disarray, Violet's goth get-up, and Bunny's inability to completely subdue her natural exuberance (her eggplant outfit had embroidery, but no beads), I worried that we'd stand out. I needn't have been concerned. Rose's friends were cat people, and despite the somber occasion, the folks who filled the big, underheated synagogue were dressed more casually than I'd expected. They all showed various signs of grief, as well, from open weeping to the kind of grim facial expression that told of sleepless nights. They were a family unto themselves, largely a sisterhood, marked uniformly by the signs of fur. Although there must have been other breeders among them, maybe even some who were suspects in the cattery thefts, I couldn't imagine any of them had wished Rose ill.

The only exceptions were in the family up front. Though the tall, elegant man didn't look familiar, nor the two younger men by his side—one blond, one darker, both with his straight brow and Brooks Brothers tailoring—the perfectly coiffed woman seated by them gave me a shock. Ash blond, with a suit that must have been made for her, she looked so much like a made-up, spiffed-up Rose that I couldn't help a quick intake of breath.

"Who's that?" Bunny saw her too.

"Must be the sister, Ivy."

"I thought you said she was older," added Violet, a little too loud for my comfort. The three of us stared, and then, realizing that we looked like a female Three Stooges, we looked away. Once we'd taken seats at the end of a row a few behind the model family, I peeked again. It was the makeup, a perfect job, that had fooled us. Closer up, where I could examine her profile, even the flawless foundation couldn't hide the eight years she'd had on her sister. Not because her eyes were swollen with weeping—they weren't—but the skin on her neck gave her away. As if she knew I was watching, she lifted her chin. But I caught her eyes straying to a slim gold watch.

"Wow, she's a cool one, isn't she?" Violet's whisper was softer now, and I couldn't help but nod.

"Rose had said they weren't close." The last time she'd had any extended contact, Rose had said, was during her chemo. Widowed young and childless, Rose had called on her older sister for help with the house and her then-fledgling cattery as the heavy-duty drugs kicked in. Ivy had responded, Rose had told me, with offers of money. The implication was that the funds would be a loan, not a gift. "It's who she is," Rose had explained, any bitterness long faded. "She doesn't get her hands dirty and she never gives anything away."

As the rabbi began his address, I tried to remember if Rose had accepted any of her sister's grudging comfort. Had she needed the cash? Had she perhaps let her older sister pay for some help around the house as she recovered from surgery or the chemo? I vaguely recalled my friend talking about that time in her life, but that confidence, made months ago, was fading from me. This fact bothered me as much as anything else as we all stood up to read from the black-bound prayer books. If her friends forgot Rose, forgot the details that made her funny and wise and just a little kooky, then she was truly gone. I found myself listing her wigs and her cats as we mouthed the prayers, trying to recall which ones she called "Pussums" and which "Sweetie."

Funerals are never a hoot, but the reception held right after seemed particularly cold, which even the day's increasingly grim overcast didn't explain. I could see not going to the grave site—I wasn't family, after all—but I'd grown up with the tradition of visiting the family of the bereaved once the funeral proper was over. "Sitting shiva," the ancient Jewish tradition that carried these visits through a full week of mourning, made emotional sense. Maybe the days of covered casseroles were finished; I sure hadn't thought of making anything. But there was still something to be said for spending time with people after a funeral. It gave everyone a chance to unwind and make the transition between traditional rites and human mourning. At times, company, just the presence of others, was a comfort.

After this service, though, it didn't seem like anyone was invited anywhere. Instead we all let ourselves be herded into the synagogue's adjoining function room, where finger sandwiches, coffee, and tea awaited. None of it looked very appetizing, and nobody seemed comfortable enough to kick back, reminisce, or even have a good cry.

Still, Ivy and her picture-perfect family held court, standing near the room's center, accepting condolences and making quiet conversation. The rest of the mourners mulled about, picking at the food. Maybe we'd all have sat and relaxed, if the family had. But they didn't. And as the overcast outdoors turned to rain, the crowd began to slip away in twos and fours. Violet and I eyed each other, but Bunny shook her head in a firm "No." Finally, the rabbi announced that there would be a notice of the unveiling, and we all felt free to leave. Free, but not relieved.

The mourning had been too formal, too far removed from the friend we had lost, and the day too unremittingly sad.

The cold little gathering had given me a chance to examine Ivy, however. "I'm sorry for your loss." The same old lines, but they came back to me as we queued up to make our exit. My own parents had been killed in a car crash just over ten years earlier. I'd learned the forms back then.

"Thank you." Her response sounded flat, automatic. Up close, the wear and tear was more visible. Ivy looked tired, I decided, rather than old. And if she hadn't teared up during the service, as Bunny and I had, she was wearing her grief around her mouth, where her powder now seemed to accentuate the lines framing those lacquered lips. I had to keep trying.

"I'm Theda Krakow. Rose was my friend."

"Pleased to meet you." An odd choice of words, but sadness takes us all in different ways. Then she looked at me, as if finally seeing me, a spark of life animating her face. "You were one of her cat friends?"

"Yeah. I mean, that's one way of putting it."

"Maybe you can help me then. I mean, you probably knew her better than I did. These last few years...." She looked off into space and grew pale. I steered her toward a chair and pulled one up beside her.

"Thank you. It's just such a shock. I mean, once she'd survived the cancer and all." I made sympathetic noises. This was the first sign of humanity she'd shown. "We weren't close, you must have known that. And now, all this." She looked around, confused now rather than frozen. "Did you know that I'm her heir?" I hadn't, but it made sense. Rose had no children, and considered her cats and the feline community her family of choice. "I'm her heir," Ivy continued, "and I've got a house full of cats to dispose of. Frankly, I'm at a loss."

The cats! I hadn't thought of those lovely, friendly Angoras. Wasn't one about due to birth a litter? That was days ago. "Has someone been taking care of them?"

"Oh yes, yes. The police put me in touch with the animal control officer, who recommended a young veterinary technician in the area. She's moved in as part of the job. The insurance should cover most of it. But I'm rather at a loss as to what to do longer term."

Her color back, she focused on me as if I'd have the answer. "These people have told me that Rose had some valuable cats and that I shouldn't just give them to a shelter." I shuddered at the thought.

"They were her life, Ivy. They are fine pedigree animals."

"So I gather." Despite her words, she still seemed vague. I wondered if she'd been listening to me. Or drinking. "In fact, I've already been contacted by some dealers who want to buy the entire establishment. I'm tempted to just unload it, once the lawyers have taken it all through probate and all. But maybe I'm being foolish. Do you know anything about this?" She grabbed my wrist and I fought the urge to pull my arm away. "How much can a bunch of cats be worth, anyway? I mean, they're just cats, right?"

◇◇◇

"She said it as if they were rats. I heard her." Violet was annotating my report as Bunny drove us home through the rain-slick streets.

"She didn't seem particularly fond of them," I agreed, wiping the wet hair out of my face. "Not a pet person." Violet snorted, but Bunny took the philosophical tone.

"Well, she's living a different life. I mean, Rose had the cats. Ivy was raising kids."

"Bunny, if you start going all suburban on us just because you're getting hitched...." Violet rose in a threatening tone.

"I would never give up my cats. But, you know, Rose did leave them to Ivy."

"Rose didn't expect to be killed." I felt worn out by the morning, and by Ivy's unexpected confidences. But it was up to me to point out the obvious, and I could almost hear Bill's tone in my voice. "She didn't expect to leave her cats like this. I told Ivy I'd ask around, find some reputable dealers to advise her. I told her to think of them like jewels, that she shouldn't just 'get rid' of them to the first buyer. That seemed to get through. She's got a while, anyway, until the house and business clear probate." I thought of the vet's aide who was boarding at the cattery. "At least the cats are being cared for by someone who knows what she's doing."

"Has she even visited those poor animals? They must be traumatized."

"I doubt she has. Can you imagine her covered in Angora?"

"Not that kind," Bunny answered. "Hey, speaking of—any interest in bridal gown shopping?" Violet and I groaned. "I'm not going nuts about it, I promise. But my mother is coming to town tomorrow and I figured she's good for lunch. And I could use the buffers."

"No way." This was not Violet's thing.

"I can't either," I said, grateful for the excuse. "Rose gave me Saturday passes to the big cat show this weekend. She was going to be judging. I figure the least I can do is go, ask around among the other breeders, see what I can find out about the Angora market." Bunny eyed me. "Not for Ivy, but for the cats. Besides, maybe someone will know something about the cattery break-ins and we can get a lead on whoever was threatening Rose." I saw Bunny open her mouth and knew she was about to warn me off getting too involved in an investigation. Time to change the subject: "Speaking of wedding stuff, I got another assignment from *I Do*."

"You're changing the subject."

"Yeah, but it's also true. So if you want any info or back issues or anything."

"You think they've run any stories on handfastings or vegan receptions?"

I was silent.

"Seriously, hon, I don't think I'll need anything from them, but I'm glad they got back in touch. They pay you what you're worth. And they're not going to cut you out for some little bimbette."

"Have you been seeing my former editor around the *Mail* building lately?"

"Let's just say some of his requests for library files have been going astray."

"You're a dangerous woman, Bunny."

"I try."

I turned around in my seat. "So Violet, do you want to go to this cat show with me?"

"Consorting with the enemy?"

"It'd be for Rose. For her cats."

"Or you could always change your mind," chimed in our driver. "And go dress shopping with me and my mother."

We heard a groan and then a thud, as Violet flopped over onto the back seat. Bunny pulled up to the shelter.

"Stay dry." I handed her an umbrella from the car floor. "And I'll pick you up at eleven."

◇◇◇

The phone machine was blinking when I came in, but all but one message proved to be from the same person.

"Theda? It's Lannie. Call me?" By the fourth message, her voice was wound tight enough to snap, so even before changing I dialed the *City* number and asked for the quizzical editor.

"Hey, Lannie. It's Theda. What's up?"

"What's up?" If anything, her voice had ratcheted up a few notches. "Death? Murder? Our millennial women?"

Rose! Lannie had seen the notice in the morning paper. After letting her spew for a bit, I tried to calm her down. Yes, I had known. I had just come from the funeral. Yes, it was horrible. I left out my own role in the discovery of my friend's body and focused instead on saving the assignment. That, rather than the death of a human being, seemed to be uppermost in Lannie's mind.

"We only have three now, and I just don't know if that will be enough. Even with the photos."

Writer that I am, I'd forgotten about the photos. "So Sunny is doing good work?"

"Well, she hasn't shot Coolidge yet. But the photos of Borgia are wonderful. Very..." she struggled for a description, "high tech." I tried to envision this and failed.

"She didn't get to shoot Rose, did she?"

"No, sadly." Regret seemed to be seeping into her voice with that realization. "We have the old photos, and they were pretty fun. Keller had also sent us some of her own press shots, judging cats? What a waste."

Indeed. "Why not use them?" I wanted to salvage the gig, but was also thinking of a last tribute to my friend. Besides, if I had an excuse to ask people questions about her, who knew what I could find out? "I interviewed her. I could still write the piece as a sort of memorial. What was going on with one of our 'millennial women' before her life was cut tragically short." She couldn't see my eyes rolling on the phone, and putting it in *City* speak would, I hoped, help.

"Isn't that a little gruesome? I mean, a murder and all?"

"It would be a fitting tribute. Besides," I was thinking as fast as I could, "readers love a real-life mystery. I even have some connections with Homicide." Not in Watertown, maybe no longer in Cambridge, but I was trying.

"True crime and a proper farewell? A moving tribute? Well, maybe." I could hear her resistance weakening, her usual perkiness reasserting itself. "You'd have to be careful about the tone, though. And Theda?"

"Yeah?"

"If your connections do find out who did it, we want the first rights."

◇◇◇

There was only one non-Lannie message.

"Theda, it's me. Bill." He sounded like he knew he shouldn't take recognition for granted. "I'm sorry about last night. Call me?"

I wanted to, I really did. But the smarter part of me held back. What would resuming our relationship accomplish, if none of the underlying problems had been resolved? I was thirty-three, too old to be spinning my wheels. Did I want anything more with Bill? I didn't belong with Rick, did I? In light of my disastrous encounters of the day before, I was tempted to write them both off, but something Rick had said stuck with me. Maybe it wasn't about what you wanted, or even who you hoped to become. Maybe it was about complementary damage, and knowing which other humans in this cold, cruel world could at least understand what you had been through. I felt a sharp prick and heard something rip.

"Ow, kitten!" Musetta, unused to being ignored, had tackled my ankle. Although the unfamiliar texture of pantyhose seemed to have momentarily thrown her, she had quickly rallied, following up her grab with a sharp nip. The run was spreading as I reached to pick her up.

"Musetta! Bad! Come here!" She bounced down the hallway as if she knew this game, and I had to confess I was grateful for the diversion. "Kitty! Kitty! Kitty!" I darted for her. She slipped by, but waited for me to follow. Finally cornering her, to her purring delight, I hugged her warm, soft body to me.

"Funeral funk, Musetta. You know how it is." She lay back in my arms as if hypnotized, letting me rub her downy white chest. "I thought being with my friends had protected me from it." All purred out, she wriggled to be let down and began to wash. Peeling off the ruined hose, I hobbled toward the phone.

"Hey, Bill." He'd answered his office extension on the first ring. "Thanks for calling."

"I wanted to. How was the funeral?"

I sighed. "It was a funeral, you know? Bunny and Violet came with me and that helped."

"I'm glad. I thought about coming over. But all things considered…" His voice trailed off into a silence that I couldn't decipher. Did he mean that he hadn't come by because we hadn't spent the night together? Or because he suspected the deceased had been killed as a result of her own crimes? Trying for a new conciliatory spirit, I didn't ask.

"You didn't know her." That would be my one dig, I promised myself. "But about last night?"

"Yeah?"

"Want to try again?"

"I'd love to." He sounded so relieved that I felt worse. I mean, I hadn't decided anything yet. "I'm going to be here till about eight," he said. "Want me to meet you someplace, or shall I just come by?"

"Why don't you meet me at the Casbah. I think I need to be out of the house as much as possible today." It was true, but I knew as I said it that I also wanted to see him on my turf. It was a test, a small one.

"Great. That'll be fun."

I hoped so. "Okay, then. See you tonight."

◇◇◇

At least Rick wasn't here, I thought as I entered the club's front room several hours later. Ralph was. Did he ever leave? But the portly writer was so focused on a young goth chick that he didn't notice me. From the way he was leaning on the bar, I suspected that he might not notice much that wasn't half dressed. The young spandex-clad female wasn't having any of it: one leg, covered to the knee in a thick platform-heeled boot, began swinging faster and faster as Ralph droned on. Finally, he must have pushed too far. Her heavy eyeliner accentuated the way she rolled her eyes as she pushed off her stool and clunked away.

"Hey, Theda. Come on over here."

Even out of kiss reach, I could smell the fumes on him. He'd moved beyond beer long ago. "Wanna join me? We can drown our misery together."

"No, thanks, Ralph. Bill is meeting me here." I looked around, hoping he'd be early.

"Ah, the faithful spouse. I need one of those."

Risa, the bartender, caught my nod and brought me a Blue Moon.

"Cheers." Ralph sloshed a half-full tumbler toward my bottle. I involuntarily stepped back.

"Whoa, Ralph. What are we celebrating here?"

"Haven't you heard? The rise of youth!" I sipped my beer and waited, not sure things were going to get any clearer. "Jessica. The great young hope of the *Morning Mail*. She's taking over the arts section. For now, anyway, acting deputy or associate or something."

So that's why I hadn't heard anything about her column—my column, that is. Not that I'd been looking. "Is that bad?" I asked myself as much as Ralph.

"She's twenty-five! She wasn't even born when the Clash played the Harvard Square Theatre." I did the math; he was right.

"Well, she'll have a fresh take."

"She'll have my hide." Ralph sat almost upright in indignation. "Youth culture for the young, that's her motto. She's bringing in all new writers to cover rock and pop."

"But you're on staff." I figured if he could get away with drinking as he did, Ralph had to be untouchable.

"I'm toast, that's what I am. They have me on human interest. Gossip." He hiccuped with a peculiar wet sound and I stepped to the side, out of the line of fire. "Know any celebrities, Theda? I'm on bloody Star Search."

Bill's appearance through the club's glass front door saved me from commiserating further. I patted my sodden colleague on the shoulder and hailed my date. Even without the comparison, he looked great. Bill must have stopped at home, to trade his customary work-day suit for the smoky-gray fisherman's sweater I loved. It brought out the blue in his eyes and felt marvelously scratchy against my cheek as I hugged him, my body relaxing. He lifted my chin for a kiss.

"Hey, you."

"Hey," I replied. So far, so good.

"Young love! So young!" called out Ralph behind me.

"Maybe we shouldn't stay here," I suggested, my earlier thoughts about testing Bill flying out the door. I wasn't sure I wanted him to fit in too well here.

"But I was looking forward to that spicy eggplant dish, and one of Risa's drafts." He was smiling, and I suspected he had guessed at my motives for having him come to the club.

"All right, then. Risa, any tables?" While pulling a pint, the dark-haired bartender motioned to a corner with her chin. Lee, the waitress, was just wiping a table down.

"Lee! Deuce!" The waitress motioned us over and Bill led me through the bar crowd. Another advantage of a tall man.

I sipped at my beer while he ordered for both of us, careful, I noticed, to check every order by me. Truth was, he knew my tastes well enough. That's the plus side of being a creature of habit. We kept the talk light, but warm, as we ate, the day's tension leaving me tired but pleasantly so. Not until Lee was clearing our plates did Bill get serious.

"Theda, I'm so glad to see you. I've been wanting to talk."

Oh, this was going to be painful. I mustered my energy. "Me too, Bill. I'm just trying to be clear."

"I know I dumped a lot on you, Theda. I'm sorry. I do worry about you, but its not that I don't trust you to take care of yourself. It's everything I see every day. Maybe the job is getting to me."

It wasn't that, I wanted to say. It wasn't his concern—I pushed a flicker of anxiety away—or his suspicions about Rose, or not just those anyway. It wasn't even knowing that I couldn't tell him what I planned on doing, that I would be keeping secrets while I looked deeper into what she'd confided in me, into what might have caused her death. My own confusion was what was holding me back. "You're wrong about her. You know that," was what I said instead. Was I such a coward?

"I hope so, Theda."

We left his car and walked back to my place, his arm warm around me in the frosty night. Musetta started twining around his ankles as soon as we entered. When she bounced off down the hallway, she looked back at him.

"She wants you to chase her," I translated. "She wants to play."

He shot me a look that made me wish I'd kept quiet.

"She does, Bill. The cat. I'm, well, I've got other things on my mind. I just need some time to figure out what I want."

"I know, Theda," he said, turning his back on the cat to hold me instead. "I've figured out that much. Look, it's been a long day at the end of a long week. Can I just be with you?"

I'm a sucker for a warm man and just nodded into his sweater. We parted only to floss and brush in relative silence, and after a moment's thought I donned my old flannel nightgown. Bill got the message and climbed into bed behind me. "It's good to just hold you," he said.

"It's good to be held," I mumbled in reply. Within minutes, he was snoring, but despite my earlier fatigue my mind had begun to race. Why hadn't I said what was bothering me back in the restaurant? Why did I let him apologize rather than bring up the real issues I needed to discuss? Was I just letting myself drift again? Suddenly, the flannel—and Bill—were way too warm.

Quietly as I could, I slid out of bed and went into the living room. Out my front window, I could see the waxing moon, two-thirds full, lighting the street with its cold, stark glow. The city looked empty, devoid of life. I sat down on the edge of the sofa, and rested my head on the cool glass pane. Maybe I even dozed, but a rustle from the bedroom roused me.

"Hey, Theda." Bill came into the living room. He was dressed and carrying his shoes. "Maybe this wasn't such a great idea, you know?"

I looked up at him, at his sweet rough face, and none of the things I'd wanted to say came out.

"Maybe we need some time. Both of us." He tied his shoes, then kissed me lightly on the lips. "We're both tired right now." He looked at me, waiting, but I had nothing to say. "Get some sleep, okay?"

I just watched as he let himself out.

Chapter Eleven

If she hadn't been waving wildly, I'd have missed her. Violet stood just off the sidewalk, her olive sweatshirt and camouflage plants blending into the dark green hedge—even if her purple 'do didn't—over by the edge of the shelter's yard as I drove up.

"Theda! Over here." She leaned out from behind one of the tall yews.

"What's wrong?" I slammed the car into park and jumped out almost before it stopped rolling. "What happened?"

"What? Oh, I just wanted to stop you." She was holding a cigarette smoked almost down to the filter. "Before you got to the house." She took another drag.

"Caro's going to catch you. You know that, and it's a good thing, too." Overtired and cranky, I was in no mood to humor my friend's habit.

"I know, I know." With a sigh she dropped the butt and ground it out with her sneaker heel. "I'm going to quit as soon as this semester is over. It's just the transition."

"Yeah right." I flopped back down into my Toyota and waited for Violet to join me. The way she'd startled me—and being back here—made my head start throbbing again. Could the attack have been personal? Intended?

"Musetta wake you with a hairball this morning?"

"Something like that."

She glanced at my face and decided not to ask more.

"Hey, look what I did this morning." She reached into the camouflage pants' big thigh pockets and pulled out a piece of paper. Looking over as I drove I could see heavy gothic-style lettering, dense with decorative flourishes.

"I'm driving, Violet."

"Oh, sorry. Here, let me read." She flattened the paper out on the dashboard and read: "Black cats got you spooked? Haunted by bats? Come to our Halloween Open House and learn the truth about your animal friends."

"I've had signs up for over a week now," she continued. "But I just found this cool typeface and made up a bunch more. Bunny might even have a web site up for us by then, too."

"By when?"

"Next weekend, silly. Halloween is next Sunday. Theda, are you awake enough to be driving?"

I growled in response and we crossed the river. This early on a Saturday traffic was light, and even though I knew we should be taking the T, I was too wiped out to be environmentally conscious. My sins went unpunished as a black SUV pulled out of a metered parking space right by the convention center.

"Why are SUVs always black?" Violet had grown bored by my silence. "Are we supposed to think they're gangsta or something?"

"Maybe it's so they don't get confused with school buses." My mood was lifting. The big, legal parking space helped. "C'mon." We got out and I beeped the doors locked. "Let's go see some cats!"

Rose's passes got us past the uniformed rent-a-cop and into the convention center's cavernous central hall, where a barrage of colors, lights, and noise finished the job of waking me up.

"Number 800 through 813 to ring three, please! Eight hundred to 813 to ring three!" A booming PA accentuated the enormity of the space, echoing into the entrance foyer. Bright yellow banners emblazoned with ring numbers hung from wires criss-crossing the high ceiling, while huge signs announcing the groupings of different breeds—Abyssinian to Turkish vans—towered above us. Even this early, a crowd of at least a hundred bustled about, half carrying cat carriers, the rest leafing through glossy color catalogues. "Number 800 to 813, please." The volume was set on low roar.

"Wow." Violet looked around at the commotion. "This is not what I'd expected."

"Welcome to the show world." Weaving between tables loaded with fliers, toys, and cat-food samples—and a dozen shoppers intent on examining each item—I led us through the first level of the so-called Mew Mart until I found one colorful booth with the purple and gold logo of Cats Fine 'n' Fancy.

"May I help you?" In a maroon jacket festooned with gold braid, the young woman staffing the desk was hard to miss.

"Yeah, thanks. We're friends of Rose Keller, and I was wondering what competitions she was scheduled to judge."

"Rose? One minute please." She shuffled through some papers. "Rose Keller? Oh, I'm so sorry. I have horrible news."

"No! No, we know already." No need to make the poor thing suffer. "We just wanted to know what rings she would have been judging."

"Ring eight. Champion and premier longhairs." Cheeks flushed, she looked down at her papers like she'd find something there. "And, and...I'm sorry for your loss."

"Thanks." She handed us a map of the show floor, and we headed in the direction of the show rings, past a display of nylon cat carriers and another of ornate, carpeted cat trees.

"This puts Pet Set to shame," said Violet, pausing by a table that held at least eight enzymatic cleaning products. "Except for the prices. Wow."

"This is premium real estate, on the way to the cats. But if you want to check out Pet Set's prices, they're here, too." Over on the right, by the corner where the Mew Mart ended and the rows of cat cages began, I could see their bright red and yellow logo.

"They come here to sell?"

"Why not? Or they may be sponsoring a shelter adoption. We can check it out later. I want to see what's going on first." I knew Rose wouldn't be in her ring, but I felt an increasing desire to see her space, to see where she should have been holding court.

"Great. Maybe I can finally find someone who can help me get a copy of that receipt, too."

"Ring two, domestic shorthairs. Domestic shorthairs to ring two!" The loudspeaker rang out as we made our way down the long rows of feline competitors. "Ring service to ring 13 with a mop. Ring service to ring 13, with mop, please!" Lined up in cushioned cages and in plush nylon carriers, dozens of show cats reclined like pashas, sleeping and grooming without any consideration for the dozens of bystanders who filed past.

"Can I pet her?" a little girl asked, watching one breeder take a puffball of a Persian from her box.

"No, honey, she's about to be judged." The child hung her head. "I've just brushed her, you see?" The breeder crouched down and ran her hand ever so gently up the cat's back, fluffing the fine, white fur even more. The little girl nodded slowly and the breeder relented. "Right after, dear. You have your mommy bring you back here."

Suddenly Mommy appeared. "The cat won't bite, will it?"

"Queen Tiki Feathersoft is a grand champion three times over." If the breeder had fur, it would've been standing up along her back. "She has been handled since birth and is a consummate professional!" With a toss of her own perfect coif, the breeder swept the pouffed puss onto her shoulder and stalked off, leaving both mother and daughter in her wake.

"Whoa," said Violet softly. "The cats don't bite but the breeders do." We walked on, slower now, stopping every now and then to look into the fleece-line carriers.

"Ew, god!" Violet had found the bald Sphinxes, and one wrinkled face was staring up into hers. I pulled her away as she collapsed with laughter. "What was that?"

"Violet!" I hissed. "Come on! Some people love those cats." Hairlessness wasn't a trait I admired in a feline, but I'd heard the diminutive breed referred to with affection by others. "Soft and warm as suede waterbottle," was the usual description, and I had to admit the big eyes and bat-like ears had a kind of charm.

"Sorry, sorry." Violet wiped away some tears as she caught her breath. "But that's not a cat, that's…that's…I don't know what it is!"

As I led her away, two more breeders quickly passed us, the cats in their arms unfazed by the noise and commotion around them.

"What's with these cats anyway. Are they drugged?" As Violet turned to look, one of the passing cats—a sleek chocolate short-hair, maybe an Abyssinian—turned his head to hiss at another. "Well, at least that one's awake. But Sibley could kick the crap out of these pussies."

"Sibley?" Violet's acknowledged favorite among the shelter cats was a noted bird watcher, but not much of a fighter.

"Okay, not Sibley. Not since he's been neutered anyway. But Cassandra could." It was true, even after neutering the tiny gray female who had come to the shelter two months prior still had the habit of slashing anyone who came too close. It was going to be a long haul to wean her from her feral ways, if it was even possible.

"You think Cassandra will ever be able to be adopted out?" Violet's shelter had a no-kill policy, but that was feasible only because Violet worked hard to place as many of her cats as possible in good homes, making room for the strays and ferals the neighborhood kids kept bringing by.

"I suspect she's going to be a lifer." We'd reached ring eight and grabbed two of the remaining folding chairs. "But what a mouser!"

Sitting in the second row, we had a great view of the judging area. In front of us twelve wire cages made up three sides of a rectangle. Each cage had a slot to hold that cat's entry number and—for the winners—any ribbons that might be awarded. In the middle of the rectangle, a table with a raised white plat-form, a squirt bottle, and a notebook waited for the judge, its edges adorned with the blue, red, and green show ribbons he or she would soon be handing out. When a short, round man in shirtsleeves hurried up, I expected him to make an announce-ment about who Rose's replacement would be, but with a few whispered words to the young attendant who had followed him he began opening cages. Lifting one heavy cat onto the white platform, he carefully extended its tail for a look, and then began to brush its thick mottled-brown fur backward with his hand.

"What's he looking for? Fleas?" Violet's stage whisper was audible yards away. I shushed her.

"Coloring, fur density. What the undercoat is like. Things like that." I tried to remember what Rose had taught me, and waited for the fussy little man to make his pronouncements. Patting down the cat's fur, he moved on to the cat's head, holding it to look up into his own round face, running his thumbs along its jaw line, and staring into its eyes. But then, without a word, he placed the docile beast back into its cage. After cleaning the platform with the spray bottle and a paper towel, he removed another cat, weighing it in his hands before placing it on the white platform.

"Isn't he going to say anything?"

"I don't know. I thought so." I was out of my depth. I'd come to ask questions, but I had no idea where to begin. The judge was stroking this second cat's fur backward again. Just then I felt movement behind me.

"Rose would have." The soft voice coming from behind us made us both jump. There, seated in the next row, was one of the women I'd seen at the funeral. Tall, slim, with white blonde hair held back in a black-velvet clip, she could have been the mirror opposite of Rose.

"Sally. Sally Frommer." She held out a manicured hand. "I'm also a judge. I helped Rose get her credentials, actually. You were at her funeral, weren't you?"

"We were friends," I replied, making our own introductions. Violet, I said in a hushed voice, ran a local shelter. We knew Rose because I'd written about her, but that was all, I added, to explain our relative confusion. I wasn't about to say that I'd come by hoping to unmask a crime ring, or a murderer. "We're not really into the show circuit. Rose had given me passes, though, and, well, here we are."

By now, the little man had hefted and stretched most of the remaining cats. After making a few notes, he hung ribbons on several of the cages and scurried off.

"I can see where you'd be confused." Sally seemed to take my explanation at face value. "He's a good judge," she continued. "He knows what to look for. But that's not how Rose would've done it. She believed in educating the public, that it was for the good of the cats for people to know what was desireable and what wasn't. She used to talk constantly, while she judged, explaining how to tell the difference between positive traits and those that aren't healthy, what she was judging on and how she was awarding points. Come on, I know who you should see."

We followed her down an aisle of cats—Siamese this time, if the quizzical vocalizations were any clue—past a group of round-faced Russian blues, and into another ring, where judging was already in progress.

"Look at the bones on this boy. Nice heft to him!" The voice that rang out belonged to a squat little woman, and the cat she was lifting, a placid Maine coon, must have weighed close to twenty pounds. "Nice conformation to the body, as well." She ran her hands along his solid form and up to his head, turning him to face the assembled crowd. "Notice the rectangular body and good, strong muzzle."

Unfazed the cat stared straight ahead and, when she placed him back in his cage, began to groom. All in a day's work, he seemed to say.

"Very beautiful tortie." The judge moved onto a swirl-patterned cat, lush with the colors of caramel, coffee, and smoke. "Excellent coat. Look at that color." Placing the cat on the white platform, she brushed the fur backward to expose the soft, rich undercoat, where shades of red glowed against the black. The crowd murmured its approval.

"You see, with judging like that, the crowd learns what to look for." As Sally spoke, the judge examined teeth and eyes and ears, leaning her two chins almost into a fine set of whiskers. "Perfectly spaced eyes. Ears right on top of the head!"

"Too many buyers just go for the name when a certain breed gets hot. Like Maine coons used to be, and Ragdolls are now. Or they go for a certain look, without thinking how the breeder has or hasn't produced healthy, happy animals."

"You mean like kitten mills?" I was remembering Violet's lecture.

"Exactly, but there are degrees. The worst are the ones that you hear about as horror stories, the ones that make the news because they keep the poor cats in all kinds of filth. Sometimes at kitten mills they'll breed the queens every time they go into heat, forcing the poor cats to produce two or three litters a year every year like clockwork until they just drop dead, sometimes with half their kittens. But there are also some unlicensed breeders who kind of barely toe the line. Maybe they don't really know what they're doing, but they'll breed too often, and also pair cats up badly, interbreeding and not looking out for unhealthy traits. All they look for is what the customer sees—nice fur and maybe a cute face—but they end up with kittens who have deformed spines or congenital heart defects."

Violet made a face. "Half these show cats are freaks anyway."

"They're healthy, happy animals." Sally could defend herself. "Descended from your working mouser. Yes, some of them are genetic accidents. The Manx, for example, especially the completely tailless ones, probably came about from some mutation. And they can have spinal problems. But when they're bred right, they're fine creatures. You just need good, ethical breeders, and the way to keep breeders honest is to educate the public. Which Rose did."

"Look at this fellow," the stout judge was saying now, holding a silver-gray Persian up high. "True to color. Excellent mascara around the eyes. Lovely head type and grand ear set. This is my best longhair premier."

"Premier?" Violet asked.

"Neutered," Sally replied. "Only unspayed or unaltered cats can be called champions."

"But isn't the point to breed them?"

"The point is to improve the breeds and raise breed awareness, not just create more cats." Sally, I thought, was losing patience with Violet. I stepped in.

"Some of these are older, right?"

"Yes, and many of them have been bred. But you don't want to keep breeding a cat, especially the females. It may not be as hard as for humans, but it's still exhausting."

"And if you limit the supply…" Violet butted in.

"It's not about demand. There's plenty of demand," said Sally. "A show-quality kitten from a line of champions already commands a price of hundreds, if not thousands of dollars."

Violet whistled.

"In fact, if anything it's getting a little out of control. I breed Weggies—Norwegian forest cats—they're like Maine coons but a little more compact, a more delicate, pointed face. And I can't keep up with the demand. I mean, I personally check out every buyer. Even the kittens that aren't show quality—I have them neutered before they leave my cattery and I make sure they're going to a good home. But it's getting harder. Show cats are becoming a big thing in Asia, Japan especially, and that makes checking out potential buyers more difficult."

"You investigate the buyers yourself?" This rang a bell. Something Bill had said.

"Of course. They're my cats."

That was it: Rose. "Sally, maybe you can explain something to me. I'd heard that before she was killed, Rose was looking to sell all her cats, or a lot of them anyway. But she kept backing out, at least from what I've heard." I didn't want to mention the cops, certainly not the suspicions Bill had passed along.

"Sell her cats? Oh how sad. She must have been harder up than I thought. I mean, despite the prices we can get, most of us are pretty much just making it, once you count in vet bills, show fees, food, litter, and everything. She must have needed money badly." Sally paused and stared off into the distance. "She could've asked me."

"I don't think she wanted anyone to know, honestly." If the word wasn't out about the extortion, I wasn't going to spread it. I did, however, want to blow Bill's theory out of the water. "But the way she was acting—offering the cats and drawing back—would that have seemed strange to you?"

"Not at all. Poor woman, it would've been like selling her children. Hard enough to let the kittens go, but especially if you were selling your breeding stock, you'd want to be careful, extra

careful where they went. Some of those unlicensed breeders present themselves as amateurs. You know, someone says, 'Oh, I just
want to get into showing. Try my hand.' But then they won't buy
a neutered cat, even a show-quality one, and you just know they're
planning something. I wonder what was happening?" She fixed me
with a stare. "Does this have anything to do with her death?"

"I don't know." She didn't blink, and I thought of the cats on
the judging table. "Honest. I think it might, though." I decided
to take a risk. "Sally, I believe someone was threatening Rose."

"Threatening her? How?"

"Someone wanted money, and they were scaring her." Sally
held my eyes with hers, but I'd said enough. If she knew anything, I'd given her a perfect opening.

"Well, then, I'm especially sorry that she didn't come to me."
She turned away and blinked, slowly shaking her head. If she was
faking her grief, she was doing a grand job. "We'd have made a
formidable front."

I was ready to give up. Maybe she didn't know about the
extortion or the cat thieves, but then she turned back to me and
grabbed my arm, her grip strong enough to hurt.

"Theda, if you're right, then I'm involved." I waited, but all
she did was press a business card into my hand. "You hear any
more about this, you let me know. She was my friend, too, and
we women have to stick together."

"Amen, sister," said Violet, and I think she was serious.

◇◇◇

We walked Sally back to her cats and made appropriately apprecia-
tive noises over them, which was easy with the elegant Weggies.
Sally had her own competitions to get ready for, and seemed to put
Rose's situation out of her mind as she got to work, combing her
cats' luxurious long, gray fur. But it was that care, and the obvious
love she felt for her furry charges, that dispelled any last suspicions.
Sally's involvement was emotional; she was on our side.

Which wasn't getting very far at all. I still hadn't uncovered
anything useful. Determined to find out something before the
day ended, I led Violet down a few more aisles, pretending to

look at cats. But when I started asking about security, about anyone's fears of their cats being stolen or hurt, the breeders stopped being so friendly.

"Theda, come on!" I was admiring a sleeping smoke-pointed Burmese, dark nose tucked into dark paws, and getting ready to approach the proud young man by his carrier when Violet started pulling at me. "Now!"

At the end of the aisle, a fussy-looking woman in pink was talking to a security guard, and pointing at us. I'd questioned her just minutes before. Taking my cue, I smiled at the Burmese's owner and we beat it, weaving through several of the displays until we found ourselves back in the Mew Mart. The security guard was nowhere to be seen, but heading back into the breeders' area seemed an iffy proposition at best. I was ready to give up. Clearly, any intrigues here were being well hidden. Plus, I was hungry.

"You know, Violet, I don't even know who else to question. Do you want anything from the snack bar? Or should we call it a day?"

"Umm, snack bar! Let's see what they have. I could spend more time here."

She turned and pointed. "Hey, that's the Pet Set booth. Let's head over there and then we can get some lunch."

The Pet Set booth, almost a little room of its own under the colorful puppy and kitten logo, was set up like a miniature store. As I'd thought, the store was hosting an adoption area, with two rows of cages and a couple of loose-leaf binders with pictures and histories of each cat.

"Hey, look at this fellow. Look at those thumbs!" Violet was using one finger to stroke the big paws of a marmalade tom—or ex-tom, as the bio clipped to his cage made clear—named Ginger. "What a sweet guy."

"He's tested positive for kidney disease," I read from his chart.

"Poor guy. But he seems healthy. He could have years yet, if someone will just take care of him properly." With longing in her eyes, Violet grabbed a sanitary wipe from the box by Ginger's cage and moved on to the next enclosure, where three tabby kittens played with their tails and each other. A sign begged passersby: *Please take us as a family!*

"Why people feel they need to breed more kittens, I'll never understand."

"I wish Rose was here to explain her theories to you." I missed my friend. "But you heard what Sally was saying: The show cats here aren't just bred indiscriminately. They're mated carefully, to bring out the best in a particular breed."

"And so darlings like these are left homeless?" Violet knew as well as I did how many unwanted, but perfectly grand animals were euthanized each year.

I sighed. "These babies will probably find someone to love them this weekend." My voice didn't quite have the conviction I sought.

"Well, what about those kitten mills, then? What about the people who aren't careful, who don't care about improving the breed? Did you see the prices listed on Sally's flier? She's getting, like, eight hundred dollars for a kitten—for kittens that aren't even born yet! You know a lot of people have got to be into it just for the money."

"Violet, these people are more likely potential marks than kitten mill owners." I wondered how many others out there had been threatened. "They've all got to know about those cattery thefts."

"Don't be so sure, Theda. Where there's cash to be had…"

"Can I help you ladies?" Something about our rising voices, not to mention the topic of conversation, had alerted the Pet Set staffers. We turned and found ourselves facing a stylish brunette, her shoulder-length brown bob as sleek as the coat of a Burmese. Her perfectly made up face looked up at us expectantly, and I felt I knew her.

"Oh, sorry." I was suddenly aware of both our volume and our subject matter. Ah well, this store was helping unwanted animals. "We were just window shopping, actually. Cute kittens."

"Yes, they are." She started to walk away.

"Wait a minute." I'd forgotten Violet's quest, but she hadn't. "Hey, maybe you can help me. Are you from the big New Hampshire store?"

"Yes, I'm the manager." Violet launched into an explanation of the missing receipt and her own tax-exempt status, and I searched my memory. Yes, this was the woman who'd been on duty the day we'd shopped there. Probably the one professional overseeing a staff of part-timers and teenagers who didn't know how to take a job seriously yet.

"I can't imagine why I didn't get your phone messages." Her tone was conciliatory, but her expression—cool, a little frustrated, overworked—made it clear she could all too easily imagine any kind of memo going astray. "What was that date again?" Violet gave her the date, rough time and amount, and the manager, Denise her nametag reminded me, repeated it all, before going off behind the red-and-gold banner. She came out with one hand firm on the shoulder of a large young man, a ripening adolescent if his red-pocked skin was any indication, and steered him to face us. He was holding a cardboard box half open as she talked to him, and I suspected he was more useful for brawn than brain. He looked over and then nodded up at her, mouth half open.

"Bruce will get a copy of the receipt out to you right away." She rejoined us. He stood watching, his mouth still open. "I've told him where to look and given him your information. I'm trying to train him, you see. But I will check up on him." If she was exasperated, she was keeping it in check. Bruce had disappeared again. "I'm so sorry, ladies."

"That's great, thanks." My stomach growled audibly—to me, anyway.

"As an apology, I'd like to offer you ten percent off anything you purchase today."

"Really?" Violet's eyes were lighting up.

"Maybe we could come back after lunch?" Soon even kibble would start to look good.

"Of course. I may be heading out, but just remind Bruce who you are. And he'll carry whatever you purchase out to your car for you."

Even if the food stand was limited to shriveled franks and neon nachos, I knew then, we'd be spending the rest of the day at the show.

◇◇◇

"Musetta, I didn't get any answers and my dogs are barking." I headed for the sofa as soon as I got home, having dropped Violet and a trunk full of kitty paraphernalia off first.

"Neh!" Those round green eyes looked up into my face as she replied, and I realized I was being rude.

"I'm sorry, kitty." I stopped in my tracks and reached down to pet her. "How was your day?" In response, she twined around my tired feet and then started toward the kitchen, pausing to rub her velvet jawline against the end table on which the answering machine rested.

"Okay, Musetta, I'll return some calls, once I'm sitting down. But would we like a can first?" She stared at me. Trust humans to have a firm grasp of the obvious. Still, when I held the small can a few inches above her pink nose she obligingly stood up, balancing on her stout hindquarters like a prairie dog. "Very good!" She shot me a look that said one moment more and she'd have batted that can right out of my hand. All grudges were forgiven, however, as I set the full bowl down by the counter. "You know none of the cats there were as lovely as you." She didn't bother to respond as she licked lustily at the moist food. "Or as intelligent." As if on cue, she sat back, satisfied, and with great concentration began to wash her face.

◇◇◇

I hit the sofa and the answering machine button in that order, but none of the messages were anything special. Lynn Ngaio, the clothing designer, had called to say Tuesday would be fine for an interview, suggested a time, and left her cell. Monica Borgia touched base to see if I needed anything else, and, by the way, had just downloaded some tunes from an Austin outfit she was sure I would love. Bunny—sounding more exhausted than I'd ever heard her—reported that "the dress" had been found and ordered, and that she and her mother hadn't killed each other, despite a few close calls. Nothing from Rick and, maybe more to the point, nothing from Bill. I didn't know how we stood after last night, but in the silence after the messages ended I knew it wasn't good.

Just then two small white paws reached up to claw for attention. I hauled Musetta onto my lap. "You want me to call him, don't you?" She kneaded my leg, which hurt. But she looked so happy I couldn't dislodge her, and soon she was purring like a bellows, all her needs met. "Kitty, if only my life were that simple." But it wasn't, so I reached carefully over my supine feline for the phone and settled in for a long gab with Bunny.

"So, tell me about it. Is it satin? Does it have frills?"

"Surely, you jest." My friend sounded more like herself than she had on her message. She credited the glass of Sauvignon Blanc from which she took frequent sips. "I gave in on wearing white, because Mom looked like she was going to cry and she's been as good as she could be about our having a handfasting, and not a church ceremony. But the gown is pretty, I'll admit. Ivory, rather than that flat sugar-icing white, with a high lace collar, like something out of an antique postcard."

"Are you going to put your hair up, Gibson girl style?" I was joking, knowing Bunny's disdain for all things traditional. Truth is, with her pretty, round face and glossy hair she could pull the look off.

"We'll fight that battle when we come to it." A pause, during which I heard more wine being poured. "Speaking of which…"

"Oh no." I had seen this coming. "I'm not doing the bridesmaid thing. In the name of all the years of our friendship, please don't ask."

"You're in the clear!" Bunny was laughing now. "You and Bill are going to stand up front with us, remember?"

Mention of my MIA beau killed my mood. "Bunny." I took a deep breath, causing the cat to jump down. "There may be some problems with that."

"What are you talking about?"

"Bill and I. We're, well, we're not exactly fighting. But we're not seeing eye-to-eye these days. Maybe it's just that the honeymoon period is over, but maybe not, you know?" Before settling in with Cal, Bunny had taken a cynical view of relationships, often stating the belief that cutting your losses was the best option when things got rough.

"Does this have anything to do with Rick being back in town?"

"Why do you have to blame him for everything?"

"Aha! That's not an answer, Theda Krakow. I hear everything, down in the bowels of the *Mail*." So someone had spotted us having coffee together. So what. "That boy—and I use that word for a reason—is no good for you."

"I know, I know." At least, I told myself I did. "The stuff with Bill is something different, Bunny. This has been brewing for a while."

"Well, I've already told Bill to expect an invitation. We consider him a friend."

"Whatever happens, we'll play nice." The thought made my stomach sink. "He's a good guy."

"So, what's the problem?"

"That's the wine asking, Bunny. You know sometimes these things just don't work out. Ouch." I reached down and detached a set of claws from my knee.

"Ouch?"

"Sorry, Musetta has developed a new habit. She's taken to using my leg as a scratching post. I think she wants my attention."

"And maybe she's just too short to slap some sense into you."

I reached down to the plump kitty and pulled her into my lap again, thus reinforcing the behavior. "I'll stick with the former. Hey, are you going to see Violet tonight?" Knowing that Rick might be there, I held my breath for her answer.

"If I'm awake at eight, it'll be a minor miracle." I exhaled, and heard Bunny rouse herself. Cheddar cheese rice cakes to go with the wine was my guess. "Between my mom and the job, I'm wiped." She crunched. I was right. "Give her my love, though, won't you? And tell her that once this planning is over, I'll be myself again."

"I hope so."

"Hey, we can't all be freelancers, can we?"

Something Rick had said tickled the back of my mind. "I'm thinking of calling myself a 'feral,' instead."

"Like the Fauve painters, huh?" I tended to forget that Bunny had an arts background. "Not quite socialized, a tendency to bite. I can see it. But Theda?"

"Yeah?"

"When you find the right hearth, you'll make a very happy house cat. Believe me on this one. I know."

"Goodnight, Bunny." My friend had clearly had too much wine. "Love to Cal."

"Goodnight, Theda. Blessed be. And have some fun."

◇◇◇

A nap, a bath, and a Lean Cuisine topped off with the rest of the leftover ice cream worked me back into a state where I could envision fun being possible. By ten, I was ready to make it happen and, pulling on my turquoise ostrich cowboy boots, felt I even looked the part. Jato's was somewhat more upscale than my usual haunts—the Casbah, Amphibian—plus it was a Saturday night. Dressed in my club best, I angled to see myself in my tiny bedroom mirror. I looked good: black jeans, black silk shirt, black leather jacket that wouldn't be warm enough going to the club and yet would be much too warm inside. Like a creature of the night, all that black made me feel independent, self-contained, a little dangerous—predator, not prey. Feral. I let the word roll around my mouth. Well, maybe I was.

◇◇◇

The club was crowded, a warm and sweaty contrast to the nippy night outside, and a low roar of conversation and laughter greeted me as soon as I pulled the heavy wooden door open.

Already, all the tables were taken, late diners hunched over the remaining candles, drinkers filling in the spaces between and lining the old-fashioned curved bar. I thought about checking my jacket, but I liked the look reflected in the mirror behind the bottles. As I hesitated a voice called out to me.

"Theda! Over here!" Tess and some of her buddies had a table over in the corner, where the bar looped back to the wall, defining a protected alcove. I recognized a few of the faces with her, and worked my way across the floor to join them.

"Hello, ladies." I ordered a beer, and found myself in several conversations at once. Tess' supervisor, someone else's day job. One of the dinner hours' remaining candles flickered between us, flashing off smiles and eyes and various piercings. Tickets to an upcoming concert, a new band someone had just heard, and a political email going around. We were all talking at once, the volume growing louder, until Dena, a bright, beefy blonde, held up a hand. "Wait a minute, wait a minute, what did I just say 'yes' to?" The ensuing round of laughter won us stares from our compatriots at the bar's edge, but none of us cared. Much as I liked feeling independent, there was something to be said for the comfort of friends.

"So, no Bill tonight?" Tess was looking right at me, the candlelight reflected off her big brown eyes.

"This isn't his thing, really." I looked down, felt the warmth of the small flame on my face. "I mean, he likes Violet, but his taste in music runs more toward jazz and acoustic. The kind of music you play, actually."

I was hedging and she knew it. But before she could press, she had to field a question about an upcoming gig and the conversation moved on. But even as she answered queries, Tess kept her eyes on me. I felt bad, but if I couldn't explain the situation to myself, what could I say to her, especially in a noisy, crowded club?

We held onto our real estate through the opening band by ordering another round. The waitress took our candle with our order, but having a table and the solid bar at our backs was worth the extra expense. We were out for fun, anyway. Once the openers, a power trio that revelled in feedback, ended, we turned back toward each other, picking up the threads of half a dozen conversations.

"I hear they're hiring."

"She's not still seeing him, is she?"

"If I went back to school in January…"

I started to tune out, wondering when Violet's set would start. "So, what are you working on?" Beni, a friend of Tess' from work, was asking.

"Nothing too exciting. A couple of short profiles." She nodded, and I noticed she was drinking Perrier with a lemon slice squeezed into the bottle. "For *City* magazine."

"Oh yeah. Cool Coolidge told me she was going to be in that." My eyebrows must have gone up because Beni raised her green bottle slightly. "I know her from around. You know?"

"Oh, yeah." I took the non-alcoholic beverage as a cue. But just because they both went to meetings, I couldn't assume Beni knew about the blackmail. "It's good to have her back."

"That it is. Oh, hey!" Beni was waving and I saw Sunny working her way through the crowd, hindered only slightly by the bulky camera bag around her neck.

"Hi, Theda! Hi, Beni!"

I was in the mood to be generous, plus I was cornered between table and bar. "Evening," I nodded. "What's your poison?"

"Nothing, thanks." She swung the bag from under her arm and fiddled with a lens. "I'm working."

"On assignment?" I hadn't heard that Violet was getting any press.

"For my portfolio. But hey, you never know." I watched her weaving her way back toward the stage and felt my breath catch. "Be right back." I put my beer down and stepped into the crowd. There, against the one bright stage spot still shining, I'd seen a familiar cowlick and the toss of a head: the kind of thing you remember without realizing it. The heat as people pushed together, closer to the stage, amplified my buzz and I felt every one of the two and a half beers I'd finished. Still, was I right? Yes.

I squeezed between two tattooed shoulders, earning the glares of a pair of punk girls, and looked up into Rick's smiling face.

"Hey, girl! What brings you here?"

"Me? I'm the one who told you about this gig." I hadn't known if he'd be into it, really, his bias running more toward the rough, garage-rock sound and boys with lots of guitars. But I had played up Violet's talents, wanting her to get the attention of course.

"That's right." He smiled down at me. "I knew someone whose taste I trusted had turned me onto it."

Just then Violet and her band took the stage. Rick put his arm around me to pull me closer to the front. Sunny would've nabbed my chair by now anyway, so I let myself be carried along and beamed up at my friend on stage. Hair freshly dyed a violent orchid purple, sleeveless black CBGBs T-shirt revealing the Celtic bands winding around her biceps. With the spotlight on her she looked every inch a star.

"One, two, three, four!" The drummer crashed down and suddenly the room was in motion. The song was one of my favorites, an upbeat political number that relied as much on heart as intellect, and I yelled along as Violet's half-screamed vocals exhorted us to stand up. For ourselves, for our sisters, for our world. Maybe not the most profound sentiment, but it was the texture, a throaty growl, that got me, that got all of us, as she screwed her face up toward the balcony and the balcony roared back. Even if we couldn't hear the lyrics, the shout-out chorus giving way to an incoherent roar of vocals, we felt the pull: Violet's voice grabbed us, her guitar forced us to our feet, and the bass kept us steady, the frantic rhythm enticing and receding as the drums built up power.

"This is killer!" Rick yelled in my ear. I nodded back, my damp hair falling into my face. This was what it was about. The next song had us in a sweat as we all bobbed in place, desperate to move. The third calmed us down, letting the bass take a meandering lead that I could feel in my belly as well as hear, with the club's giant speakers right beside us. I wiped a sweaty curl off my forehead and closed my eyes, swaying into the sound, trusting the crowd around me and loving the sensation. When the next song started us all dancing again, I looked up and couldn't help but notice how close Rick was. Even in the sweaty heat, I could feel the extra warmth of his body beside me and see the perspiration gluing his hair to his face, just like mine. This was his music, too. This was what we had shared. Would Bill and I ever feel this close? Did we need to? I must have been staring because I realized Rick was looking back at me, that quirky cowboy grin all confident again. This music, this night: this is where we'd always come together.

He pulled me toward him and I looked up, trying to read his face. All around me was motion, people dancing. I thought I saw Tess waving, her long slim arms reaching over the crowd. Then the band broke, Violet handing off her instrument to take up a second guitar, and Rick kissed me. He felt sweet, and he felt familiar. But as his mouth opened onto mine, my body stiffened up. There was too much history here, too much that would need to be said first. I pushed him away.

"What?" I saw his mouth form the question in disbelief, his lips still smiling and still moist. Why did all the men in my life assume so much of me? I shook my head, the magic of the music broken, and began to edge away.

That's when I saw Tess again. She was definitely waving to me, jumping around in an agitated manner. Catching my eye, she then glanced at the exit and that's when I saw him: Bill. Hunched over so his usual height could barely be made out among the revellers, those still caught up in the sway, he was pushing through the crowd, toward the door, and out.

I made my own way through the crowd and to the door.

"There's no readmittance." The doorman put his arm up to stop me. I shoved by him.

"Bill!" Out on the sidewalk, I was glad for my jacket. The night had grown frosty and hard, my sweat suddenly cold. "Bill!" I looked up and down the street, trying to figure out which way he was headed, but all I saw was empty sidewalk. A late-night bus careened away from the opposite curb.

"Bill!" He was gone.

Chapter Twelve

The rest of the night passed pretty much in a blur. Perhaps because he could see how distraught I was, the doorman let me back in, and I found my friends. Tess had figured out what was up and greeted me with a hug, which helped. Rick, as had been usual for him when we were together, had disappeared. He never did like dealing with me when I was upset. I didn't seek him out.

The Violet Haze Experience had brought the crowd into a frenzy, and objectively I know the rest of the set sounded as great as those first few numbers. But even as Tess' watchful eye was distracted from me, was taken up by the whirl of color and sound our mutual friend made on stage, I couldn't get back into the groove. When the set ended, I made my farewells and headed home. Tess would let Violet know why I wasn't waiting around. Nobody else would care.

Nobody but my kitty, that is. Or so I thought the next morning, when I awoke strangely early and strangely stiff. Even her rounded black back leaning up against me couldn't keep the memory of the night before from crashing down.

"Musetta, it's just you and me again. Just you and me."

She grunted in response, stretched a white mitten out in a yawn, and went back to sleep. So much for empathy. On such a cold autumn morning I should be grateful that she sought me out for warmth.

I willed myself to go back to sleep, since nothing much else was happening, and must have succeeded. When the phone rang, the clock said noon. A reasonable time.

"Hang on," I said to nobody, but the cat looked at me as if I'd insulted her and jumped off the bed.

"Sorry," and then, into the phone: "Hello?"

"Hey, Theda! What a show last night! That crowd was something. And weren't we hot?" Violet's energy level didn't sound at all diminished from the night before, and I wondered if she'd slept.

"Hey, Violet. Yeah, you were. The new drummer is amazing. She had this crazy polyrhythmic beat going that had everyone dancing. I thought the roof was going to come down, the way the place was moving."

"I know, I know. Caro was right up front and she said she was checking the pillars, just to make sure." Violet laughed.

"Hey, I'm sorry I didn't hang around after your set."

"No problem. Tess told me something came up with Bill. And Caro saw you with some other guy, a blond? What's the story with that?"

I reached over and pulled the blanket up around me. "Rick. My ex. He's back in town."

"Uh huh?" Quiet now, she waited. I had to explain.

"There's nothing there. At least, I don't think so. But we always shared the music and I'd told him about your band. We were club buddies once, you know?" She didn't answer.

"And I don't know what's going on with Bill. Sometimes I feel like he's making too many assumptions about us. That I'm being carried along in something that I didn't agree to, and it pisses me off."

"So you get back with the ex you don't feel anything for? I wonder if that knock on the head did more damage than we thought." I hadn't realized Violet liked Bill that much. Either that, or she'd heard more of my stories about Rick than I'd realized.

"I'm not back with him. I was dancing with him. We were hanging out."

Silence.

"And then he kissed me. Just as Bill came in, I guess. But I didn't want him to. I mean, maybe things aren't cut and dried but there's too much that we haven't spoken about, you know? I mean, why am I always supposed to follow their agenda?"

More silence. "Violet? You there?"

"I don't know what you want me to say, Theda. I really don't. I sort of feel like you just gave me a cue to bash men. Like I'm supposed to go on about their insensitivity and all that. I can't say I want to defend the madness that the XY chromosome drives men to." Here I heard a little bit of a laugh sneak back into her voice. "That's not my trip, either. And I don't know this guy Rick. But it just seems to me that if you're not feeling heard, there might be another reason behind it. Maybe it's time for you to speak up and say what you need."

I did not need this. "Thanks so much, Dear Abby."

"C'mon! Cut it out. I mean, as far as I'm concerned, you can have 'em both. But on your terms. Let them know what you want, girl."

"But that's the problem, Violet. I just don't know anymore."

"Well, I do. For a start, anyway. Coffee."

I grudgingly agreed to meet her in a half hour at the Mug Shot and somehow crawled out of my nest. A shower helped, as did a good petting session with the cat. But I still felt raw. Maybe I did need to express myself better. With that in mind—thinking "express, not explain"—I tried Bill's number. I didn't want to apologize, just to talk. But when I got his voice mail my mouth went dry. Coffee first, I promised myself, and hung up without a word.

◇◇◇

Caffeine did help, and after about a half hour Violet's leftover energy became more inspiring than annoying. I still felt like the sludge on the bottom of the pot, but at least I was warmed-up sludge, and so I let her drag me back to the shelter. The lure was a visit with the fluffy mystery kitten, the sib of the two who'd gone missing. The still-nameless baby was a healthy little furball now. The Siamese-like points on her paws and tail and ears had darkened to a delicious chocolate against her creamy fur, and playing "bat the feather" with her was good for what ailed me. But work, Violet had decided, would do the rest, and she set me to laboring with paste, scissors, and paper. She and Caro were putting together materials for the Halloween open house.

"Hand me the glue, will you?" Her denim carpenter's overalls sparkling with green and gold glitter, Caro had taken over decorating the "fun facts" fliers she and Violet would be handing out. I was in charge of the pumpkin, bat, and cat cut-outs that we'd be hanging on the walls. Already, two glittering piles of black and orange paper had grown between the three of us, as we sat cross-legged on the living room floor.

"We're going to need more for the masks," Violet noted, a slight edge in her voice, and I saw Caro write something on a somewhat sticky pad to her left. I made my own mental note to be a little less generous with the gold glitter, and swept some of the purple back into its tube. Bats didn't need that much highlighting, and I wanted to be supportive. This was a new venture, the holiday party, but Violet was committed to having everything be perfect from the start. She'd already explained her plans for the day, which she hoped would draw children and their parents from around our Cambridgeport neighborhood. A little talk about Halloween superstitions and where they came from would start the party. From there Violet would lead into pet overpopulation and the need to spay and neuter, even the "neighborhood" cats that nobody owns. With the heavy stuff over, she'd made a countdown list of how cats help us. "I mean, if you have a choice of a cat or bubonic plague, which would you choose?"

To keep the holiday fun—and to keep the kids' attention—Violet then planned a mask-making workshop with lots of sparkles and pipe-cleaner whiskers, and, of course, supervised visits with the calmer of the shelter occupants. The sleek gray Cassandra, known for striking claws out at anyone who tried to approach, would not be among the official greeters.

"Watch it!" Sibley, a more personable inmate, had come to watch us, which was fine until his long spotted tail began to flick over freshly glued sparkles. "Kitty!" Caro dragged him away.

"So are you going to get into the Druid stuff?"

"You mean, am I using any of the material Bunny gave me?" Our Wiccan friend had responded to Violet's request for help with about fifty Xeroxed pages of religious history.

"Yeah." I reached for the magic markers.

"Some of it. You know, the bits about Hecate, the Roman goddess who they made into the ruler of the witches, pretty much just because they didn't like women having power. And Freya, with her sleigh pulled by flying cats. The kids will love that. But I'll stop there, with the myths and legends. Not the modern stuff."

I wasn't sure that was exactly the intent Bunny had had in mind, but Violet knew her audience best. She must have noticed my eyebrows rising, though.

"Hey, it's the parents, not the kids I'm thinking about." She put down the sheet of orange construction paper she'd been gluing. "I've gotten them to accept me and Caro, not to mention the cats! If I start proselytizing that we should all become witches, whatever Bunny wants them to be called, this place would go up in flames."

It was a joke, but we both stopped.

"You don't think that's what the break-in was about, do you?" Her face had grown pinched and pale.

I shook my head, reaching up to touch the spot where I'd been hit. "I don't know, Vi. It still doesn't make sense." The spot no longer hurt, but it didn't feel quite right yet, either. With all my men trouble, the thought that I might have been gay bashed made me smile. It was bitter, but at least I still could.

"Do you think the cops are any closer to finding out who killed Rose?" She voiced the next question in both our minds.

"I don't know. I don't even know if they believed me that someone was threatening her." I wished I could talk to Bill about this.

"You can't ask Bill, can you?" Maybe Violet really was a witch.

"I'll be lucky if I can talk to him about anything after last night." The cold pit in my stomach started growing again, and the glitter in front of me blurred. I got up. "'Scuse me."

A quick trip to the bathroom to wash my face kept the tears at bay, but walking back I couldn't resist picking up the hallway phone. No answer, just his machine. Before the second beep cut me off I managed to croak a message: "Hey Bill. Can we talk? I'm at Violet's." I could hear Caro and Violet whispering in hushed tones in the next room, but they were my friends and didn't ask why it took me so long to come back in.

Nor did they comment on my sorry output the rest of the afternoon. Four basic cat masks assembled, ready to be decorated, a few more seasonal silhouettes, and I knew I had to go home. Caro was making a big pot of split pea soup, but I didn't think I could manage conversation for as long as a meal. Besides, I wanted to see if anyone had called.

One message. Bill? I hit the replay button.

"Hey, Theda." It was Cool, herself, without Ronnie interceding. But she didn't sound happy. "I wanted to ask you something. I need some advice. You know that thing I told you about? Well, I haven't heard back yet. Frankly, that's not what I expected. I mean, they said 'by the weekend.' And, well, it's making me even more nervous. Call me?"

I did, but the hotel switchboard told me nobody in her suite was responding. Why should I have assumed otherwise on this miserable day? A dinner of Raisin Bran and milk served to make me feel even sorrier for myself, and I retired early, not that sleep followed suit.

Chapter Thirteen

"Cambridgeport cat house!" The morning had broken bright and clear, and I had enough coffee to make a pot. I still hadn't heard from Bill. Then again, my message had said that I was at Violet's. Telling myself that I just needed to hear a friendly voice, I called the shelter. The one that answered was gruff, loud, and just a little off the wall.

"Morning, Caro! You sound lively today! Hey, thanks for the creature comfort yesterday." I fumbled for the pot, needing a refill already.

"Think nothing of it, my girl!" Caro was practically yelling, and I could hear her bustling about the living room as she spoke. Gathering her tools probably. "But you'll want to be speaking with Little Ms. Studious, the Carbon Queen herself."

That's right, I'd forgotten. Violet was due to get her Organic Chemistry midterm results today. A few seconds later, my friend's higher voice was singing into the phone.

"We're feeling pretty good about ourselves today, aren't we?" I smiled despite myself and pulled my Café du Monde mug closer. "What's up?

"Aaaaaaye-Minus!" Violet sang back in a "Here's Johnny" cadence. Behind her, I could hear Caroline hoot and clap. The cats must be going nuts.

"And why the minus?"

"Hey, Caro!" Violet yelled, not bothering to put her hand over the receiver. "Theda just asked me the same thing!" More hoots ensued.

"Seriously, Vi, that's great. Congrats. So, you getting ready for that steak dinner?" I was not going to be jealous of my friend's happiness.

"Am I ever! We're going tonight."

"Well, you've earned it." I stopped myself from saying anything more by downing half my mug. How could I rain on her parade? But although Violet hadn't been my friend long, she knew me well.

"Have you talked to Bill yet?"

"Uh uh." I forced the coffee down. "He didn't try to reach me at your place, did he?"

"Sorry, no, and we've been up for hours. Call him again, Theda. You guys have to work this through."

I sighed. What could I say? "Maybe there's nothing to work through, Vi. Maybe this has just run its course and I should let it die a natural death."

"That's last week talking, Theda. A lot happened, and you forget, I've seen you together. You two have fun together. I think you click, on a molecular level." I could hear a grin sneaking back into her voice. "Sorry. The chem test has gotten to me. But it's true, kid, I like him for you."

I bit my tongue.

"Oh, cut it out." She heard what I wasn't saying, although the words were sticking in my throat. "This isn't because of me being with Caro or anything. You think I'm Bunny, wanting to marry you two off?" That was news to me, if it was true. "I wouldn't blink an eye if a friend wanted to march down the aisle with one of my cats. Well, as long as it wasn't Sibley. He's mine, my own cow-spotted baby. But you and Bill are just so easy together. He relaxes you, I've seen it. And I think you're the happiness in his life. His sunshine."

How could she know that was one of his pet names for me? The unspoken words had turned into a lump too big to swallow.

"I've reached out to him, Violet. I left a message after…well, after the whole thing with Rick at your gig. He can call me if he wants to."

"Ever think he's afraid to? Worried about what you might say?"

It was more likely he just didn't want to speak with me, but that thought made me queasy. "I don't have time for this, Vi. I really don't. I've got to get to work."

"Well, don't let it go too long, Theda." I had to get off the phone.

"Enjoy your steak, kiddo. You earned it."

"Thanks, Theda. Remember, you pushed me to go back to school and I fought you on that. Sometimes you've got to listen to your friends."

◇◇◇

My next call was to Cool, and this time I got through. Sure enough, the blackmailers had never called back. It sounded like cause for rejoicing to me, but to Cool—and to Ronnie, I gathered—the silence was strange and in some ways more menacing than the initial threat.

"I mean, what if they're planning something worse?" Her deep voice sounded tight. "Something big?"

"What else could they be thinking of?" My mind reeled for a moment. "Hey, Cool, are you sure you won't consider talking to the police? I know a cop. He's really a nice guy—" A snort cut me off, and what sounded like a swallow. "Cool, you're not indulging in anything now, are you?"

"No, no, no. This is water, honey. Poland Spring. I'm going to a meeting almost every night. That's where I was when you called yesterday. And I've been working out and seeing a shrink, too. Actually, I'm the healthiest I've ever been, at least in years." As if to reassure me, her voice dropped down and opened up to its more usual boom. Maybe she'd just been thirsty.

"So you're really okay?" How in control was she?

"Yeah, but I keep waiting for the other shoe to drop. I mean, Theda, I'm even writing again. Good songs, too. So how can I go public now?" I could hear the edges of panic creep back in.

"How can I perform? How can I go back into the studio when I don't know when they'll call again?"

I bit my lip to keep myself from repeating the only advice I had, and let my silence answer for me.

◇◇◇

My mood wasn't going anywhere, but what could I expect for a Monday? Determined not to let the entire day be a waste, I made a few calls to florists, explaining to the inevitable machines that I wanted to talk to them for a bridal magazine. I added that the story was for the January issue, timed to help June brides plan their nuptials. They'd call back, all of them, if they wanted what amounted to free advertising. However, none had by the time I finished my lunch-time Raisin Bran, so I forced myself to buckle down on my profile of Rose. It was going to be hard enough summing up a life in seven hundred fifty words, especially the life of a friend. But after such a death—and with so many unanswered questions—the assignment seemed impossible.

Who was Rose Keller anyway? I'd always accepted her at face value: a struggling single woman, trying to make a living in a competitive and offbeat world. I knew she'd loved her cats. Each time one had a litter, Rose stayed home until she knew the queen and the kittens were all healthy and nursing. And each cat went out with a guarantee: show quality or pet, if the new home didn't work out, Rose would take the feline back. In fact, she made all her buyers sign a statement—though whether that was legally binding I had no idea—saying that they promised never to just drop one of her Angoras off at a shelter if they didn't want or couldn't keep it anymore.

Plus, I had learned to respect her as a dedicated professional. It takes a lot of effort, both study and networking, to get as far as Rose had. When she had qualified to be a judge, she'd called me and I'd responded with a bottle of domestic bubbly. I remembered her talking about how much time she'd put in to earn that title. The breeder we'd met at the show, Sally, had spoken about Rose as one of the top in the field, dedicated to her profession. Maybe I could use Sally as a source in the profile. But thinking of her also brought back the rest of our conversation: Rose never had money to burn, and if her passion for cats was costing her more than it was bringing in, well, how far would she have gone? Could Bill's suspicions that Rose was somehow involved in the cattery thefts have any basis in fact?

Somewhere, I knew I had Sally's card. Telling myself that I really just wanted a quote for the piece, I dug through various pockets until it surfaced in Saturday's jeans. Just as I reached for the phone, however, it started ringing of its own accord. Could it be Bill?

"Hello?" I tried to keep the breathlessness from my voice.

"Hello. Is this Theda Krakow?" A woman's voice, a little coarse, and not one that I recognized.

"Why, yes. May I help you?" Whenever dealing with strangers, my mother's training kicked in.

"This is Ivy. Ivy Gellinane. Rose's sister?" Of course. The demanding voice of the suburban matron I'd met at the funeral didn't fit with her polished appearance, but it did jibe with that air of entitlement that had surrounded her.

"Hi, Ivy. How can I help you? Are the cats okay?" If she'd fired the veterinary assistant who was looking after them, I wasn't sure what I'd do.

"You know you said you'd look into breeders for me?" I already regretted agreeing to that.

"Yeah?"

"Well, I've got more now and I don't know what to do with them."

"Excuse me?"

"Cats, kittens. I got a call from the young lady who has been watching them, and I guess one of the cats had its babies."

"Ah, congratulations! But you call them a litter. Have you seen them? They must be adorable."

"I haven't had the time. But I guess there are more to sell now."

"Well, there's more to it than that, Ivy." I thought of Rose's meticulous records, of her careful screening of potential buyers, and her guarantee. "I was actually about to call a breeder, though, and I will ask her if she has any ideas." The thought of buyers made me wonder what else might be in Rose's neat files. "But Ivy?"

"Yes?"

"Can you look through Rose's papers for me? She used to keep records of everyone who'd ever bought a cat from her. That might help us." I wasn't going to tell her that I wanted to look at those files for any other reason.

"You mean, maybe someone would want another?"

"Something like that." I was just casting about, but sometimes that's how I got the best material for a story. Ask questions and read background material: you'd be surprised at what popped up. Maybe those records would reveal something about Rose's murder. Something off, something suspicious. Something that an outsider—a non-cat person, a cop—wouldn't recognize as fishy. Could another breeder have been behind the threats? Someone who had spent a lot of money at her cattery? I had no idea.

"Well, I could call the young lady. She sounded busy what with the new cats, and all. But considering that we're talking about financial records, it would be better if a family member were there."

I bit my tongue to keep from commenting on her priorities, and scrambled for words she might respond to. "I'm sure you can handle the business aspect, but I might be useful in translating the industry lingo. Besides, if you go over there, you'll get to see the kittens. I bet they're just the prettiest things!"

"I'm sure they're fine." In the background, I heard a day-planner slamming shut, another item crossed off her list. "But I'll look through those files, see what I can send you, Theda. And you'll call me about breeders?"

"You bet. And congratulations again. You're a grandma!" I just couldn't resist.

She sputtered a bit, and the line went dead.

◇◇◇

That was fun, I thought, letting her attitude about the cats absolve me of any guilt. And I would ask Sally about breeders.

Who might want to take over an entire cattery full of Turkish Angoras? Who could have wanted to take out the woman in charge?

Sally answered on the second ring, and remembered me right away.

"Did you stay late on Saturday? I didn't see you at any other events."

"We browsed…and bought." I recalled Violet's shopping spree, aided and abetted by the careful attentions of the Pet Set manager. She'd recognized a good customer when she spied one and barely let us out of her sight. "How did you do?"

"Not too badly." Happy pride warmed her voice and I was glad I'd asked. "I've now got two grand champions, and some of my little ones got ribbons, too."

"Congratulations. I'm sorry we didn't get to see them."

"You should come by sometime. We're out in Newton."

"Thanks, I will." Without telling Violet, of course. Despite her warming to Sally as a person, I suspected her bias against show cats would never completely disappear. "But I'm actually calling about Rose."

"I figured as much, and figured you'd get to it in your own time. What's up?"

"Well, do you know about the cattery thefts, the break-ins that have been happening?"

"Do I ever! That's all my breed organization is talking about, and a few weeks ago I installed a state-of-the-art security system. Why?"

I tried to remember what I'd told her on Saturday. "Did Rose ever mention the robberies?"

"No." I could hear her thinking, going over past conversations. "I don't think so. But she wouldn't have, would she?"

"What do you mean? Why not?"

"Well, her cats weren't the type being stolen."

"They were longhairs, and pedigreed."

"Well, yes, but Turkish Angoras are sort of a…" The phone went quiet for a moment, and when Sally came back her well modulated voice was a little quieter, and more careful. "Well,

Rose would hate me for saying this, but Angoras just aren't in that high demand. It's not that they're a dying breed, just more of a boutique cat. I mean, they're lovely and they've got fantastic temperments. But they're not really considered top cats anymore. That was one of Rose's problems. She adored those cats, but their prices were plummeting."

This wasn't news I wanted to share with Ivy, but I'd get to that soon enough.

"So, Rose was probably having money problems?"

"She definitely was. I mean, I'm sure she'd have weathered the storm, but she was facing some hard times."

That was grist for the cop rumor mill. If they knew. I trusted Sally's insight, but couldn't see sharing her information with Bill. Not yet. It was too damning to my late friend. Besides, who knew when, or if, my beau and I would speak again? But enough of that.

"So, which cats are in danger?"

"The big ones, heavy cats in the Persian mode, like Ragdolls or Maine coon cats and even the English shorthairs, because they've got those wide faces and husky bodies. Norwegians qualify, too, though I tend to think of my cats as more delicate than those big babies."

"Have you gotten any threatening phone calls?"

"Calls? No. But I do think someone tried to break in about a month ago. I was showing cats in Oregon, and when I came home my locks had been tampered with—that's why I got the new alarm system. Thank god my partner was around. I stopped posting my show dates on our website after that. Why give the bad guys notice that you're going to be away?"

It was a good question, and I remembered something from the news reports.

"The other break-ins, they happened when the owners were out of town, right?"

"Right. The latest was a judge who was making a special appearance."

"So it had to be somebody who knew the circuit." My brain was warming up.

Sally stopped it cold. "Not necessarily. I mean, a Google search can uncover a lot of this information. Even, probably, potential buyers! But the thieves have been careful. Nobody has been around while they hit these places."

Not during the successful robberies anyway. But what if that had been the plan at Rose's cattery, only she'd been home when the thieves came? Maybe the calls were designed to scare her away.

"So, you didn't get any phone calls? Nothing to ask you to pay up or anything?"

"No, I don't know anyone who has." Sally's voice rose, puzzled. "So someone was calling Rose and threatening her cattery? Why would someone do that? I mean, why would thieves broadcast their intentions?"

For the second time that morning, I had no answers. Before we rang off, though, Sally was able to give me a good quote about Rose—and some info to pass along to Rose's sister. Although Rose's lovely, lithe cats were no longer the height of fashion, they were represented by several breeding societies, of which Sally knew the names of three. I debated doing the legwork for Ivy, and came down on the side of getting my own work done.

Where had I put her number?

"Ivy?" The cool voice that greeted me was a recording. I repeated some of what Sally had told me about the cats' value, but concluded by saying I had the contact info for several Turkish Angora breeder associations. Rose's sister seemed to have the money sense that my friend had lacked, and I knew she'd call me back.

◇◇◇

Without much heart, I made myself hack together some eight hundred words on Rose. I'd trim them back later, but cutting anything out now just felt too hard. Having something down on paper did give me a feeling of satisfaction, however, especially since the assignment wasn't due until Friday, and I congratulated myself on my professionalism.

"Hey, kitty!" Musetta had made herself scarce for much of the afternoon. My writing, at least when it was uninspired—or unaccompanied by gestures—bored her. "I'm a pro. Did you know that?" No response was forthcoming and I realized that I missed having a real human to talk to. Not that Bill ever scoffed at my love for my cat. In fact, he said that the conversations I conducted with the black-and-white feline were one of my more endearing habits.

Okay, that way melancholy lies. It was time I left the house.

Darkness was falling by the time I finally got out, and we wouldn't turn the clocks back for another week. Telling myself that dusk always came early on late October afternoons didn't go far in making me feel less like a social reject. Hey, I had friends, didn't I? On days like this, I almost regretted quitting my day job. With little thought, I headed toward the Casbah, where camaraderie of some sort could always be found.

◇◇◇

I had the bar to myself at that hour, but Risa, the bartender, made for good company. Since it had just turned five, I let her draw me a Blue Moon and she pulled up a stool to chat while I waited for what I realized was going to be my first actual cooked meal in two days.

"So what's up with you?" Risa hiked up the low-rise bell bottoms that threatened to slide even further once she sat down and fixed me with her kohl-rimmed eyes. She'd already told me about her latest studio class in life drawing.

"Nothing so interesting." I reached for a lemon slice for my beer. "In fact, the only nudes I'm likely to see are in your next show."

"Don't look for that." She smiled and reached for her own pint glass. "I'm working them all into abstractions. The lines are fascinating to me. There's so much movement."

I was used to Risa's enthusiasms. A natural, if unfocused, artist, each semester had found her a new medium to love. The previous autumn, it had been video and the back wall of the bar had flickered for months with colored lights and shapes that she called an installation. A new tattoo—a coiled snake—wrapped around her wrist couldn't quite hide the burn scar from her brief infatuation with soldered metal work, last spring. Drawing, at least, sounded safe.

"I look forward to them."

"Next month, you'll get an invitation." The college celebrated the end of classes with a big show and sale. "Bring your boyfriend. I like him."

So much for my buzz. "Well, there may be a problem there. I'm not sure we're still seeing each other."

"Bummer." Risa rolled her coaster around on its edge to avoid meeting my eyes, but she recovered quickly. "Plenty more where he came from, though, huh?"

I nodded an agreement I didn't feel.

"There's that guy you used to see. Blondie, what's his name?"

"Rick." She was trying at least.

"Yeah, he always had that sexy farm-boy vibe going on."

"Among other things."

"Hey, I didn't say you had to marry him." She made a face. Risa was barely pushing twenty-five, so it might have been the idea of a permanent union that got her, but I suspected it was the subject himself. Bartenders see a lot.

"I don't need Mr. Right…"

"Just Mr. Right Now," she finished the line and pushed off the stool. Someone from the kitchen had put a plate on the bar's far end, and I could smell tomato, garlic, and onion as she brought it over. "Bon appetit."

"Thanks." Even the rice, steaming and flecked with parsley, looked scrumptious. When had I last had a real meal?

"Oh, someone else was asking for you."

"Huh? Not Rick?"

"Not the farm boy. Some big lug."

Who would look for me at the Casbah? Without thinking I swung around. No, nobody was behind me.

"You okay?"

"Just hungry." Appetite and loneliness were getting to me.

She handed me the pepper mill without my having to ask. "Anyway, he looked kind of young for you." This was an odd moral position for a bartender, which Risa belatedly realized. "But, hey, who am I to question? I mean, as long as he's legal, that is."

I smiled.

"Anyway, I thought he might be in one of those new emocore bands, and wanting you to write about him. So I told him if he had a package or a CD, he could just leave it for you here. He didn't."

"I hope he wasn't from some band that you trashed." She looked up at me, worried. I guess she hadn't noticed that I hadn't been writing about music lately. "I mean, he was big. Scary big. You ever have problems after that happens?"

"Nothing too serious." Critics become used to being cursed out on stage. Female critics, in particular, get sexual threats at times. But it's just noise, some boy in a band verbalizing his pain. It was all part of the life, and I'd take the hassle if I could get the gigs again. "Thanks for not telling him where I live, though!"

"Hey, I'm young, but I'm not stupid." Just then, a couple walked into the bar. The after-work rush was starting. Without asking, Risa topped off my pint and moved to serve them. I lost myself in the pleasure of well-seasoned pasta, and for a little while my life was good.

Chapter Fourteen

The next day dawned too quiet for my comfort. Despite my determination to have an early night and a good sleep—I'd turned off the phone's ringer—there were no messages waiting. So much for virtue rewarded. Even Musetta seemed distant, having abandoned her usual spot on my pillow for the windowsill before I got up.

"Okay, kitty, I can take a hint. Time to get my own house in order." Calling Bill again would be a good start. So would finishing up what I could on the *City* story or reaching out to more florists for the *I Do* assignment. Then there was cleaning the apartment or getting in shape...given the choices, a run beckoned. I creaked a bit as I reached for my sweats and retrieved my sneakers from under the sofa, but once out in the crisp air the effort began to seem almost worthwhile.

"Ah one, two, three, four!" I sang aloud with the Beatles, and within three blocks my legs began to thaw. This was the first time I'd exercised since I'd been attacked and it took a good while before I began to feel like I had muscles again. A contagious beat helped, and before I was a mile from home I could imagine myself a jaguar, racing through her jungle territory—if jaguars sang out loud, that is. At least my jungle was still a colorful one. Following the recent rains, the last of the season's bright foliage had been battered down, and leaves lay plastered on the sidewalk below me. They made the running treacherous, just damp enough to slide when you least expected, but preserved the bright reds and oranges as a tapestry carpet.

"Here comes the sun." As if on some celestial cue, the song I needed just then came on. And if the sky didn't exactly follow suit, the cloud cover did lighten a bit.

Half hour later, I rounded my own corner and bounded up the stairs feeling loose, fit, and charitable. I'd even call Sunny, I'd decided while pounding down the home stretch. My agreement with *City* magazine to coordinate this story with the annoying photographer had barely been honored, and I knew that was largely my fault.

"Hey, Sunny! It's Theda." As soon as I was showered, I'd dialed her number and stood in my bathrobe waiting for the inevitable machine. Instead, I heard a grunt and then a shuffle.

"Oh hey, wait a minute. I'm here!" All perky myself, I'd neglected to check the clock. Clearly, I'd woken Sunny.

"Sunny," I said, talking slowly and clearly. "It's Theda. Should I call you back?"

"No, no, I'm awake." She sounded doubtful. "It's just my head. A bunch of us went out last night." I remembered my quiet dinner and felt a twinge.

"Where?"

"Oh, some loft party. Jessica from the *Mail* thought it would be a scene."

"Was she doing a column on it?" My column, that is.

"No, Ralph went with me." That explained the hangover. "She sent us both. She's assigning stories now. They just named her to be the permanent deputy arts editor."

I whistled silently while this bit of news sunk in. Had Bunny known about "baby Jessica's" promotion and just not wanted to tell me? Did this mean they'd finally be looking for someone to write the column that I had proposed? Maybe that girl had more than her bustline going for her. And maybe I shouldn't have burned my bridges quite so thoroughly.

Enough crying over spilled tempers. At least I still had a few clients.

"Wow, well, actually I'm calling about the *City* gig." I waited for Sunny's grunt of assent. Good, she was still awake.

"I'm going to interview Lynn Ngaio this afternoon. Want to come? You can shoot after I've talked with her, or maybe just scope the place out."

"What do you mean by that? Why would I need to scope it out?" God, Sunny's namesake disposition did not hold true this morning.

"I mean, just get the lay of the land. See what you might want to photograph."

"Oh, okay. Sorry. What time?" I gave her the info, and directions to the designer's South End loft space, and heard her shuffling about to write it down.

"Just let me do my interview first, okay?" Already I was regretting my generosity.

Once we rang off and I'd dressed, I turned once more to the brief profile of Rose. If I could finish this up today, at least get it done in some form, I'd feel I'd accomplished something. But as I looked down at my own words—detailing Rose's establishment of her cattery, her care and study of the Turkish Angora breed, and her determination to become a judge—I also remembered Sunny's pat dismissal of her. What had she said? Was it that Rose was too old, or didn't make enough money to be important? That was the kind of thinking that could backfire on all of us. I mean, Rose was easily into her fifties, so she had a good two decades on me. But already, at thirty-three, I'd been passed over for that *enfant terrible* Jessica. And if you were looking at financial success as some kind of benchmark, well, Sunny was the one always cadging drinks. Usually, anyway. Honesty compelled me to admit that Saturday, when Violet had played, the thirsty photog had turned down my offer of a free beer. Maybe she was trying to be less of a parasite. And maybe I should try to be a little less judgmental.

"Am I getting old and cranky, Musetta?" Now that I'd settled down at my computer, she'd taken her usual place on the chair behind me.

"Meh!" She yawned, showing her pink tongue and sharp white teeth. I'd have to be content with that.

Determined to start treating myself better, I took myself out for lunch on my way to the South End. The weather was just cold enough so a big bowl of mushroom barley soup at City Stop Café hit the spot, and their news rack gave me an opportunity to peruse both the local papers. Settling in first with the *Mail*, I spotted Ralph's byline right on the arts front. Clearly, he was on his new beat. The story, complete with pictures of famous faces, was a puff piece on a Hollywood actor who was shooting a new movie north of the city, in one of the sailing crowd's favorite resort towns. He must have loved that, hanging around the set just to get quotes like the one that was blown up large over the photo: "We're looking for that authentic New England atmosphere. That's why we had to build an entire nineteenth-century seaport here." But then if editor Jessica was also sending him to loft parties, maybe he'd find a way to work back into music writing.

I decided not to waste too much sympathy on Ralph and turned instead to the news section. Nothing about Rose, which could mean that the cops had nothing to report or just that there wasn't anything that they cared to make public yet. At least there were no stories of new cattery thefts. It seemed a little strange that after eight or so break-ins in the last few months, the crime wave would have stopped completely, but I was sure that Sally and her compatriots wouldn't complain. Maybe all the breeders had upgraded their security systems just as she had.

Switching over to the tabloid *Independent*, I let myself linger over the page-six photos: some movie hunk had been caught with his married co-star. The fact that I didn't recognize the names of any of the players couldn't keep me from enjoying the photos. Obviously staged, their glares of shock and anger as fake as the story, they looked as posed as stars of the silent screen. And as pretty. Perhaps, in that world, you leave your bungalow every morning in full makeup? Well, good for them, if this is what they needed to do to raise publicity.

The pull-out arts section was a good idea, one the *Mail* would be smart to copy. It almost fell into my lap as I flipped through the rest of the paper. And right there, on the bottom of the arts front, was the Violet Haze Experience! One of the tab's columnists had been at the show, and he liked what he heard. The column seemed to be a round-up of local bands, but Violet's was first, with her name and the band's in bold type. "Psychedelic guitar driven by relentless rhythms, the Violet Haze Experience updates the 'riot grrrl' sound for the 21st century." I'd have to call her as soon as I got home, though I bet her phone had been ringing off the hook since this issue hit the streets early in the a.m. In addition to the plug for my friend, it was nice to see that someone was paying attention to local music. Now if I'd gotten the go-ahead for my column, the *Mail* would be giving the *Independent* a run for its money. Their loss.

Warmed by the soup, as well as Violet's write-up, I turned back toward news. Graft, politics, war, all covered as usual in the tabloid's florid prose. Then I saw it: "Local woman's murder tied to crime ring." "Rose Keller, 57, of Watertown, murdered last week in a brutal home invasion, may have been linked to a big-money crime circuit," the tabloid's lead began, and from then on got worse. Keller, as the reporter called her, was known as an "ambitious but cash-starved up-and-comer in the notori-ously cut-throat world of cat breeding," it said. Notorious? Cut-throat? Bad enough that the story made ambition sound like a bad thing. "Sources say that police are investigating her murder in light of a series of stolen show cats, expensive purebreds that could have been sold illegally to put the struggling Keller back on the map." Where did the reporter get this stuff? Who were these sources? Nobody was named, but the information—including that Rose had been trying to sell the majority of her cats, and quickly—echoed what Bill had told me. I found it hard to believe that something so gossipy could have come from the cops. But who else could have leaked it? For the umpteenth time that day, I wished I could talk to Bill.

I could, however, talk to the reporter. He must be a regular on the cop beat, covering crimes like this. Maybe he had sources that I didn't. Regretting, for the first time, that I'd given up my cell, I ran out to the street. There, on the corner, was the last working pay phone in the city. A handful of change got me the *Independent* newsroom and, finally, the reporter.

"Hi, my name is Theda Krakow. I'm calling about your story on Rose Keller today."

"Oh great, another one." The voice on the other end of the line sounded young, and bored. "Let me guess, you're a cat lady?"

I wasn't going to say yes. Besides, in journalist terms I had something better to offer. "I'm the friend who found her body." Sure enough, the voice perked up.

"Oh really, Ms. Krakow? And would you care to answer a few questions?" I heard the ping of a computer roused from its sleep mode.

Damn, there went my career with the *Mail*.

"No, no, I have nothing to say for the record." How often had I been on the other end of this type of conversation? But this was important. "I do have a lead for you though. You cannot use my name. I am not really involved in this anyway." God, I could only hope he'd respect my request—I mean, here I was talking to a journalist and then asking to be kept off the record. "But I do think you should look into Rose's finances further. That's where your story is. Think about it, if she'd been behind the cattery thefts, wouldn't she have been flush with cash? So there's every reason to believe that she wasn't. That, in fact, she'd been trying to raise a large sum of money because she'd been threatened. Maybe even threatened by the criminals behind the break-ins. I don't mean to tell you your business." Which, of course, was exactly what I was doing. "But I think if you poke around you'll find out that she was more likely the victim of this crime ring than a member. Just ask the cops."

"Ask the cops, great." I didn't hear him typing anything. Probably as soon as I said I wouldn't be quoted I'd lost him. But I had to try. "What do you think I've been doing? I got this story because every single woman in the western suburbs has been calling to ask if they're going to be next. The cops aren't talking. This one hint is the only thing anyone's given me at all."

"Well, ask them about threats, about extortion. She wasn't just a random victim, you know." She was my friend, I almost repeated. But then I risked being discredited. Disinterested observer, that's what I had to play.

"Be a lot easier if I had a statement from someone who was there." He was fishing.

"I'm sorry, I really am." For more reasons than he knew. "But go with this, maybe you'll get an even bigger story out of it."

"Right."

"Thanks," I said, and hung up. So the cops were going with the theory that Rose had brought about her own death. At least, that's what someone had leaked to the *Independent*. All the warmth of my morning dissipated, and I set out to do my own work.

◇◇◇

Sunny had beaten me to Lynn Ngaio's studio. When the designer buzzed me in, the slight photographer was already wandering around the large, airy space, taking light meter readings and jotting down notes on a small pad.

"So you must be Theda?" The woman who greeted me could have been a model, if she hadn't already introduced herself as the designer. At least three inches taller than me, with waist-length midnight-silk hair and the kind of almond eyes that perfume advertisers die for, she made the jeans and man-tailored blouse she wore look like haute couteur. "Your photographer is already here. It's Sunny, right?"

I agreed that indeed it was and let her walk me across the concrete floor to where Sunny had begun to browse through what looked like a rack of dresses.

"I see you've found my spring evening wear," said Lynn, deftly maneuvering herself between Sunny's less than spotless hands and the silks and feathers on the hangers. "These are just samples, but I'm very excited." She took two of the hangers off the rack and held them up for us. "Several of the Newbury Street boutiques have already placed orders, and some of the department store buyers may be coming by, too."

"For this spring?" I tried to imagine a Boston in which wealthy women wore colors as bright as these, and couldn't.

"No." She had a musical laugh. "Not so soon. It takes a year at least for everything to go into production. But if they like what they see, then somewhere down the line they're going to place an order, and…" Her eyebrows arched.

That was my opening. I pulled out my miniature tape recorder, and a pad and pen for good measure, and started in. "So you're still looking ahead for a break, even though you've been in this business since the '90s. Tell me, how long does it take to get established in the fashion world?"

"You really want to know?" I nodded, and she burst into a very unladylike guffaw. "Oh baby! The stories I could tell you…."

We talked for a good hour after that. With Sunny still blessedly preoccupied, I got all my questions answered and lots of colorful detail, literally, as Lynn led us around her atelier. A lot earthier than her ethereal good looks implied, she dove into cabinets and drawers full of notions, showing us how she was working a variety of fabrics, beads, leather, and even feathers into updated evening wear. Elegant, sure, but with a sense of fun.

"I've got a friend who would love this stuff." I was fingering a length of rose-colored lace and thinking of Bunny. As soon as the words were out of my mouth, I realized what my comment had sounded like. "I mean, I do, too. Of course!"

Another guffaw. "It's okay!" Lynn laughed almost as much as she talked. "I can see that maybe this isn't your style." Talk about understatement, but that was a kind way to refer to the jeans and long-sleeved T-shirt I had on. "But why not bring your friend by? I'm having a trunk sale, selling off some of my samples, on Friday."

"Well, I don't know."

"I have special prices for people I know." Those elegant eyebrows were raised in suggestive invitation.

"My friend isn't exactly built like a model."

Lynn slapped her own slim thigh. "Well, good for her! But don't worry. I do samples in a variety of sizes. I think it's important for clothes to be wearable by women with real bodies. And more and more, the stores think so, too. So I go out of my way to show them that bright turquoise with feathers"—she held a draping top against her own slender torso—"and purple and gold and green as well as basic black look just fine on full figures. Even zaftig ones." At her use of the yiddish, even I laughed. Only Sunny was silent.

"Okay, Sunny?" Ralph must have done a number on her. I worried that she'd fallen asleep.

"Over here." Ignoring the bright fabrics around her, the photographer was standing by the window, looking through the ancient glass down onto street.

"You okay?"

"Yeah, just tired." She smiled and seemed to rally. "Are you ready for your close-up now, Miss Ngaio?" I was happy to hear that she'd taken a cue from my pronunciation of the designer's name, and left them to it, with Lynn reaching for hangers and Sunny's flash popping in a whirlwind of color and light.

◇◇◇

Four messages awaited me when I got home. None were from Bill. Musetta performed some balletic leaps as I returned two, from florists, and set up visits to their shops for the following week. The third was from Monica Borgia, the web whiz. She had called to chat as much as to inquire about the story, and I ended up on the phone with her longer than I'd thought, telling her about Lynn and, with some editing, about Cool and Rose, as well.

"God, that's awful about your friend."

"Thanks." It was nice to get some straight sympathy, without hearing Rose blamed for her own murder.

"But I'm glad you're still writing about her. Maybe it's more important now, you know?"

Those had been my thoughts too, and I found myself warming even more to the young entrepreneur.

"Hey, do you have any interest in fashion?" I'd been toying with the idea that it might be fun to get some of my "millennial women" together. Cool wasn't likely to come out and play, but Monica and Lynn might just hit it off.

"Well, as you may have noticed, I'm no size six!"

"So much the better." I relayed Lynn Ngaio's defense of full-figured fashion and finished by telling her about the trunk show.

"Sounds like fun," she'd said, before we hung up. I left a similar message—along with glowing descriptions of Lynn's bead and featherwork—on Violet's machine. Maybe she and I could splurge on something extravagant for Bunny, call it a handfasting shower gift. The hell with the boys; we'd have quite a girls' outing on Friday.

There was one boy left to deal with, though. The last message had been from Rick. Sounding a little embarrassed, a little pleased with himself, he'd said he wanted to see me again.

"So, that was some show the other night, huh?" He'd made no reference to our kiss, but his meaning was clear. "I thought there were some sparks in the air. Call me, kiddo, will you?"

I hit the erase button and went to feed the cat.

◇◇◇

If only real life were that easy. Memories of my dinner the night before had me walking over to the Casbah a few hours later. But instead of the quiet that would have let me unload on Risa, I found the club's front room packed and noisy. Making my way to the bar, where a few stools still stood empty, I heard a familiar voice.

"Well if it isn't our fellow feral!" It was Rick. Seated right next to him was Ralph, both of them looking like they had a good head start on me in the beer department.

"Hey, guys," I said, looking around for an empty table.

"Oh no you don't." Rick slid over toward the *Mail* critic and patted the empty stool next to him. "What are you drinking?"

"I'll have a Blue Moon." I resigned myself to the inevitable. Maybe with Ralph here the talk wouldn't turn personal. "But I'm looking to order some food, too."

"Food? What a concept." This from Ralph.

"Hey, how's the 'youth initiative'? I hear you've got a new boss."

"Oh, man, that's too painful to talk about. I need another beer. *Garçon!*" Ralph leaned over the bar to signal Risa.

"That means 'boy.'" Rick corrected him before I could, and then turned toward me. "I'll share some baba ganoush with you, if you'd be willing." I nodded. What was one appetizer between old friends?

"Risa?" The bartender was already refilling Rick's mug and Rick placed our orders, asking for a menu for me.

"You don't have to," I interrupted. I didn't want to drag out this encounter. "I'll follow the baba with the shikel mishi. Thanks." She walked away and I found myself hyper aware of the man on the stool beside me.

"You know Risa's into drawing now. She's got a show at the museum school next month." My eyes followed our bartender as she moved toward the kitchen.

"Really?" Rick didn't look at the bartender once. I didn't even know if my words had registered.

"Yeah, she's gotten really serious about her art since you went away. Been trying different media and everything."

"Theda?" He put one hand over mine and I fell silent. "I wanted to talk to you about the other night, about Saturday."

Why couldn't Ralph butt in when I needed him to? I looked over Rick's shoulder, but the ponytailed writer was busy surveying the crowd for available females.

"Rick, that was a mistake." Whatever was going on with Bill, I knew I wasn't ready to dive back in with Rick.

"It was. My bad. I should have been more sensitive." This was new. I looked up just as he pushed his hair out of his eyes. He reached for my other hand.

"Theda, I should never have gone away and left you like I did, all alone. I was confused, I know that now."

I tried to swallow, but my mouth was dry.

"You know I had problems out there, in Phoenix. But they're not the only reason I came back. Theda, I came back because of you. I missed you. I screwed up, and I want to try again with you."

I didn't know what to say. Two years of back-and-forth, followed by eight months of absence, weighed against the warmth of his hands, the pleading in those big, brown eyes.

"Rick, I've been seeing someone." It was time for full disclosure. "I don't know what's going on with us, but he's been pretty important to me since you've been gone." As I said it, I realized how true my words were. "He's, well, he's sort of outside our circle." I remembered our time in this very club, but images of afternoons in bookstores also sprang into my memory. Of the Cambodian restaurant in Jamaica Plain that he'd introduced me to, and the quiet evenings when he'd put some blues on the stereo and we'd both curl up and read. None of which I knew how to explain. "He's a cop," I said instead.

"A cop!" Rick threw back his head and laughed, then leaned close to me, his long forelock once again falling into his face. "Theda and a cop. No, no, no." He shook his head, and although he was trying to sound sad, I could hear the smile creeping back into his voice. "That won't work at all."

I started to protest that until a week or so ago it had been working just fine, but he put up a hand to stop me.

"Theda, darling, this is what you call a rebound. You can't be serious about a cop. You just can't be. You're never going to fit into the straight world, remember? We're the ferals. I know you, and you are just like me."

Just like him? Since when did he know me, and how did he know I hadn't changed? With that thought, it all came back: to Rick who I was never mattered. Us being together was always on his terms, and always had been. When he wanted, what he wanted, how he wanted it, and nothing I did or said came into play. Why had I even tried to explain?

"You're wrong, Rick. You're wrong but you won't ever believe me. Yeah, I quit my job to freelance. And, yeah, I may be having some career problems, too. But I'm a hard worker and I am willing to change and to grow. I'm going to make my own place in the world—in the straight world even—and I'll do it on my terms."

"With a cop?" He was openly chuckling now, a wide grin on his face.

"I don't know. I don't know what's going to happen with Bill. But I do know that I'm not going to waste any more time on a man who is only there when he wants me, and never when I want him. I'm going to be with someone who listens to me and takes me seriously, or I won't be with anyone at all."

"Have fun, darling. Call me when your cop gets too boring." He raised his beer in a mock salute and swivelled his stool away from me. I fumed for a moment, trying to think of a good parting shot, and then just signalled to Risa to pack my food up to-go.

Chapter Fifteen

I could call it righteous indignation, but the more likely truth is that I needed to prove something to myself. Either way, Wednesday saw me diving into my assignments and clearing a lot of work off my desk, or at least my computer screen's desktop. Two interviews with florists, one of whom provided the requisite white bouquet, were conducted and transcribed, and all my notes on Cool, Monica, and Lynn were if not publishable at least on their way, all put into some kind of prose by early afternoon. I should have been content, but the day yawned ahead of me like a hungry beast, and I had nothing to feed it.

"Musetta?" The kitty, sleeping on the window ledge, opened one eye and shut it again. She wasn't coming to my aid.

Truth was, I felt helpless. After weeks of indecision I was ready to hash things out with Bill, only now I couldn't reach him. And one week after Rose had been murdered, I had the horrible sneaking feeling that her death was already forgotten by everyone but me. The cops were looking to blame her. Her sister wanted to get rid of what had been her life's work. My own feeble attempts at detection had introduced me to Sally, who at least seemed to understand. But that was it—except for nearly getting me and Violet tossed out of the cat show. At least Vi had gotten some more shopping done, and maybe her unlikely rapport with that pet-store manager, a Mutt and Jeff pairing if ever I saw one, would pay off for her shelter. That would be something. But I needed more—revenge, action, some way to attack. I was sick of being spooked by shadows and waiting by the phone. I wanted to fight back.

Just as I was reconsidering my career choice yet again, I was saved by the bell. The phone rang.

"Theda, I've got some papers for you to look at." It was Ivy. I must have been getting used to her brusque delivery because she sounded almost warm on the phone. "I need someone who understands the lingo and whatnot. Can you come over and read them here?"

"Sure, where are you?" I expected her to give me an address on the North Shore. Beverly or Peabody, one of the nicer suburbs.

"Oh, I'm at Rose's. I'll be here all afternoon."

My curiosity was piqued. For her to commit several hours, there must be something at Rose's to hold her interest besides the cats. Besides, maybe I would find something that would give me a clue about who had killed my friend. I promised that I was on my way and, giving my own sleeping feline a quick ear scratch, grabbed my coat and headed out.

The foliage was sparse and brown, but driving up Rose's quiet street brought a flood of memories. I realized I was tearing up by the way the street numbers started to blur, and was grateful for the glossy green holly that marked her house. But as I was waiting at the door the horror of that last visit came back as well. As I rang the front bell, shivers began to climb up my back. Why wasn't anyone answering? Had tragedy struck twice?

Just as I was deciding whether to try the garage door—or run for the cops—I heard footsteps and then the click and sliding of locks.

"Sorry about that." The woman who answered the door couldn't look less like the polished matron I'd seen at the funeral. Sure, her corduroy jeans were from L.L. Bean, and the floral smock she had over the fine cotton shirt looked just as upscale. But the Ivy who stood in the doorway couldn't have seen her own face in hours. Her mouth was bare of lipstick, her mascara had settled raccoon-like below her eyes, and any foundation she'd once applied had been sweated off to reveal a healthy pink glow underneath.

"Ivy?"

"Come in, come in. We're busy."

I followed her into the entrance hall, noting how she carefully locked the new deadbolt behind me. She led me to the left, away from the living room, and into the small, converted sunroom that had served as Rose's business office.

"Here you are. Everything we got back from the police."

On an antique rolltop desk, a present to Rose from their father, sat a pile of papers, Xeroxes by the look of them, all with official looking markings.

"From the police?"

"They took everything at first. They seemed to think it wasn't just a random break-in." I'd forgotten that Ivy might not have heard the rumors and murmured something noncommittal. It would be great if the police found who had been threatening Rose, but it seemed more likely they were following up her contacts in the hope of uncovering disgruntled co-conspirators.

"How'd you get these back?" I started leafing through the pile. Records of litters born and breeding fees. Notes on buyers and potential buyers. Rose's meticulous handwriting, even in these pale copies, made me smile. Looking through these would be bittersweet.

"Our attorney." I looked up at my hostess and recognized, even in the rumpled *hausfrau*, the steel matron I'd seen before.

"Attorney?" I was becoming a parrot.

"They wanted to hold onto everything until the investigation was complete. Small-town cops." She sniffed. "We had our attorney explain that this was an ongoing business and its value once through probate depended in large part on access to records. All the records." Ivy reached over and patted the pile of paper. "We had to remind them again yesterday. Rather firmly. But these copies arrived by messenger a few hours ago. I trust we'll get the originals back in good time."

There were advantages to confidence and an iron will. Not to mention the money to hire what must be powerful lawyers. I wasn't going to complain. Thanking Ivy, I reached for the chair beside the oversized desk, took out a pad and pen to make my own notes, and settled in to work. The letters about judging assignments, including several from out of state, looked promising. Had Rose cancelled a trip that would have taken her from harm's way?

"You don't mind if I start with these here, do you?" It occurred to me that Ivy might want to lock up and leave. I assumed the vet tech had her own keys.

"Not at all. I'll be in the other room for a few hours yet. There's lots to do."

The idea of Ivy, even in her modest outfit, cleaning out her sister's house seemed out of place. Maybe doing chores was her way of mourning, or doing penance. "Cleaning out closets?" I remembered doing that for my parents. It had been difficult, but full of sweet memory as well.

"Taking care of the kittens!" With that Ivy turned on her heel and left me alone with a huge pile of paper and a stunned look on my face.

Two hours later, I conceded that it was hopeless. I'd only gotten through the judging requests and first three inches of unsorted papers, bills of sale for the most part, but these hadn't shown anything out of place. Rose had been scrupulous about her breeding and judging schedules, making no plans at all whenever one of her cats was coming to term. What she had done was keep careful account of where her cats went. In addition to the address and contact numbers of her buyers, she'd jotted down Social Security numbers and brief descriptions of the people and their own pedigrees: "Childless couple. Last year had one grand champion, Russian blue," read one entry, stapled to the back of a bill of sale. "Bit boisterous but very gentle with the cats. He seems afraid of people, knows his longhairs very well," read another, which came attached to a phone bill that showed a long series of what must have been follow-up calls on that particular cat. I thought of Sally's description of Rose's judging, the careful noting of important characteristics, the desire to educate those in the audience. I could see the same impulses at work here, the desire to find good homes for her cats matched only by her wish to enlighten the human populace. Had either of these traits gotten her killed? It all seemed so unfair.

Especially when there were kittens in the house. Using my long reporter's pad to weigh down the remaining papers, I went off in search of Ivy and the new litter.

"Ivy?"

"Up here!" Climbing the stairs, I followed her voice into what I remembered as Rose's second bedroom. Ivy and a young woman I didn't recognize were sitting on the floor inside, next to the open door of what seemed to be coat closet.

"Theda, this is Joy, from the veterinarian's. Joy, Theda—a friend of Rose's." For Ivy, her voice was soft. Joy and I exchanged quiet greetings and I got down on the floor to join them. There, just inside the closet, was the kittening box. An old cardboard box, the size that would have held a sweater as a Christmas gift, had been filled with newspaper and what looked like some wool socks. Whether it was what Rose would have chosen, it looked warm, cozy, and safe, and I could see the vet tech had been keeping it clean and dry. In short, perfect for the new family.

"May I see?"

"Sure." Joy moved over to make room for me. I knew that Rose had insisted that all her kittens be handled from the day of their birth, but I didn't want to disturb the new family. Sliding closer over the wood floor, I saw four little kittens, eyes still closed, curled up against their mother, who looked up at me with sleepy eyes.

"Good girl. What a litter!" After extending my hand to have the momma cat sniff it, I gently touched the kittens, smoothing two fingers along each downy back. One dark little presence woke and kicked. His rounded, flat face looked up toward me briefly, perhaps sensing a new admirer, and then turned back toward warmth and a nipple. The others merely nestled in, taking up any slack their sibling's motion may have created.

"They're gorgeous," I whispered, hushed by the scene. "They're all okay?" Joy's continued presence could signal a cause for concern if she were here in her professional capacity.

"They are now," she smiled calmly. "We had some worries about that little fellow." She pointed to the kitten now nursing, the darkest of the four except for his minuscule pink feet. "He was a little weak at first and we had to warm him up. But he's been making up for lost time ever since. I think they'll all be just fine!"

I believed her, but the tiny kittens looked so vulnerable it was hard not to feel like a protective momma cat myself.

"You know you can't sell them for weeks yet." I looked up at Ivy, remembering her financial interest in the cattery. "You shouldn't even think about it for two months!"

She reared back as if slapped. "What kind of monster do you think I am?"

"Well, you'd talked about selling them before they were born." I was trying to keep my voice down, and hoped she would take the hint. The queen had already woken up and was washing her progeny with single-minded intensity.

"That was before." Ivy's voice grew soft again. Maybe it was the shadowy light, but I thought her face did, too. "Before I saw these little darlings. Now I wonder how Rose could've parted with any of them. They're so cute. And their momma is such a beauty. Aren't you darling?" She reached over to rub the queen behind her ears and the cat lifted her head appreciatively, moving so that Ivy's fingers slid under her jaw. "Yes, you are."

The sound of purring filled the room. If only Rose were here to make the family complete.

It would've been impossible to go back to the tiny office after that. But when my butt grew numb from the wooden floor and Joy moved to gather more clean bedding, Ivy surprised me yet again. Even before I asked, she told me I could take Rose's papers home. "Just make sure you get them back to me," she'd said, albeit quietly and with just a vestige of her former sharpness, when I finally creaked to my feet to leave.

Carrying the bundle out to my car, I thought once more, sadly, of her sister, my friend, who had made this little cattery so homey and just maybe had made Ivy more human, too. It was so unfair that she wasn't here to share all of this. Even the day had turned beautiful, clearing to a classic October crispness. The trees might be almost bare, but driving home I noticed several jack-o-lanterns decorating porches, some carved into childish faces, others obviously helped by adult hands. Someone, somewhere was breaking in a fireplace or burning a last load of leaves, as well, the tang of wood smoke scenting the air. I'd try Bill one more time, I decided. He'd understand why days like this mattered.

◇◇◇

"Bill," I rehearsed what I'd planned on saying. "We need to talk. Our time together deserves that much." No, that wasn't going to work. I'd have to wing it. I reached for the phone and dialed. As I'd expected, his voice mail picked up.

"Bill, it's me. Theda." So much for great beginnings. "I'm going to Central Café tonight, going to get some dinner, stay for the music." The little restaurant had been one of our favorite hangouts, with good food and interesting acoustic acts on Wednesdays. "I'd love to see you, and I think we need to talk. If you think so too, you can find me there."

"Do you miss him, too?" That was to Musetta, who was trying to body-check my shins by throwing her full weight against them, purring her grunty little in-out purr all the while. "Yes, we do, don't we?" Lifting the elastic feline into my lap, I settled in for a good petting session, working on her ears with one hand and leafing through Rose's papers with the other.

Two hours later, Musetta had fallen asleep and I was close to joining her. To say that Rose had kept careful records was an understatement. Financial records for her home and car, various insurance policies, and complete histories of both human health and veterinary care were in perfect order. The details on the cats, particularly, bordered on obsessive: Each kitten sale, it seemed, was followed up by copious notes, many of them made after the cat had settled into its new home and Rose had called or visited to check on its well-being. Each stud fee was noted along with facts about the male cat who had stayed in the little cattery, as well as numerous health certificates, and for the queens that Rose's studs had impregnated, descriptions of the catteries and the accommodations where the mating couple had spent their brief honeymoons. Several of these files ran to twenty pages or more, with receipts and phone bills stapled in, along with copies of Rose's hand-written notes.

I pitied the clerk or secretary who'd been stuck by the copier, Xeroxing all of this and trying to keep it all in order before restapling it, and could only imagine the clout Ivy's high-priced lawyer had brought to bear on the department to expedite it so quickly. But none of what I was reading sparked any suspicions. As far as I'd gotten—up to the week before she'd died—Rose seemed to be making ends meet, barely but solidly, with no unusual deposits or wild expenditures on equipment, food, or new cats. And all the kittens she'd sold looked like they were bred in her Watertown home. There was no evidence of suspect cats, or even other breeds besides her beloved Angoras, being sold. No outside cats had been placed as pets or show cats. If Rose had joined a conspiracy to steal and sell show cats, she'd done it just days before her demise.

I'd wanted to get through all the papers, and clear my friend's name. But by seven the numbers were beginning to blur. It was time to put the files, and my own snoozing kitty, aside. As scary as the thought of facing Bill was, the need for something besides financial records—something that would include food—served as spur enough.

◇◇◇

The air had turned from nippy to downright cold, but that enticing smell of wood smoke lingered as I retrieved my Toyota and headed over to Jamaica Plain. Maybe the café would be grilling pizzas. Bill and I could share one, if…. Not wanting to think too much about the confrontation ahead, I turned on the radio. My favorite college station was playing the news, so I let the tuner drift. A commercial, another commercial, and some sports. Then, suddenly I heard a familiar voice. It was Cool, crooning into a torch song, only her guitar and a bit of piano behind her. She sounded like a young Billie Holiday on this song, from her first album. Her timing, her phrasing—sexy, but hurt—called for you to pull over and listen.

I kept driving, but did catch myself singing along. Which made it all the more jarring when the song ended and the DJ back announced the cut with a question. "That was Cool Coolidge from her debut CD," he said, his smooth FM voice conveying some mild form of unhappiness. "Now what ever happened to her?"

I'd have to call Cool tomorrow, or tonight if I ended up home early enough. She seemed so strong now, so pulled together. But even if she kept it together, and had heard the last from those would-be blackmailers, could she recapture her audience? The idea of being washed-up before forty seemed preposterous, especially for someone who had such a gift. But that DJ had probably voiced the feelings of a lot of her fans: wistful, maybe, but ready to move on.

Was that how Bill and I would be? I pulled into an almost-legal space on Central Street and hesitated for a moment before getting out of the car. Is that what I wanted, how I wanted it to end with him? Just a week before, I'd been wondering if things were moving too fast. Then Rick had re-entered the picture, confusing everything for a moment. That wouldn't work, I knew that now. Rick was still the same charming boy, but I wasn't going to be content to be his sometime girl, his club buddy, no matter how much we loved the same bands. Still, I had to keep the obvious in mind: Rick and Bill were not the only options out there. Was I missing Bill just because I didn't have anyone else around? Because he took care of me when I was hurt and scared? Or was it something special about the gray-eyed man I'd come to know?

These were the questions that I chewed over as I sat in the café and waited for the music to start. I'd grabbed a two-top, wishful thinking perhaps, but positioned myself facing the small corner that served as a stage. The café wasn't so crowded that I was keeping anyone else out of a seat, and in a few minutes I'd give in and order myself a solo dinner. Bobby Rains would be playing soon; he'd greeted me in the bar area on the way into the café proper. His rockabilly would sound a lot more like country with just himself and one guitar, but one look at his greased-up hair and flashy Western shirt and I knew he'd put on a fun show, albeit quieter than usual. Bill or not, I could still enjoy a few hours here.

"Another pint?" The waitress broke into my solitary thoughts.

"Thank you, yeah. And I'd like to look at a menu, too."

"Be right back with both." I watched her as she took my empty glass through to the bar and caught my breath as, right after, a familiar face appeared. Bill, looking around and not yet seeing me, his long face a little hesitant, a bruised look around his eyes giving evidence of a couple of days of hard work, or lack of sleep.

"Bill! Over here!" I couldn't help yelling, nor jumping out of my seat. Even the old fisherman's sweater, which I'd tried to patch in a moment of domesticity, made me smile.

"Theda." He nodded and made his way over, but the weary look remained.

"Hey." I could feel myself smiling and felt absurdly happy. "How are you? I've missed you."

"I'm okay." He said it tentatively, like at any moment something could break, and ran one large hand over his salt-and-pepper hair. I realized then that he was as nervous as I'd been.

"Bill, before you say anything, let me explain." Damn, I'd meant not to use that word. "Saturday night. When you showed up, what you saw.... That wasn't supposed to happen."

He jerked back as if I'd slapped him.

"No, I don't mean that you weren't supposed to be there." This was getting all confused. "I meant that Rick wasn't supposed to kiss me. I don't think of him like that anymore. I don't. I really don't." As I said it, I realized just how true that was.

He looked down at the table and picked at the tablecloth. Only when he looked back up could I see how close to tears he was. When he spoke again his voice was low, almost a whisper. "Would you be saying that if I hadn't run into you there?"

"Yes. Yes, I would. He and I are over. That was just..." I scrambled for the right words. "It was making sure that we no longer fit."

"You looked awfully happy." Bill sounded more like his regular gruff self suddenly, but that also meant more like a cop.

"I *was* happy." Would I ever get over my defensiveness? "Violet's band was playing, and they sounded great. I was out with my friends. I was dancing. I didn't even know Rick would be there. I mean, I had told him about it." Honesty pulled that last bit out of me.

"You didn't tell me about the show." Bill looked down at the table again and for a moment I was speechless. Then he looked up, laughing. "Christ! Can you believe I just said that? I'm sorry, Theda. I don't know what's been up with us. But, why didn't you tell me about Violet's gig?"

"I didn't think you'd like it." That sounded lame. "I mean, I think you just put up with half of my music just to humor me." I tried to remember what I'd been thinking. Had it only been four nights ago? "Plus, well, things have been sort of strained between us."

"Yeah, I know. That's why I went over to the club that night. I mean, you're right. I like Violet, but her music...." He shook his head slowly.

"I think she's great."

"I know, I know, Theda." He reached out now, palms up, waiting. I put my hands in his. Now was the time to broach the big subject.

"You see, Bill. That's one of the things I've been thinking about. I mean, for so long that music, that community has been my life. It's not my entire life, but it's a big part of it, and I don't want to give it up."

I looked up into his face, into those gray eyes, and realized he was watching me intently. "I, well, I know that you and I have a connection, Bill. And I've never meant to hurt you. But I can't give up part of myself because it doesn't fit into your world. And I can't keep dragging you around trying to force you to fit in."

His smile lifted half his mouth. A start. "My eardrums thank you."

I didn't share the humor and pulled back, my hands balling up into fists. "That's what I mean, Bill. I'm saying that I don't feel heard. That you're not hearing what I am trying to tell you about my friends, my crowd, my scene. That—I don't know—maybe it's because you're older than me or because you're a cop. But sometimes I feel like you just brush me off, like I'm being some silly kid." Was I overreacting to a joke? Probably. "Okay, maybe I am overreacting," I said aloud. "Maybe I am silly, too, but that's who I am right now."

I opened my mouth to continue, but realized that I'd said it all. The big issue—the age disparity, the power, the presence—the whole ball of wax. And he was still sitting there, listening.

He waited a moment. My hands unclenched and I flattened them out, palms down, on the table. Was he watching to see if I had more to say? Finally, he leaned back, but slid his own large hands forward a little until just the tips of his fingers touched mine. "I'm sorry, Theda. That was just a crack, and a stupid one. I said it because I'm nervous. I'm nervous in part because you keep poking your nose into things that could be dangerous, and someone has already attacked you. And I'm nervous because each time I try to hold you back, try to protect you, I know I'm also pushing you away."

I looked up at him, at those sad gray eyes and his dear battered nose, his wide mouth now set in such a serious line. He leaned forward again and took my hands between his thicker, rougher ones. "I do hear what you're saying, Theda. You're saying I don't love the things that you love, that I don't fit into your world, and sometimes that's true. And you're saying that I try to protect you, which is also true. But you see that as a sign that I don't trust you, and that's wrong. I worry, but I do respect who you are. Maybe I have to work harder at showing it. Maybe I have to try a little harder at understanding your world. But I want to. I will, and I do love you."

◇◇◇

I tried to speak again, but nothing came out. Then the gentle placement of a pint glass on the table reminded me that we were in a public place and I looked up to take the menu from our waitress as Bill put in his order for a draft—and a second menu.

"So, you're staying for dinner?" I could ask that.

"Looks like. I mean, I'm hungry. We're here." He was smiling now for real, his long, dear face crinkling up.

We ordered and drank and greeted a couple of familiar faces. Sunny had even stopped by, long enough for Bill to get her a drink on our tab. She was shooting tonight, but I guess her proscription against drinking while working hadn't lasted. The music, when it started, was not what I'd expected, but good: Bobby Rains doing his best Roy Orbison. Despite the distraction, our conversation kept replaying in my head. I was still confused. "Bill?"

"Yes, my dear?" The smile had reached his voice.

"How are we going to work this? I mean, you and I are very different. I know that, but half the time I don't even know what I want these days."

"You wanted to see me. You called me."

"Yeah. But Bill, I can't make any promises. I'm just full of contradictions right now."

"You're a complicated communicator," he said, quoting one of my favorite Liz Phair songs. I coughed up a little of my beer in surprise. When had he heard that? I raised my eyebrows in surprise, but he only tipped his glass toward mine in salute, took a sip, and turned back toward the stage.

Chapter Sixteen

I woke up alone, with Musetta pressed against the back of my head. But a pleasant hum in my body and the coffee keeping warm in the coffee maker reminded me of the reconciliation Bill and I had enjoyed the night before.

"Watch it, kitty." Rolling over to sit up, I nearly flattened her, and she stretched a paw toward my mouth. I eased my way around her and reached for my robe.

"Off to work, sleeping beauty! Talk to you later." The note propped up on my favorite mug might be corny, but it made me smile. I tucked it into my robe pocket as I poured myself some coffee, and realized that life seemed a lot simpler this morning.

First thing, I realized, I should call Cool. It didn't matter if she listened to my advice about calling in the cops. Just like it didn't matter if she was going to meetings. Cool was a friend who was facing a difficult time. Even if I had nothing concrete to offer, I wanted her to know that I was around for her.

Then I needed to call Ivy back. I had an idea for a photo for my story, and I wanted to strike while her mellow mood lasted. And finally, I decided, as I pushed some papers aside to make room for my mug on the table, I'd finish the *City* assignment and plough through the rest of Rose's paperwork. There wasn't going to be anything in that pile of notes and transactions, I was already pretty sure. I couldn't do the police's job for them. But I owed it to Rose to give it an honest shot. I'd not rest easy until I did.

"Hey, Ronnie! It's Theda." As soon as I'd refilled my mug, I'd started making calls.

"Good morning, darling. You'll be wanting to speak with Miss Cool, I'd imagine?" Gone was the hesitation, the guarded wariness of the week before. "She's just coming in now."

"Hey, girl, you're up early!" The Cool I remembered rarely rose before noon.

"I've been up for hours, Theda. Pilates and a run, then an early meeting."

"I should get a run in. I've been, well, not as regular as I should be with my exercise." To compensate, I took a long pull off the mug.

"Well, do it soon, Theda, and then come on over! Sunny is going to shoot me for your story, and it would be good to have you for company. Besides, we could talk after."

Supervising photo shoots wasn't my regular practice, but I remembered my resolve. For emotional support, I could lend an hour or so. Cool told me the shoot was scheduled for noon, and I promised her I'd be there. It sounded like she knew Sunny, either from the old days or even that original "Women of the Millennium" assignment, but I could understand being a little more comfortable in the company of a friend. Besides, I'd also promised myself that I'd collaborate more closely with Sunny, no matter how annoying she was. Maybe all that friction would spark some good ideas.

Calling Ivy was a little more difficult. Her home voice mail had so many options it sounded like a business line, and I left my name and number on extension four, hoping that was right. On a whim, I tried Rose's old number and had to catch my breath when a voice answered: "Rose Blossom Cattery."

"Ivy?" For a moment, I thought a ghost had answered. "Is that you?"

"Yes, who is this please? We're very busy."

"Sorry, sorry." That brusque delivery was definitely Ivy. "It's Theda. For a moment there, I was, well...."

"Oh I'm sorry, dear." Her voice softened. "I must have given you a shock. Mother always said we sounded a lot alike."

"It wasn't just that. The way you answered...."

"You mean, identifying the cattery? Well, Theda, I've been thinking."

Count on Ivy to keep business front and center. As long as she had cats to place, including the new litter, she'd be keeping the cattery open, and that meant staffing the office and phones.

"I'll do as much of it as I can to keep expenses down. Though I've got my own obligations, of course."

"Of course. But speaking of those kittens, I have an idea I wanted to run by you."

She waited. I shuffled my thoughts into a form that would show a profit. "You know that I'm doing a story and that Rose was supposed to be part of it?" As I gave Ivy the rundown on the *City* assignment, she made the kind of happy murmuring sounds that made me think she was impressed. After all, suburban matrons make up most of the magazine's readership. "Well, my editor agreed that we could keep Rose in it as a tribute. Salute all she was able to accomplish. And so, especially because you're looking to sell the cattery, and find proper buyers for those adorable kittens, I thought that maybe a photo of you and the new kittens would be a great way to close the story. Sort of 'Rose Blossom Cattery lives on.' It'll be irresistible—to buyers, I mean."

"Hmmm, the cattery's next generation. I like it." Ivy sounded subdued. Perhaps she was more affected by her sister's death than I had given her credit for, or simply computing those increased profits. "It gives me some ideas. But, yes, sure, that's fine. As long as the photographer doesn't bother the kittens or the mother cat, that is."

"Great, I'll run it by my editor and if she okays it, I'll contact the photographer." I thought about passing Ivy's phone numbers along to Sunny, then thought better of it. Ivy needed to be handled with care. "If this works out, I'll call you back and we'll set something up. When it's convenient, of course."

That done, I read through what I'd written the day before on the "Millennial Women" profiles, and decided that they weren't too bad. Twenty minutes later, the prose was as polished as it was going to be—and three minutes later, the story was filed. I put a call in to Lannie at the *City* offices and left a message telling her to check her email for the piece, one day ahead of time, I was proud to add. I also quickly explained my idea for the cattery photo before her voice mail cut me off. Which left Rose's papers. Or a run. Not that Cool had made me feel like a slacker or anything, but the light shining in my windows was too clear and beautiful to do nothing more than illuminate some papers. Pouring the rest of my coffee into the sink, I went into the bedroom to find my sweats. It was time to hit the road.

An hour later, I was a completely happy animal, wet with sweat and newly in love with the world.

"It's beautiful out, Musetta! Too bad you're a confirmed house cat." Woken by my outburst, the cat on the sofa stretched and grunted. "Neh," she repeated as I approached her, and rolled over on her back.

"Oh, don't be so blasé about everything. It's a marvelous day." She deigned to open one eye as I chucked her chin, and licked my sweaty hand. I resisted the temptation of that fluffy white belly and let her resume her beauty nap as I went off to shower and change. One toasted bagel later, I was ready to face Rose's remaining paperwork.

"Musetta, what's this?" I'd been starting on my second bagel when I'd reached a particularly thick file. Brushing the crumbs aside, I worked the staple out and prepared to start reading. Musetta, now at my feet, reached her claws up.

"Oh no you don't." I leaned over to hold her paws before they could find purchase in my leg. "That's a bad habit, little girl. If you want my attention, you'll have to find another way to get it." I released her and she jumped onto the chair beside mine. "Much better, Musetta. Much more civilized." Then she reached over and started pawing at Rose's files, threatening to tumble the growing pile I'd already read. "Kitty!"

I moved fast and must have startled her, because with one quick motion she leaped over the edge of the table, taking with her the stack of papers I had just loosened. I grabbed at them too late and they fluttered to the floor.

"So now you want to play?"

Two green eyes peered out from under the sofa, daring me to reach for her. But all I had time to do was gather the pages and restack them. I was due at Cool's. "Later, kitty. I'll make a foil ball and we'll bat it around. I promise."

◇◇◇

"I may as well have spent the morning playing with the cat," I found myself telling Cool twenty minutes later, as I watched her button up an emerald green raw-silk blouse. The stiff collar gave shape to her rounded cheeks, and the subtle sheen of the fabric played up both her eyes and hair. "There's nothing in those papers to help me. On the other hand, there's nothing there that says she was a catnapper, either."

While Sunny fussed in the suite's main room, arranging lights and furniture, Cool and I were getting her dressed, which meant that I talked while she pulled out clothes and makeup. Despite her fame, she'd nixed the idea of a professional makeup artist with a broad "Oh, please!"

"A catnapper?"

"The cops seem to think that Rose was involved in some kind of band of thieves, that she got herself killed. But I don't see anything in her records that gives a shred of evidence for that."

"You sure you don't want me to call someone in?" Sunny stuck her head through the door. "I know a makeup artist who lives in Back Bay."

"That's fine, darling. If I can't paint my own face by now I'm hopeless." Sunny opened her mouth to object—facial highlighting for a photo shoot, after all, is a far cry from a Saturday night sprucing up—but Cool interrupted her. "You know how many of these I've done, darling. Don't worry about it."

"You two know each other?"

Cool was applying the second layer of a dark red lipstick, but she made a noise that sounded like an affirmative.

"Of course, from the old days, same as with me." I was thinking aloud, as if Cool were my cat. "Anyway, do you mind that I'm telling you all this?"

"Mmm-mmm," or some other sound I chose to interpret as "go ahead" came from behind the lipstick.

"Well, anyway, I'm just trying to figure out what I can do next. I tried talking to people at the cat show last weekend."

"And?" Cool had moved on to her eye makeup. I felt a surge of sisterhood to see that she, too, opened her mouth while putting on mascara.

"Nothing. Almost got us kicked out, too. What I'd really like to see are her phone records."

"Calls she made?"

"Calls that came into Rose's home phone. Rose told me that she'd been threatened. That someone called demanding money. But the cops looked at her records and said there hadn't been any calls that didn't have a good explanation."

Sunny stuck her head back in. "I'm ready for you whenever, Cool!" It was amusing how polite and deferential the petite photographer became in the presence of fame.

"One more minute, sugar." Cool reached for the powder. "So tell me about these phone records."

"Well, that's just it. I'd like to look at them. There's one fat file of papers left, and I'm hoping there's a copy of all her calls in there."

"You think you'd find something the cops missed?" Picking up a gold, gauzy scarf, Cool walked into the living room and settled on the sofa, one hundred percent a star. I followed and Sunny jumped to attention, adjusting lights and pillows.

"Well, I'd like to take a look at them anyway. Maybe they didn't check everyone out."

"They called me." I looked up in surprise at Sunny, who was holding what looked like a huge silver balloon.

"The cops did?"

"Oh yeah. I had to tell them about this assignment and that I was supposed to photograph her. Joe Cacciatore over at *City,* the art director? He backed me up."

"I thought you hadn't gotten in touch with Rose." I remembered Sunny's dismissal of my friend. In contrast with her deferential treatment of Cool, here and alive today, it still got me riled up.

"Did I say that? I'd called her. Never got through, though. But the police checked me out all the same. Hey, Theda, would you hold this?" She handed me the inflatable reflector and moved me to where the lamp shone right in my eyes. So this is how the people outside the limelight were treated. I tried to remember if anyone had vetted me. After all, I'd telephoned Rose on the very day that she said she'd been threatened. My statement must have covered all that, not that any of what I'd told the officer on that dreadful day was clear. Between my friendship, and the assignment—not to mention my obvious shock at finding the body—they must have cleared me of any possible involvement. Unless, of course, I was a suspect. Would I even know?

"Hold!" The flash blinded me and left floating rectangles of blue and white inside my eyes. I'd have to ask Bill about that phone log as well as my own status in the investigation. Still squinting, I let Sunny move me again, this time remembering to blink.

◇◇◇

Two more outfits and ninety minutes later, Sunny was wiping her forehead as she packed up. I was still seeing bright shapes. Only Cool seemed as calm as if the day hadn't started yet, but when I moved to help Sunny carry the lights down to her car, she put an arm out to stop me. "Do you have a minute, Theda?"

"I'll be right back," I promised. I might be blind, but I could still be a friend.

Two trips later and I could almost see. Cool, meanwhile, had washed off her heavy stage makeup so that her skin glowed.

"You look great." I flopped on the sofa in a much less graceful pose than my friend had assumed.

"Pilates." She took the chair next to me, sensing that I wanted to put my feet up. I did. "Organic food. And a clear conscience."

My eyebrows went up. "Something new?"

"Nothing, which is strange." Her clear brow knitted for a moment, then she leaned over and took my hand. "The black-mailers never called back. But that doesn't matter."

"Do you think it was a hoax?"

"No, no. They—she, it, whatever—sure sounded serious. But I don't care anymore. It doesn't matter."

I sat back and waited. Cool was building up to something with the same timing she'd use for a song.

"I'm sick of it, Theda. Sick of the hiding, of the secrecy, and of feeling ashamed."

"Yes?"

"I'm going to go public. I haven't told my label yet and, to be honest, I'm not sure how they'll react. But I need to do it. For me, you know?" She pulled back, her serenity briefly clouded by doubt.

"I think so." I sat up and this time I took her hand. She sighed, a long, deep sigh. "Do you think the label might drop you?"

"Yeah, they might. I've broken a lot of promises to them—and to everyone. But I'm sick of hiding. Sick *from* hiding." She sat up straight. "I'm healthy now, and I'm not going to run from who I am, or who I have been, anymore." As she spoke, her eyes sparkled, making her look like some kind of Celtic goddess. I could see, finally, how much the fear had been weighing on her.

"Just by looking at you, Cool, I can tell this is the right move for you." Lord, I hoped I wasn't just spouting nonsense. "However it plays, you know I'm here for you." More of a safe-guard would be nice, though. "And, well, since you're going to go public anyway, would you consider talking to the cops? You haven't met my boyfriend Bill, but I'm sure he could set you up with someone."

"No, no, I don't want to deal with the dark side—the down side. That's the whole point of just being open and honest. I'm going for the light, not the darkness."

"But just making those calls was a crime. They threatened you. Don't you want to know who did it? Make them pay?"

"I did it to myself, Theda, in my own way." She must have seen my confusion. "I made myself vulnerable. I'm the one who did things to be ashamed of."

"But, but…" I was struggling here. "How can you stand not knowing? I mean, you thought you were hiding out here." It hit me: "Cool, it has to be somebody here in town. Who else would know?"

"Or someone back in LA. Or on the road." She was shaking her head slowly, sadly, back and forth. "I was pretty gone for a while."

I wasn't giving up. "No, it has to be someone who knew you were here, because they knew where to reach you. And it has to be someone who knew you had pulled yourself together enough to be worried by what you had done. Someone who knew you had a career to lose again." The possibilities began to assemble in my head. "It could be someone you deal with every day, Cool. Someone you trust. Your personal trainer, maybe?"

"Not likely. I'm too good a customer. And with me as a reference, she's pretty much got it made."

"What about your shrink? No, I guess not." She was laughing at me now, but it was a soft laugh and gentle.

"Okay, then, what about someone from one of your meetings?"

She shook her head firmly, the laughter gone. "That couldn't be. You know our motto: 'What you say here, stays here.' It's the only way the program works. I believe in that. But, Theda, this is pointless. I know you're trying to help, but honestly I don't care if those calls did come from someone I see every day. I'm letting go of the shame and the blame. I am choosing to put all of that behind me."

I sighed and reached forward to give her a hug, because that seemed to be what she wanted. Maybe I wasn't as evolved as my friend was, or maybe I was more suspicious. I believed in letting others live in peace when they left you in peace. But when people try to hurt me or try to hurt my friends, at the very least I need to know who they are.

◇◇◇

When Bill and I hooked up later I was so close to telling him that my jaw ached from clenching it. It wasn't my secret, though, and so I swallowed the stiffness, along with a large serving of black beans and rice that my beau had whipped up in his Inman Square loft. They tasted of garlic and vinegar, with a bit of red pepper bite, and along with some pan-fried trout and nutty brown rice made up the healthiest meal I'd eaten in recent memory. Would Bill ever cease to surprise me? He mostly talked while I ate, catching me up on some office politics that lost me after a few minutes. I appreciated the effort, though. The man was trying to let me in.

"So, if Tai gets the promotion, what happens to the new position?"

"The promotion is the new position." He scooped us both out generous seconds and fixed his eyes on me. "I'm boring you, aren't I?"

"No!" I nearly tossed my spoon in protest. "I mean, well, I'm a little confused, but I really appreciate you telling me what goes on in your day to day. To be honest, it doesn't sound that different from what went on at the *Mail*."

"But you've got something else on your mind." It was a statement, and he looked at me to run with it. "How is that head of yours anyway?"

"It's fine." I nodded—no pain. "But it is pretty full of questions." I sucked the remains of some savory beans from my spoon, trying to figure out just how much I wanted to reveal. "First off, am I a suspect in Rose's murder?"

"What? No. I mean, I seriously doubt it." He had his work face on now, his generous mouth set in a grim line, but he seemed to be telling me the truth. "Why would you be?"

"Well, Sunny—the photographer on the story?—said the cops talked to her to find out why she had called Rose before she was killed. I gather her phone number showed up on some records. She said they checked her out pretty thoroughly."

"Well, you said that she'd been receiving threatening phone calls."

"I didn't think they took me seriously."

Mouth full, he still managed to look up at me with cynicism. It must have been the eyebrows.

"I mean, when I told the cop who took my report that her cats were threatened, he looked like he was going to rip out the page he'd been writing on and throw it away."

"Theda, Watertown may not be Cambridge, but it does have a good police force. Believe me, someone in Homicide went over everything in those statements."

"Well, if they're so good, why are they leaking things to the paper that just couldn't be true?" I thought of the story I'd read about Rose. "Rose wasn't part of any crime ring, Bill. I've been over and over her financial records—bank statements and everything—and there is just no proof of that." It hit me then that if someone had illegal profits, that someone might have hidden them. No matter. "Besides, I know Rose. Knew her."

That last bit wouldn't hold much water in terms of evidence, but it was true—and it was why I was so convinced. Bill opened his mouth to speak, closed it, then tried again.

"You've been over her records?" His voice caught a bit on that.

"Yeah, the cops returned her papers to Ivy, Rose's sister. I was hoping I'd find something, I don't know, evidence of a threat. The police's log of her incoming calls. What I found were meticulous, detailed notes on every single financial or feline interaction she had. And all of it, all of it, looked perfectly normal. I know this stuff."

"Better than a forensic accountant?" At least he looked amused.

"Maybe in this case. But you're not answering my question. How could such a nasty rumor be leaked to the press?"

"Spoken like a true journalist." He ate some more while I waited. Then he looked up. "Theda, do you believe everything you read?"

"You mean it's not true?"

"This isn't my investigation, Theda. You know that. But let me say it wouldn't be the first time that incorrect information was leaked in order to tease someone out of hiding."

"So you do think that Rose was killed by the cattery thieves! Or, the Watertown cops do."

He sighed. "I really can't get too involved in this, Theda. But let's just say that I would still be looking at all angles."

"Such as?"

He shook his head. "Theda, I love you. But someone out there isn't afraid to be violent. Please, leave it to the professionals." For the sake of peace, I didn't answer. He was being as good as he could be, and I wanted to meet him halfway. Besides, it would be so incredibly satisfying if I could surprise him. Over dessert, we talked about a present for Bunny and Cal, and decided to skip coffee in favor of bed.

Chapter Seventeen

"I'm home, kitty. I'm home!" The biggest problem with staying at Bill's was the guilt I felt at leaving Musetta alone. She had probably been fine before I got home around noon, after a detour for a long-overdue grocery trip. But my voice, as I worked my way down the three locks on my front door, had agitated her until her pitiful mewing nearly broke my heart.

"I'm here, kitty girl. Come to momma!" But as I put down the bags and reached for my black-and-white furball, she turned on her heels and dashed down the hall. It wasn't company she wanted. It was play. And I still owed her.

"Okay, kitty, let me get my coat off." I dumped my jacket and bag and looked around for anything that would roll or bounce. Musetta beat me to it, however, dribbling a crumpled-up piece of paper like a soccer star.

"Mia Hamm doesn't have anything on you, kitty." As I reached for it, she sent it flying underneath my CD case and looked up at me in anticipation.

"Uh, goal? Hang in there, kitty." Grabbing a coat hanger and poking under the shelf I was able to retrieve the paper ball, which came out trailing a dust bunny that was nearly rabbit-sized. "Hold on, Musetta. Let me clean this off." Pulling the dust off the impromptu cat toy made me glad that Bill hadn't stayed here last night. Though, truth was, if he was going to love me, he'd love me, housekeeping deficits and all.

I threw the makeshift ball again and Musetta winged it into the back room. I followed, and that's when I realized that I hadn't locked the window overlooking the fire escape since opening it the earlier in the week. Was it Monday, the last fine warm morning?

"Oh, good move, Theda." I thought of the three locks carefully attended to up front. "But no harm done. What?" Musetta had knocked the wadded-up paper back to me. "We've found a good one, haven't we girl?" She looked up at me expectantly. "What is this anyway?"

I'd become too oblivious to my surroundings and decided to uncrumple the paper we'd been kicking about. There was type on it, and I flattened it out to see what it said. "Kittens for sale," I read, and recognized Musetta's toy as the flier that Violet and I had first seen, almost two weeks ago, posted by the Pet Set store. I also remembered what Sally and Violet had been telling me, about kitten mills and home breeders. Was this sign for one of their unhappy litters?

"Hold on, kitty." Reaching into a kitchen drawer, I ripped off a length of aluminum foil and balled that up for her. One toss—a ricochet against my right speaker—had her after it. I heard the skittering as she knocked it down the hall. She'd run herself tired and sleep half the afternoon.

I, meanwhile, had other things to do. Without any real plan in mind I reached for the phone.

"Hello? I saw your flier about the Ragdoll kittens?" I should have done this when I first saw the flier.

"They're all gone," said a gruff male voice. His gender—and his answer—threw me. But maybe that was for the best.

"Oh, um, do you expect any more?" If this was a kitten mill, wouldn't they say yes?

"No, no more. We're out of business. Who's this calling anyway?"

"Never mind." I hung up and tried to puzzle it out. I wondered if that harsh voice could belong to an innocent home breeder. Or, I hoped for the cats' sake, the breeder's alienated teenage son. It hadn't been a pleasant voice. But that reference to "business" didn't sound good, certainly didn't sound pet friendly. Could the kittens have gotten sick? A kitten mill would be especially vulnerable to an outbreak of distemper. The thought made my breath catch. Dozens, even hundreds, of kittens could die.

Was there any way to report a suspected kitten mill? A suspected former kitten mill—in a neighboring state? It seemed unlikely, and I knew my local animal control officer was busy enough with her own Cambridge turf. I should let it go. If it had been a mill, and it had been wiped out by distemper or something like it, I was too late. I should have called last week.

Besides, I was due to pick up Violet and meet Monica at Lynn's trunk show. I balled the paper up again and tossed it for Musetta to find in case the foil ball grew tiresome. But as I went to change out of last night's clothes, one question kept dogging me: if the advertised sellers were operating a kitten mill and it was truly out of business, whether from money or disease, what had happened to the mothers of those kittens?

◇◇◇

"So tell me again what this is?" Violet smelled of cigarettes, but she wasn't smoking when I picked her up so I didn't say anything as she hopped into my Toyota.

"Lynn is having a trunk show," I explained. "It's kind of like an open studios for clothing design."

"Does she make anything in black?"

"Not much. But she does do purple," I replied. "Actually, she does a ton of stuff with beads and spangles and feathers. I thought maybe we could chip in and get something for Bunny."

I heard a grunt of assent. "Oh yeah. No feathers, though. I'm not spending cash on a sweater that turns into a glorified cat toy as soon as it gets home." Bunny's two cats were rarely disciplined.

I agreed, and as we headed over to the South End, told her about the flier and the phone call—and about all the kittens being gone. Just as I had, she found the whole exchange ominous.

"You sure you heard him right? He said 'the business was closed'?"

"Yeah, that was pretty much it, anyway. He definitely used the word business. But even if it is, or was, a kitten mill, what can we do?"

"If we knew for sure, we could call the local animal control. It's illegal to keep animals in unsafe conditions, you know. Even in New Hampshire."

"But we don't. And we don't know where they are. But here we are." As I'd feared, even this corner of the onetime industrial area was busy on a Friday afternoon, and between the traffic and the lack of parking, it looked like we were going to have to circle.

"There's a…no it's a hydrant."

"I'm going to try the dead-end up ahead." We waited at a light.

"I've been thinking." Violet broke the silence.

"Well, that's good."

"No, seriously. What if we're looking at this the wrong way. Maybe the kittens didn't all get sick and die. I mean, that wouldn't necessarily put a kitten mill out of business—they'd have another litter on the way, sooner even because the mothers wouldn't be nursing. What if they'd sold all the cats, not just those kittens, but sold the whole shebang?"

I shot my friend a look and almost missed a pickup truck pulling away from the curb. "Huh?" Braking, I grabbed the space, much to the annoyance of an SUV driver behind me.

"Well, you remember what that breeder lady, Sally, was saying. There's big money in cats. Maybe the entire outfit was bought out by someone who wanted a ready-made business, a bulk of cats."

"But if someone wanted to sell their whole enterprise, why would they advertise on a telephone pole in New Hampshire?"

"Oh yeah, right."

We trotted up the stairs and into the Ngaio atelier. Over in the corner, Monica was chatting with the designer.

"Hey, Theda! Glad you could come!" Lynn looked surprisingly elegant for a woman wearing what seemed to be a feather duster on her elbow.

"Wow, Sibley would love that," said Violet, almost under her breath.

"Who's Sibley?"

"No, he's not getting it." I interrupted, before Violet could explain. "Actually, we're thinking of a wedding gift for a friend. She loves fun clothes."

"Oh, that's great." Lynn was in her element. "What else does she like?"

"Cats." Violet was not going to be suppressed. "Cats, cat toys, and computers."

"And shiny stuff," I jumped in. "Because of the cats, maybe we should stay away from the feather trim."

"How about these beaded pieces?" Lynn led us over toward the large window. There, a dozen long, tunic-like jackets sported enough sparkle even for Bunny. Monica pulled a turquoise and black patchwork piece over her sweatshirt. Even Violet was intrigued.

"One problem solved." She pulled one jacket off its hanger and headed for another.

"Any of these come in size sixteen?" I asked.

"No problem," Lynn jumped in. "All my clothes come in real-world sizes."

The petite Violet looked up at the tall, lean designer, but she was smiling with approval.

"Good for you, girl. Good for you. Now if only you could help us with our other problem."

"Maybe I can." Lynn was smiling.

"I doubt it." I had to be the voice of reason. "It's probably impossible and has nothing to do with clothing. And, well, it's not really based on anything much."

Violet interrupted me: "We're trying to figure out why a kitten mill would close suddenly. Like, with a going out of business sale." The term "kitten mill" didn't seem to be registering, but before I could explain, Violet broke it down: "Where would anyone unload a whole bunch of cats?"

"Like, a foreign country?" Violet looked up expectantly, but Lynn continued. "Well, in China they eat cats."

Monica gasped, and Violet dropped the jacket she was holding. I quickly grabbed it and brushed off the nonexistent dust.

"Hey, don't look at me. I'm from Lowell," said Lynn. Violet was still staring. "And my family is Vietnamese, not Chinese."

"It was just the idea," I interrupted, not wanting to have to stop a fight.

"No, no, maybe she's onto something," said Violet, stepping away from the rack. "Remember what that breeder said about the Asian market?"

"She was talking about the Japanese. They eat sushi, not cats."

"I know, I know." Something was coming together under Violet's purple mop. "But they're wild about collecting. They go crazy over certain breeds. What if those kittens are going to Japan?"

"Without papers?"

"They're a fad, there, right? The buyers don't care about breeding. They love the looks!"

She could be right. Maybe.

"This could be crazy," I thought out loud, but Monica was already turning toward Lynn. "Do you have a T-1 line?"

She looked a little worried. "My web guy might. But he's in Hawaii right now."

"Show me your computer."

Lynn led the four of us off to a corner, where a shoji screen hid a high-powered home office. Propped up on four filing cabinets, a large tabletop held a flat-screen computer, a fax-printer, and a scanner. Monica pulled up a chair and began to type.

"Password?"

"Clotheshorse."

"How do you spell? Forget it. I'm in. Okay, what are we looking for? Fads for cats?"

"Try pet-store owners or articles. Anything on Ragdoll cats."

A flurry of rapid typing pulled up a few notations, all in Japanese. "Hang on." A few more keystrokes and Monica had the documents translated. "Ragdoll beauties" exclaimed one headline. "Dolls of your heart," another.

"We already know they're popular." I had to state the obvious. "That doesn't mean anyone is smuggling cats into Japan."

"They don't have to be smuggling them." Monica typed a few more lines of commands and the screen went blank. The machine whirred. "What we're looking for are announcements of cats for sale."

"There are always cats for sale. Breeders take orders years in advance."

"That won't work in Japan. I remember how consumer crazy their markets are. If these cats are hot, people will want them now. Like this." Sure enough, she'd pulled up an ad from a Tokyo paper. Translated it said: "Peach-puff soft, fuzzy furballs." Beneath the headline was a basket of kittens, long fur fully fluffed, blue eyes shining out of round, chocolate-tipped faces. "New shipment of American ragdolls this week! Dozens to choose from!"

"Do you realize how farfetched this is?" I was getting caught up in this, but some part of my mind recognized that it didn't make much sense. "That's like saying 'American blue jeans.' Those kittens were probably bred right in Tokyo. Or, or in Singapore."

"Singapore?" Violet shot me a look. "Maybe. But do you want to take that chance?"

"And what do you suppose we do?"

"Call the Customs hotline," piped in Lynn. I'd almost forgotten we were in her office. "There's an anonymous tip line the Feds have set up for anyone who may know something about illegal imports. The kind of clothes I do, I get offered a lot of strange things. Exotic animal skins, feathers from endangered birds, you name it." She pulled a business card out of her Rolodex and handed it to me.

"But that's for imports. These animals might be going out of the country."

"Give it to me." An exasperated Violet snatched the card from my hand and stalked over to the corner of the office to make the call. A few minutes later she was back, looking a little sheepish. "Okay, that didn't go so well."

"They didn't care about cats being sold illegally?"

"Well, they wanted details. Like when and where the cats were leaving from. How many there were, and who was shipping them." She looked up at me. "I realized I couldn't really tell them anything."

"That's okay, kiddo." We all stood there, looking at the computer screen. "Ragdolls of the Heart! Here Soon!" Those round faces looked so innocent. Monica typed in the commands to power the machine down. The image disappeared.

◇◇◇

"You think maybe those kittens just all got placed?" Violet and I were driving away. We'd managed to find an outfit that Bunny had to love. It lay wrapped on the back seat, forgotten.

"Maybe. Or distemper wiped them out."

"No, the mothers would have survived."

"Maybe it wasn't a kitten mill, then. Maybe the kittens are just gone, sold or given away. And Groucho and his equally sunny family are left with the kitten's mother, and she's just a regular house cat."

"Maybe this time they'll get her spayed."

"Maybe." Neither of us believed a word we were saying.

Chapter Eighteen

I'd already told Bill that I wanted to check out one of the bands playing Amphibian that night, and he'd sworn that it would be his pleasure to join me. So even though I was still somewhat disheartened—and two more calls to florists had done nothing to lift my mood—I took my cue from the frou-frou I'd been looking through all afternoon and tried to make myself somewhat fancier for the evening. In my case, that meant brushing my hair and putting a little eyeliner on, as well as cleaner jeans. But I was pretty pleased with the result.

"What do you say, Musetta?" As if on cue, my cat rolled on her back to take my measure upside down. With her mouth half opened, one white fang visible, she looked a tad demonic. "Good enough for rock and roll? Close enough for jazz?" She blinked, which I accepted as acquiescence, and after a quick belly rub I was out the door. "If any of those damned florists call back, ask them why they don't want free publicity, will you?" I thought I heard a chirp—"mrup!"—as I locked the door, all three locks, behind me.

The stage was barely set up when I arrived at the downstairs club, but I wasn't taking any chances. Sara Linda, a singer I'd loved back when she'd fronted the Crullers, had been added in the earliest opening slot. Whether I ever got to write about the local scene or not, this was my world. I didn't want to miss any of it.

"Hey, Theda!" Sara waved from the impromptu stage, where the sound man had just rigged up monitors. "Glad you could make it."

"There'll be more of us." I knew Bill was likely to miss Sara's set; Fridays he tended to work late. But I'd told everyone I'd run into this week about Sara's gig.

"Theda!" I had just taken a seat and was both pleased and surprised to see Cool descending the stairs, past a cut-out carica-ture of a witch and another of a black cat. God, I hoped Bunny wouldn't notice those if she came by. Sara, a few years younger than either of us, was star-struck into silence. Her mouth slightly open, she sort of resembled my cat.

"Hey, glad you made it." I really was. Cool had said she'd try to come out, adding that since her decision to go public, she'd felt safer and freer than she'd been in years. Still, an opening set in a tiny basement? Cool Coolidge?

"Cool, this is Sara. Sara Linda. Sara, Cool Coolidge." Once more in the green silk shirt from the photo shoot and a pair of chamois pants that fit like a second skin, Cool could have stepped right out of a big-bootie video shoot, and I couldn't blame Sara for stammering her hello.

"Pleased to meet you," Cool smiled at the younger singer. "I think I remember the Crullers. You had that radio hit, right? And Theda says you're just grand."

"That'll throw her off for the first three songs," I whispered to my friend as we went back to our table.

"She's got to get used to it sometime, poor fool." The waitress came with our drinks, a draft for me, San Pelligrino for Cool, and we settled in. Sure enough, Sara did choke on the first song, repeating a verse twice. But she pulled herself together by the next tune, and soon was singing unselfconsciously, working her lovely soprano along with her finger-picked guitar.

"Brava!" Cool and I stood and clapped and yelled when the set was over, trying to make enough noise to cover up the fact that we composed fully a third of the audience. Making a mock bow, deep enough for her shoulder-length dark hair to fall over her face, Sara acknowledged us and slunk off. But she didn't look unhappy.

"Trial by fire for that girl," said Cool, still standing. "She'll be okay. So, where's the bathroom around here? If I'm going to keep drinking bubbly water…"

"Behind the stairs." I pointed and as she wandered off I saw Sunny descending.

"Sunny!" My mood had been lifted by the music, and by Cool's company. I headed toward her. "You missed Sara's set! She was great."

"Damn. I know when they add a fourth band they start early, but…ah well."

The waitress walked by and I signalled her. "Sam Adams, right?"

"Yeah, thanks, Theda. You with your boyfriend tonight?"

"He might come by later. I'm with Cool."

"Oh!" She looked even more shocked than Sara had been.

"Yeah, she decided it was time to start checking out the local scene again." Until Cool said anything else, I wasn't going to. Besides, Cool was walking back toward us by then. "Hey, Sunny."

"Hey, Cool." Even after hours of shooting her, Sunny couldn't look our famous friend in the face.

"San Pelligrino? Blue Moon? Sam Adams?" With so few patrons, our drinks had come quickly. Feeling flush, I ponied up for the round and moved toward the table. When I got there, I realized I was alone. Cool and Sunny were still standing, looking at each other, but silent.

"Hey, Theda. I'll be down later. When the music starts." Sunny nodded toward me and headed toward the stairs. Cool came back and took her seat.

"What was that about?" I asked. Cool was shaking her head.

"Nothing I can talk about." She looked sad, but then she turned toward me and smiled. "Hey, I know better than anyone that denial isn't just a river in Egypt."

That sounded familiar. "Sunny's in the program? You never told me that."

"And I'm not telling you now. Some things are private."

"Yeah, I know: 'What you say here, stays here.' But that doesn't fit with the Sunny I know." I thought of all the drinks she'd cadged over the years. Cheapness isn't an addiction, but had she gotten that many? And since when had she been trying to quit? "I mean, I never thought of her as someone with a problem."

Cool just smiled and lifted her San Pelligrino in salute as the second band, three guys centered around a vintage electric organ, kicked in.

◇◇◇

Wow, I had to be pretty out of it, I thought as the organ wheezed and roared. Violet always said I had a naive heart, not noticing when certain musicians were nodding out or so high they couldn't talk. But someone I'd worked with? Three songs in, I murmured a "be right back" to Cool and went in search of Sunny.

I found her at the upstairs bar, looking at what I imagined was that same bottle of Sam Adams.

"Sunny, what's up? Why didn't you ever tell me?"

"Hey, Theda. Tell you what?"

I didn't know what to say. Suddenly all the beers I'd bought for Sunny over all the years came back to haunt me. Had I made things harder for her?

"Just, well, I just feel bad. I didn't realize you were dealing with things and I probably just made everything worse." I wasn't making sense, even to myself.

"What are you talking about?"

It was time to spill. "I didn't know that you had a problem. I mean, that you were in the program." Sunny looked up and started to speak. I raised my hand. "Cool didn't say anything, but, well, she did sort of give you away. So have you been trying to quit drinking?"

"It's private, Theda." She was right. Why was I pushing?

"I know, I'm sorry. It just totally took me by surprise." Something was coming together in the back of my brain, but I couldn't make out just what. "I mean, the other night you were saying you didn't want to drink because you were working. We didn't push you, did we?" That wasn't it.

"Uh-uh." If anything, Sunny looked more downcast than before.

"It's not the whole thing with Rose, is it?" I was reaching, but such violence did have repercussions. "I mean, you didn't know her, but that was still pretty harsh. Was it that?"

"No. Well, yes. Maybe. It was just so stupid, you know? The whole thing. So stupid." Sunny looked up at me and I realized that this wasn't her first drink of the evening. She wasn't slurring her words—not yet—but there was something unfocused in her gaze, like she was looking two feet past my shoulder. Maybe she did have a problem.

"Yeah, it really blew me away too." This I could relate to. "Just out of nowhere."

"And over so little, too. It was nothing."

My heart stopped, then started again so loud I could barely hear myself. "What did you say?"

"Just that it was so stupid."

"No, you said 'so little' like you knew that someone was squeezing money out of her."

"Well, she was telling everyone about the threats."

"No she wasn't. She was afraid to tell anyone. And you said you hadn't talked to her—hadn't been able to reach her." Suddenly it all came back to me: the phone log that supposedly hadn't revealed any suspicious calls. Sunny explaining how she'd justified her number being on it to the cops, using our joint assignment as an excuse. Sunny telling me that she'd only left messages, when I knew Rose had been staying close to home because of the kittens being due. Even Sunny's intense interest in the assignment, as more than just a well-paying gig. And she was going to Cool's meetings?

"Wait a minute." I grabbed her wrist. I didn't know if Sunny would try to run or slap me or just laugh in my face, but I had to get it out, see if it made sense. "You made those calls to Rose. You did, because you figured if she was going to be in the story, she must be making money. When she balked, you figured out that she was small potatoes—you told me that—but you still thought she might be worth at least twenty grand. And you've been going to Cool's meetings. I bet someone spotted her, someone who recognized her, and tipped you off. You've probably been going since you heard she was back in town. Not to give up your own drinking, but to get the dirt on her. On our old friend. For money. It was you!"

I was ready for anything. Braced for a fight. Everything was coming together. Everything except Sunny, that is. As I stood there, blocking any exit from her barstool and holding her wrist, she seemed to collapse. Her face turned inward, her mouth opened, and she let out a bawl like a three-year-old.

"Wah!" She started to wail, the volume rising. With my free hand, I grabbed some bar napkins and shoved them toward her. I wasn't going to let go.

"Sunny! Pull yourself together!"

"Tired...broke..." Nothing else that sounded like adult English was forthcoming, and I felt myself begin to melt. Almost.

"Sunny! Sunny!" Dropping the napkins I grabbed her other wrist and began to shake her hard. "I understand the money. But why did you have to hurt Rose, Sunny? Why?"

"No!" Her head was hanging against her chest, but the way she shook it back and forth was very clear. "No," her sobs wracking her body now. "I didn't, I didn't." But clearly she had. Still, I wasn't going to get any sense out of her, and every face at the bar was looking at me as if I had three heads. Even for clubland, we were making a scene.

"Theda, here, let me take over." It was Bill. I couldn't tell how long he'd been there, but he was putting away his cell phone as he walked toward us. Nodding to me, he wrapped an arm around the distraught girl, protective but also very hard to resist. "Come on, Sunny. Let's wait outside." He raised his voice for everyone to hear: "Nothing happening here, folks. Go back to your own lives." I followed them into the cold night and waited until the cruiser pulled up. One of the uniformed cops cuffed Sunny and read her her rights, while Bill talked softly to the other.

"I didn't kill Rose, Theda. You've got to believe me." The cop had his hand on Sunny's head, starting to maneuver her into the patrol car, but she had turned to me. Her face was wet with tears and mucus and half-covered with her hair, but her eyes were wide and desperate. They caught mine, and I looked away. "I never hurt anyone." I could still hear her. "Never!"

◇◇◇

"You okay?" Bill was standing beside me on the sidewalk and I realized I was shivering, despite his coat around my shoulders. The cruiser had left several minutes before but I was still seeing its lights. Seeing Sunny's face—and Rose's. Maybe I nodded. I meant to.

"C'mon, let's get you back inside."

The noise and warmth broke my daze. "Cool!" I looked up at Bill. "She's downstairs. I've got to tell her."

He looked at me hard for a moment, holding my face in his hands. He brushed one thumb along my cheek. Had I been crying, too? But I must've passed muster. "Okay, I'll meet you downstairs in a few." He'd pulled out his cell again and was heading toward the quiet of the street as I turned toward the stairs. "And Theda? Please don't say too much. I mean, we don't yet know exactly what happened."

I walked stiffly back down to the music room. Amazingly, the keyboard trio was in the middle of a song, three voices raised in harmony. According to my watch, less than twenty minutes had passed since I'd gone upstairs.

"What's up?" Just looking at my face, Cool could tell something had happened. I wiped a sleeve across my eyes and realized that they were still damp. Where to begin?

"It was Sunny, Cool. Something she said just clicked. It was Sunny who was blackmailing you."

She was shaking her head, pretending like she hadn't heard me. "No way."

"The drinking and the not drinking. The way she's been acting."

"I don't believe it. I've known her, well, as long as I've known you."

"And you suspected me at first." She looked up. "Be honest."

"But she was in the program."

"She pretended to be. I mean, I don't know that much about it, but did she seem to be really committed?"

Cool sat back in her chair, chewing on her lip as she thought it through. "Well, she never spoke. But a lot of people don't at first. It's hard. And she never identified herself. I thought, well, I thought she just wasn't ready. But she certainly knew me, even though we only use first names."

She paused and closed her eyes. When she opened them again, she looked a lot less certain. "Theda." Cool leaned toward me; her pink cheeks had gone pale. "Can this be? Can she really have betrayed me, betrayed the group like that? This blows the whole program out of the water. I mean, how can I trust it?"

I leaned forward and took her hands in mine. "You can trust the program because it works for you, Cool. You know that. Look at yourself." I was paddling as quickly as I could. "Look at how well you're doing." She nodded slowly. Something was getting through. "And in all fairness, I'm not completely sure that Sunny was the one calling you. You said the voice was disguised, right? But I am pretty sure she was the one threatening Rose. She just as good as admitted it."

"You think she killed Rose?"

"I don't know. I mean, it's hard to believe, but…" I leaned back in my chair and tried to put it all together. Sunny's denial, her wet beseeching face were clear before me. But what did they count for? "Wait, when did you get the last call?"

"Monday. That was the one that said to get the money together by the weekend."

"And Rose was killed sometime Wednesday morning. Something must have gone wrong. Hurting Rose must have been an accident, that must be why she gave up on the whole scheme."

"But why? I still don't understand. We were friends once, Theda. At least, sort of. Club buddies, back in the day."

I couldn't explain it, beyond the most basic level. "She needed money, Cool." It was all I could offer. "She's just been scraping by. And I think she's jealous."

That seemed to floor her. "God, I really need a drink. A big double shot of whiskey with a frosty draft chaser." Now it was my turn to be alarmed.

"But I won't." Cool smiled at me. The big, easy grin that lit up so many album covers had returned. "I'm okay, now."

"Yeah." I reached over and patted her hand. "You are."

Chapter Nineteen

Bill took longer to return than he'd anticipated, but that turned out to be just as well. I needed some time to sit and listen to music with my old friend. I needed the familiarity of clubland. I didn't know if I was digesting what had happened, or simply distracting myself, but by the time the third band had finished I'd begun to breathe normally. We both did.

Despite the shock about Sunny, the evening proved perfect for Cool. People trickled in slowly, many of them having been around long enough to have known her from the old days. She got attention, sure, but it was more of the friendly "Where have you been?" variety than anything nasty. And little by little she told them. All of it. By the time my guy did come down the stairs she was sitting in the center of about a dozen people. Sara, the opening act, had joined us, too, looking pleased as punch to be invited. And the bar was sending over complimentary bottles of San Pellegrino with every round. Cool was back, the queen of the underground.

◇◇◇

The next morning it all seemed so unreal as I woke up to the sound of Bill making coffee. Musetta jumped to the windowsill, pushing aside the curtain and letting the sun stream in. Sunny as a blackmailer? My cat stretched out, reaching for the window catch, the bright light revealing red highlights in her fur. Sunny as a murderer? I tried to imagine her killing Rose. If she were threatened, maybe a desperate fight had broken out. Maybe she'd even willed herself to forget it, admitting to the crimes she planned but not to the accidental one. Which brought me around to my own head wound, which still made no sense. Was that, and the break-in at Violet's, somehow related? Had Sunny been trying to keep me from talking to Rose? I preferred to think perhaps the cops on the scene had been right, and that attack had been the result of my interrupting an unrelated robbery. I sighed, letting out tension I didn't know I still had in me. Tomorrow was Halloween, and maybe some pranksters had simply started early. Musetta settled onto the sill. I wondered where those two missing kittens were, and slipped back into sleep.

"You up for a phone call?" I came awake with a start. "It's Violet." Bill was standing in the doorway, holding a mug.

"Yeah, sure." I reached for my robe and shuffled toward the phone. "Hey, Violet. What's up?"

"It's an emergency, Theda. I wouldn't ask otherwise."

My sleepy thoughts of kittens vanished. "What? What's wrong?"

"It's the van, Theda. It's dead. Caro thinks it's the transmission." I breathed out what must have been an audible sigh. No point in yelling. She couldn't know what had happened last night. "This is serious, Theda. The open house is tomorrow and I've got a ton of supplies on order, waiting for me."

Bill handed me a mug of coffee. I put my hand over the receiver and mouthed "car trouble."

"So you need a ride? Where to?" I dreaded the answer.

"Uh, that Pet Set again, in New Hampshire." I sipped. "Denise is being really nice. She may even take some of our kittens for her next cat-show adoption center. But she can't waive the delivery fee, not for out-of-state."

"It has to be today?"

"The open house is tomorrow."

I looked over at Bill, who'd already started on the paper, and at Musetta, who'd jumped down from my window and claimed the business section for a nap. They looked so relaxed. I sighed again.

"Okay, give me a half hour."

◇◇◇

It was closer to an hour by the time I showered, dressed, and bolted down the oatmeal Bill had made. But Violet was so grateful she didn't mention it. As we sped up I-93, past the bare hillsides that define "stick season," I filled her in on the events of the previous night.

"Man, I knew I should have headed out for Amphibian."

"Sounds like you had your hands full." Despite all her planning and Caro's help, Violet had ended up working till past midnight, cleaning the shelter's big ground-floor living rooms and finalizing plans for the neighborhood party.

"So, you think Rose's death had nothing to do with the cattery thefts?" She hit on the same point I'd been wondering about.

"I guess not. I guess the whole idea of a kitten mill was just imagination."

"Oh they exist." Violet relaxed, putting her feet up on my dashboard. "But, well, maybe we did get carried away on that one ad."

"I'm glad we weren't able to sic those Customs people on anybody, after all."

"Yeah really!" She began looking through my CD case. "Do you think there's a fine for false reporting of a cat sale?"

◇◇◇

Denise wasn't there when we got to the big mall, but the well-groomed manager had left detailed instructions about Violet's discounts along with a note for us.

"This is so nice." Violet read as a scrawny teen piled sacks of litter, flats of food, and two bulk bags of cat toys, especially set aside, into our cart. "She says she can't promise to place any cats, but if we have any particularly cute kittens, she'll take them to the next cat show for the Pet Set booth."

"The woman knows a good customer when she sees one." Pity she wasn't nicer to her staff, I thought. We'd gotten to the register by that point and the taped-up photo of a plump orange tabby reminded me of our last visit. What had that cashier's name been? Sandy? The girl working today was undoubtedly more to the boss' liking: slim, pretty, and quick about ringing us in without any chitchat. But I didn't see any photos of her pets taped to the register, and that made me miss the heavy girl we'd met before.

"Well, I'm grateful, anyway." Violet was looking over her receipt. The discount had saved the shelter almost forty dollars. I wheeled the overloaded cart through the electronic door and waited while she unlocked my trunk. Looking around, I was hit by deja vu.

"Hey, Violet. Is that the same sign?" Someone had stapled a handmade poster to a telephone pole. The big letters, in black magic marker, looked familiar.

"Hang on." Violet ran over to read. A moment later, she'd ripped it down and had shoved it in my face.

"Look!"

"Halloween Kittens," the sign read. "Just in time for Halloween Fun." A crude map indicated a site not five blocks away.

"Let's get this stuff in the car," I barked. "This time we're not going to let this go."

◇◇◇

The map left out a few streets and misspelled some others, so it took about twenty minutes before we found ourselves cruising in mostly angry silence through a rundown industrial area with large patches of scrubby brush and leafless trees. Looking for building numbers had us going at a crawl, and it would've been hopeless if I hadn't spotted a handmade sign, magic marker on cardboard this time, announcing "Halloween Kittens." Following the arrow at its bottom, we made our way down a rutted drive to a dingy white ranch house. On the steps sat a heavy young woman, a girl really, who looked up as we got out of the car.

"You here for the kittens?" I was fully prepared to hate her, and Violet didn't seem much better disposed, but the face that looked up at us was swollen with weeping. One eye, peeking through lank brown bangs, was also blackened and nearly shut. The rest of her was unformed, doughy and shapeless. She couldn't have been more than sixteen.

"Wait a minute, don't we know you?" Even with the bruising, that round pale face looked familiar. "You're the checkout girl from Pet Set. Sandy, right? The one with the orange cat?"

"Bootsy." She sniffed and wiped her nose on the back of her hand. It wasn't any cleaner than her face, just wetter. "Yeah, he's my cat. But do you want to see the kittens?"

Clearly something was going on here, but I wasn't sure what it had to do with cats. "Yeah, sure." At least we could keep the girl talking.

We followed her into the house, which looked as scruffy as its surroundings. Passing through a nearly empty living room, we came to a kitchen. In a large box, probably fresh from the Pet Set warehouse, were five kittens, all black.

"These are the Halloween kittens." Sandy nodded toward the box, as if she were afraid of picking them up herself, her hands jammed into her baggy jeans pockets. "They're black, special for the holiday. Twenty dollars each."

"Twenty dollars?" Violet had already reached in and picked up two. "What are you talking about? You should be happy to find these guys a home." She passed one to me. The round blue eyes that looked up at me were lined with mucous, but the face was alert. As I held him to me, he sneezed.

"How old are these kittens and when were they taken from their mothers?" Violet put hers back in the box and reached for another, flipping him over to run her fingers over its belly. "They're undernourished." She turned the kitten to peek at its bottom. "I wouldn't be surprised if they've got worms, either. Poor babies."

Sandy scuffed her sneaker toe into the grimy linoleum. Violet tried to hand her one of the squirming kittens, but she kept her hands in her pockets. "Twenty dollars. They're for Halloween. I'm not supposed to say anything else."

"What do you mean, 'not supposed to'?" The kitten I was holding had climbed onto my shoulder and begun to nurse on my earlobe. The big girl hung her head and didn't answer. "Who's making you do this, Sandy? And who gave you that shiner?"

She started to sniffle again and ran her arm over her face. I feared a full-fledged bout of tears was on its way.

"Wait a minute." Violet stood up, holding the fourth kitten. "Wait a minute." She took it over to the window where the midday sun was shining in, even through the dirty glass. "Theda, come here. Hold that kitten up, too."

I did, and as we examined both the mewling babies in the light I saw what had alerted her.

"These kittens aren't black." It seemed preposterous, but as I started brushing the little one's fur backward it was clear. "They've been colored. Dyed or something. What did you do to these kittens?"

Sandy was crying in earnest now, both hands over her face, and I handed my kitten back to Violet. Maneuvering Sandy into one of the two folding chairs that constituted furniture in the room, I pulled the other up beside her. I put my arm around her broad, heaving shoulders and tried to talk as slowly and calmly as possible.

"Sandy, something's going on here. Somebody has hurt you, and somebody's doing something funny with these kittens. I want you to tell me who hurt you and what exactly is going on here."

She shook her head, dark hair hanging in strings over face, fresh sobs wracking her round shoulders. "I can't."

Time for another tack. "You like kittens, right? You love Bootsy! Bootsy was a tiny little kitty once. Right? So help me help these little, tiny kittens. Look how cute they are."

Violet handed me one of the kittens and I placed it on the girl's lap. Her hands, down from her face at least, clenched. She was going to put them back in her pockets. But just then the kitten sat up and batted at a stray lock of hair.

"Oh!" One hand came up, one finger extended to touch the little paw. The kitten reared back to smack at it, and lost its balance. Tumbling backward, it fell into Sandy's other hand and then she was holding the kitten up to her face. "So cute! Such a pretty little kitty."

"Sandy." If this moment of bonding didn't open her up, I had no idea what would. "Sandy, honey. Don't you want to help this kitty? Won't you tell me what happened here?"

The face that looked up at me was a mess, but the eyes that met mine were clear. "It's Bruce. He's my boyfriend." I recalled the hulking teen who'd been helping out at the Pet Set booth. "He said I had to stay here and sell the kittens. He said I wasn't to play with them or anything. Just get what I could. He said ask for twenty."

"He dyed them?"

"Yeah, he used something from the grocery store, said it would make them good for Halloween parties and all."

"Bastard." Violet was now on her knees examining the other kittens. I motioned for her to be quiet.

"And he hit you to make you do it?" She shook her head no. Her tears had slowed to an occasional sniff.

"He said I had to get rid of these today. Three of them are sick. I wanted to take them to the vet, but he said no. I tried anyway, tried to sneak them out, and that's when he hit me. The other two, he just wanted to get rid of them quick. They weren't good or something. He said get some money for them or he was going to kill them."

I thought of the options, and realized these babies were the lucky ones. "Were there other kittens, Sandy?" I tried to keep my voice gentle. "Do you know what happened to them?"

"Yeah, there were lots. The healthy ones. They took them away."

"They? Bruce has a friend in on this?" I imagined a group of large, brutish boys alone with cats, and shuddered.

"His boss! His boss was the one who said to color the kittens, the ones they left behind. She said they could make some more money that way, without taking them away."

And keep them from getting sicker and dying en route to wherever "away" was. The boss' mercenary decision may have saved these kittens' lives. But to what end?

"And the others?" Violet was standing behind me now, anger coming off her like heat. "Where did they take them?"

"They had a big order, and they were scared someone was onto them. They said they'd better stop after that."

I looked at her, holding my breath, willing her to continue.

"They drove them down to Boston, to the airport this morning. They had boxes of kittens. Dozens. Some really young, and still with their mommas."

She looked back down at the tiny animal in her lap and began stroking it. I was afraid we'd pushed her too far, but she kept talking. "They left most of the momma cats behind, though." That was a blessing.

"Listen, Sandy, do you know Bruce's license number?" Violet was all business now.

"Uh uh." At least the girl seemed calm. "But they rented a truck, does that help?"

"Bingo!" Violet jumped up. "Sandy, is there a phone around here?"

"You going to call the cops?" I felt as confused as the girl.

"Even better!" Violet fished a business card out of her jacket pocket. "I forgot to give this back to the designer yesterday. I'm going to call the Feds!"

◇◇◇

Sandy showed us to a phone, back in the other room, and gave Violet all the details she could dredge up about the truck, Bruce, and the boxes of cats he'd loaded in that morning. Violet, in turn, alerted the Customs hotline about an orange rental truck that would be carrying cats, possibly sick and certainly without papers, into Logan. They'd left less than two hours before, she worked out from Sandy's story, which meant that they'd probably be at the airport within the hour.

"They said they'd get them!" Violet looked triumphant as she hung up the phone. "They're going to put the agriculture department on it. Turns out there are laws against breeding and selling without licenses, and the guy said they'd probably get them on animal endangerment, too."

"Yes!" Violet and I traded high fives, causing all the kittens—and Sandy—to look up.

"But what about the momma cats?" Despite the bruising around her eye and the gray smudges on her face, the teen now looked positively kittenish.

"I forget to tell them." Violet looked back at the phone.

"No, wait. Sandy, do you know where the mother cats are?" She nodded enthusiastically. The girl was coming back to life. Working with us was helping her. I turned to Violet. "Even if Customs lets Bruce and his buddies go, we're going to have hours before they get back. Why don't we go liberate some cats?"

Chapter Twenty

We loaded the box of kittens into the Toyota's back seat with Sandy and set off to the old warehouse where the girl had last seen the cats. We were in holiday spirits, congratulating ourselves on a job well done, and the warehouse was off in the boondocks, so it wasn't long before Violet and Sandy each had kittens out and were playing with them.

"Look at this baby. I think I'm going to call you Smokey." The girl did not have the greatest imagination.

"I wonder if you'll be smokey, too, when we get this stuff off of you." Violet was holding one of the blue-eyed kittens again, rubbing her fingers through its long, soft fur. "Sandy?" Violet held the fur bundle up to her face to examine more closely. "What color were these kittens before Bruce dyed them?"

"The two fluffy ones? They were sort of white and brown. Like Siamese, you know?"

Violet looked across at me. "The kittens from the shelter."

It made no sense. "Sandy, did Bruce steal these kittens?" I tried to imagine why someone would break into a shelter to steal kittens.

"The kittens and their momma, too." Their mother?

"Wait a minute, Sandy. Let's go slowly here. Are these the kittens from Violet's shelter?"

I could see her nodding in the rearview mirror. "There were lots of kittens, but three got sick and Bruce was going to drown them. I said we should just take them to the animal hospital and leave them there, but Bruce was scared. I figured if I took them far away, I thought nobody would recognize them and it would be okay. So I got a nice carrier from the store, took my dad's car, and headed into Boston. I've got a learner's permit."

"How'd you end up at Violet's?"

"She comes in a lot and she always seems so nice." Sandy looked up at me like I was her last hope. "I got lost, once I was off 93. But there were signs up about a Halloween party with lots of cats and kittens. It sounded like so much fun. Then when you came back to the store, I knew I'd picked the right people. I knew the kittens would be safe with you."

"Did you tell Bruce where you'd taken them?"

There was silence from the back seat, but finally I saw her nod. "Uh huh. I had to." Seeing the bruises on her face, I didn't doubt that Sandy had been forced.

"And then Bruce broke in to take the kittens back?" And walloped me in the bargain, I realized. I was getting happier and happier about that call to the Feds.

"Yeah, the boss said we had to, especially once I told them about the carrier."

Violet and I both turned to look at her. "You know, the zip-up basket-thing I left them in? They were so sick, I wanted them to be warm for the trip. I wanted you to see that, you know, someone had cared, so I took one of the new ones."

Violet looked up at me. "The carrier. It was a classy, fleece-lined carrier."

I filled in the obvious: "And it came from Pet Set." Everything was making sense. Sandy nodded, biting her lip. "It isn't even for sale yet. She was really furious. When you started calling she, like, lost it."

"She?" Violet and I spoke at once.

"Bruce's boss. She's the one who said that the kittens could be identified and that with the carrier people could figure it all out. She thought maybe you knew something. She sent him to get the kittens back."

"But there was one more kitten," Violet said. "The littlest one."
I didn't say anything. A horrible idea was growing in my mind.

"Oh yeah, the last one. Miss Denise was positively frantic."

"Denise?" Violet sounded shocked. My thoughts were spinning in a different direction.

"She told Bruce he had to find that last kitten, right?" He'd followed me, I realized. He must've gotten the truth out of Sandy soon after she brought the kittens down that Friday. If he'd been watching the shelter, he'd have seen that Violet had been in virtually all weekend—except, of course, for that suspect trip back to New Hampshire, up to Pet Set, and who knows what motives he attributed to that? But if he'd been keeping watch, he'd have known that I made that trip with Violet, and that I was in and out of the shelter. And that I'd rushed over to Rose's the day after driving to New Hampshire with Violet. I'd raced over to Rose's and snuck in the back. That night, when Bruce had broken into the shelter and hadn't found the third kitten, he must have thought I'd taken it and hidden it somewhere. Had he searched my place? I remembered the open window. I'd been in the hospital for hours, and the next morning my apartment had seemed even more of a mess than usual. It was possible. And if he hadn't found the third kitten in my apartment, he might have thought I'd brought the kitten over to Rose's cattery.

I'd led a killer to Rose.

"It was Bruce." I had to say it out loud. "Bruce was looking for the third kitten. He's the one who broke into Rose's." Violet turned to look at me, realization and shock growing in her face.

"She must have been there." Of course. She would not have left the house with a cat due to deliver, or not for long. She must have surprised him. I filled in the blanks. "Rose must have thought he was going to hurt her cats. Like the phone call threatened to."

"Like Sunny threatened to." But Sunny had been all talk. I believed her now, in retrospect. She'd been out for a buck, but not to hurt anybody. No wonder she stopped calling Cool, stopped her game. Sunny must have been terrified after one of her victims ended up dead.

"What's with these kittens anyway?" Violet turned back to Sandy, fixing the girl with a stare.

"I don't know. He just brought them in, with their momma."

"They weren't born in the warehouse?" Sandy shook her head.

"Wait a minute." Bending over the kitten in her lap, Violet slowly worked her thumbs up its back. When she got to the loose skin between its little shoulders she stopped. "I feel something. This kitten has been microchipped. I bet all three were." She looked at me. "That's why he didn't want them going to a regular animal hospital."

Just then I saw our turn and pulled off, parking the car on what used to be a paved lot. "Those are pedigreed kittens, aren't they?" I had to ask. Violet nodded. "Bruce and Denise, they're the cattery thieves."

◇◇◇

The building in front of us looked deserted, its windows painted over and crusted in dirt. But Sandy showed us to a door around back, nearly hidden by some dense, prickly shrubs, and it let us into a cavernous space. Far from empty, in the supposedly deserted space we passed a tower of folded cartons, clean and stacked as if they'd just been emptied. A few steps in, shelves rose high above our heads, stacked with more boxes, mostly unlabelled. Some seemed to hold machine parts, others pet goods. We ran down one aisle, and then another, turned a corner and saw more boxes.

"What is this place?" Violet's voice echoed in the dust.

"Some place Bruce found. I don't know who else uses it."

"Talk about a thieves' den," I read one label: Ink Jets, Two Gross. "They were into everything. So where are the cats?"

"There's a hidden door someplace." She disappeared down an aisle and we followed. "I was only here a few times."

"Are there any lights?"

"Not in most of the building. Bruce always said it would attract too much attention. He'd bring a flashlight when we came by."

"Great." Then I thought about the cats. "Is there any heat here either?"

"I don't think so. It was pretty cold in here last week."

No wonder those kittens were getting sick. I'd be happy when we found the remaining queens and got out of here.

"Theda? Sandy? Where are you?" Violet's voice came from behind a corrugated metal wall. I tried to find my way around it.

"Violet? How did you get in there?"

"I ducked under something that looked like a tractor. I thought I heard something."

"Hold on." Following her voice I crawled under a Harvester that was taking up the space between two stock shelves, and found myself in a small, cleared-out room with one bookshelf and a desk. A high window let in a little light. "Now maybe we're getting somewhere." A moment later, Sandy joined us.

"Yeah, I remember this. This is Denise's office. Where she made the deals. But her laptop is gone."

"Guess they really were going out of business," said Violet. "Maybe we did scare them off."

"More likely, they figured the cats wouldn't survive the winter." My earlier euphoria had disappeared with the realization that I'd led a killer to Rose's door.

"Well, they will now, honey. We just have to find them." Violet was running her hands along the fake wood panelling. "There's got to be a real door here, maybe more than one. I can't see that woman crawling on her knees. And I swear I heard something move or click just a minute ago."

"You know, it's not too bad in here." Sandy had stopped rubbing her arms. She was right, maybe it was because three of us were together in the little office, but it definitely seemed warmer than it had a few moments ago.

"So they were just going to abandon the mother cats?" I asked, as I examined a wall of bookshelves, hoping for a hidden catch or a switch. Sandy was poking at the panelling. I kneeled to look under the desk and then sat up.

"Does anyone else smell smoke?"

◇◇◇

Violet looked at me. We both turned to Sandy.

"Sandy." I grabbed her arms. "What were they going to do with the mother cats?"

"I don't know." She shook her head, tears springing into her eyes. "They were going to get rid of them. They just said they were going to clean everything up!"

"And they're out of town. Both of them. The perfect alibi." I turned toward the exit. Violet was ahead of me, halfway under the farm machinery that had blocked off the office alcove.

"No good." She squirmed back to us. "The smell is stronger out there, and it's hotter too. I think the fire must have started over in those boxes." I remembered the stack of cartons next to the door. All that cardboard, piled high over our heads.

"But how?" Sandy's voice was rising into hysteria. "I don't understand!"

"A timer, something like that?"

"That must've been what I heard. Damn." Violet kicked the wall.

"Call for help!" Sandy was yelling now. "Call for help!" Even Violet looked at me expectantly.

"No cell phone," I responded, coughing. "I gave it up. Vi?" She shook her head. Sandy wailed.

"There's got to be another way out." I looked around. "Sandy's seen a door, and this was Denise's office so there has to be one. There's got to be another way out of the building, too. This was a real warehouse, once. Warehouses have loading docks, right?"

"There is another door. Out where the cats are!" Sandy was crying now. "I remember! That's how I took the kittens out!"

"But where are those cats?" Violet started pulling books from the bookshelves and I went back to the panelled wall. This couldn't be too solid. It looked too cheap. But could I break through—and what was beyond it? Smoke was beginning to fill the air. Sandy's sobs turned to coughs.

"Here." I ripped off my scarf. "Hold this up to your face. Breathe through it." Violet pulled off her sweatshirt and tied it around her mouth. I lifted my own sweater's neckline up, to cover my own nose and mouth, and as I did, a rumbling came from the space behind us, the space we'd crawled through. Then a crash. My knees went weak and I leaned against the wall.

"Mrow!" Faint but unmistakeable, the sound came through the panelling. "Mrow!"

"The cats! The cats are on the other side of this wall! But how?"

The three of us threw ourselves against the fake pine, punching it and pulling at its edges with our fingernails.

"It's no good." Tears were running down Violet's face now. My own eyes were streaming. The smoke was getting thicker. "They must have put this up before they left. I bet they sealed them off. And us, too!"

She leaned against the wall and sank to the floor. Sandy stumbled into the desk chair.

"Mrow!"

"Wait a minute! Get up!" I grabbed the chair. "Violet, stand back." I swung it. Nothing. I swung again and Violet grabbed one of the metal supports from the bookshelf and began stabbing at the cheap panelling. Little by little, sure enough, it began to crack, to give way.

"Mrow!"

"We're getting through!" Holding the chair legs outward I started stabbing at the wall and soon we had a hole to see through.

"Give it to me!" Violet grabbed the chair as I collapsed, coughing. Years of hauling amps had made her wiry arms strong: four more blows and there was room enough to squeeze through. Sandy, Violet, and then myself. We were in a big room, on what must have been a loading dock, complete with metal dolly and some wooden flats. A wall of grime-encrusted windows let in enough light to show us two large metal doors, but they were hung with chains and padlocked.

"Those are the only doors!" Sandy was near hysteria, her round face bright red with panic.

"Step back!" Violet grabbed the dolly and swung. The old metal must have weighed as much as she did, but my fierce friend let it fly and the windows burst, letting in sweet clean air and the afternoon light.

"Mrow!" Behind us now we could see sat dozens of cages, empty except for eight big, fat, fluffy cats, one of whom looked exactly like her newspaper portrait.

"Quickly!" I took off my sneaker and knocked out the remaining shards of glass, while Violet started dragging wooden flats over to the window and piling them up. "What about the cats?" Sandy was staring at the cages. The animals had started pacing, the smell of smoke breaking through their customary languor. Violet and I ran to join her and quickly formed a plan. Boosting Sandy through the window first, Violet and I started unlatching the cages. One by one, we handed each cat through to Sandy in relay, before climbing out ourselves. Smoke was pouring through the windows behind us, oily and black in the slanting light, and the cats were clearly spooked. Huddled together, they watched us as we stumbled, coughing, onto the cracked pavement, only mewing softly as we grabbed them two at a time under our arms and ran them over to the car. All, that is, except for the Ragdoll queen. Docile, now, and silent once again, she sat up proudly while she waited her turn, her back to the burning building, as if to let us know that she'd been in control all along.

Chapter Twenty-One

I like to think the fire trucks would have gotten there in time. That the smoke would have risen above the woods and alerted somebody somewhere in civilization before the old warehouse— and those of us trapped in it—had succumbed to the heat, the flames, or that oily, insidious smoke. That's what I kept telling myself once we got to the nearest strip mall and talked a kindly bookstore owner into letting us call 911, the Customs hotline, and Bill, in that order. I like to think we would have been rescued. But even that fantasy couldn't keep me from shaking like a leaf once the New Hampshire state troopers got around to taking our statements, my teeth chattering so fiercely that I could barely speak. Which may be why the emergency medical technicians insisted on wrapping me in a blanket and strapping an oxygen mask over my face.

The trooper, a very nice woman named Grace, also called animal control while Violet, Sandy, and I were being bundled and monitored and, in Sandy's case, sedated. Which was just as well. Botty and her sisters—along with one tired-looking tom—may be impeccably behaved under most circumstances, but it had been a trying time for the eight liberated cats, not to mention the five kittens. Being stuffed into a Toyota as sirens and lights swirled around can upset anyone's aplomb. When the animal control officer showed up, with a van full of carriers, Violet and I ran through our theory again: These lovely cats, all long-furred and portly, were the missing pedigree dfelines. Animal control would be scanning for microchips and checking DNA, but it seemed clear to us that these cats—Ragdolls, Maine coons, and a sleek gray beauty who resembled Sally's Norwegian forest cats—had been stolen for their ability to produce beautiful kittens. Back at home, with their papers in place, their offspring would bring close to a thousand dollars a kitten. But even on the black market—and it seemed certain now that the ring had a connection with Asian dealers—their fat, fluffy kittens would fetch at least a hundred a pop.

Why they were closing up such a profitable scam remained the only outstanding mystery. By the time we'd been checked out by the EMT crew, Grace was able to tell us that a rental truck had, in fact, been stopped at Logan airport; six dozen cats, including several litters still nursing, had been taken into custody. The officers, acting as agents of the Animal and Plant Health Inspection Service of the United States Department of Agriculture, looked at the tiny cages and the animals' matted fur and charged Bruce and Denise, who'd been driving, with animal cruelty. Neither had been able to produce a commercial breeder's license, either, which added another charge, and grand theft would probably follow. Cats and kittens alike had been rushed to an animal hospital, though it seemed like dehydration and hunger were the worst of their ills, and already, Grace said, the nursing queens were being matched up with reports of stolen cats. But why those fertile queens were being sold, rather than giving the kittens a few more weeks and shipping them weaned, and why the remaining cats had been left to die, nobody understood.

"It's a lot of risk for one short-term score," noted Grace amiably. "Something must have spooked them."

She and Violet and I were sitting in the back of an ambulance, the other having already taken Sandy off to the closest hospital. Between smoke and shock and what the EMT thought might be a fractured occipital lobe, the battered teen had been fairly incoherent when Grace had showed up.

"They must have known we didn't have a microchip scanner," said Violet. She and I had already filled Grace in on the identifying chips inserted in the loose skin at the back of the cats' necks. "Even Sandy must have known that."

What the teen knew or didn't would be for the courts to figure out, as would her degree of complicity. We believed, and had told Grace, that the young woman had risked serious harm in her attempt to rescue the kittens. The bruises and possible broken bones of her face proved that. Whether she'd been aware of why her brute of a boyfriend hadn't wanted the sick animals to go to a bigger animal hospital, where they might have been scanned, was another question.

"So why end it all?" I was thinking aloud. The bigger question—why kill Rose?—echoed in my head, but I didn't know if that would ever come out.

"Maybe it wasn't anything you folks did." Grace was trying to be helpful. "Maybe trying to sell them here, one by one, wasn't working out."

"But they didn't have to." This wasn't making sense. "It seems like they were only selling the rejects, the sick ones. The rest they had a good market for overseas."

"Maybe someone else was honing in on their business?"

"Or they thought someone was. Violet." I turned to my friend. "When did you start calling the store?"

"Sunday, almost as soon as you dropped me off. Why?"

"I bet they thought we were onto them. Somewhere in there they found out that Sandy had brought the kittens to you and they must have thought you were trying to get in on it, or that you were doing your own little bit of blackmail."

"But I don't know anything about pedigreed cats."

"Denise didn't know that. Bruce certainly didn't. And your name is on the license for the shelter." Another memory came back to me. "She saw us at the cat show last Saturday, too, and we were talking about selling kittens."

"The pet store woman was at a cat show?" Grace was intrigued now.

"Yeah, as a vendor for the store. And they bring cats for adoption."

"Well, that explains how she knew about the judges and the breeders. She probably found out in advance who would be showing, and whose place would be vulnerable."

Vulnerable. I thought, again, of Rose. If I hadn't visited her, Bruce would never have suspected her of hiding the last kitten. If I'd convinced her to call the police, he might have been caught, or seen them and been scared off. I tried to imagine what the confrontation had been like: A hulking, overgrown boy, probably starting to pry open a window like he'd done at Violet's. Rose opening her door to see what was causing the commotion. Had he said he'd come for the kitten? Had she rushed him to defend her animals? Had they struggled? My head hurt and I felt dizzy again.

"Head down, Miss. Now, breathe in." Violet had been replaced by the medic, who put one arm around me and with the other gently lowered my head between my knees. "Just breathe. Everything's all right now, Miss. Everything's all right."

Except it wasn't, of course. It wouldn't ever be.

◇◇◇

"You didn't kill her, you know." By the time I got us home, driving at a shaky forty miles per in the right-hand lane, Bill was waiting. He now had me tucked into my comforter, on my sofa, with a mug of hot cocoa liberally laced with brandy in my hands. "You didn't kill Rose. And if it weren't for what you did, her murderers might have gotten away with it."

He was too much of a cop for me to believe that. "You're lying, Bill. Am I that much of a basket case?"

"Close." He smiled and sat down next to me, pulling a pliant Musetta onto his lap. "But in this case, I mean it."

I stared him down. Musetta started to purr like a little engine.

"Okay, okay. Let's just say that from what I'm hearing, Watertown Homicide wasn't anywhere close. Nor were the Feds. I don't think Rose was ever really a suspect in the cattery thefts. But the investigators were looking at other judges and breeders, people who had inside knowledge of the show schedules, and they leaked what they thought might draw out the real perps. From what I can tell, they hadn't even considered the vendors yet. I mean, I'm sure they would have—and you did take a hell of a risk—but—"

"But we caught them," I interrupted before he could slip into lecture mode. "Poor Rose. She was right to be afraid, even though the real brute wasn't the caller who had threatened her." I thought again of the smoke and the rising heat, of that awful search for some way—any way—out. "We didn't know we were walking into a trap, Bill, I swear. If anything, we thought we'd find some horrible kitten farm and we'd end up calling animal control." Once I'd seen Sandy, I'd also wanted to get my hands on her bully of a boyfriend, too, but that was hardly information to share with my own beau.

"Well, you did more than that." He leaned over the coiled cat and kissed the top of my head. "And I'm proud of you."

◇◇◇

My throat was sore and my body felt battered when we woke the next morning. It was too late, right? The sun had me pegging the time at noon. Musetta had already made herself scarce, abandoning her place on the bed to catch up on her own business. But Bill was making breakfast, and not taking any excuses.

"C'mon sleepyhead. You got an extra hour already cause we turned the clocks back. And we've got an open house to go to. Caro's already called."

I groaned. How could I deal with kids or cats?

"That's the adrenaline run-off talking. It leaves you stiff. Have some eggs." He'd made eggs? "Some food and the company of your friends will do you good."

He was right, of course. The fake smile I'd plastered on my face became real enough after an hour at the shelter. The open house, by any measure, was a huge success. More than two dozen kids showed up, many dragging parents, some leaving with the paperwork that would result in the adoption of one of the shelter's inmates. Bunny told stories of good witches, and Violet and Caro showed the children, and some of the attendant adults, the correct way to pick up a kitten and pet a cat. Monica came by with her boyfriend, Tess brought a guitar, and Cool thrilled the parents by a quick visit and impromptu singalong. Even Lynn showed up, surprising everyone with a bag of rainbow-colored feathers that promised to make the Halloween costumes even wilder. Once the kids were settled into their mask making, with Caro supervising the use of glue, Violet and I had a moment's break.

"So, I've told Caro. And if I tell you, then I've really got to do it." We were standing off by the kitchen, where some of the less social cats had taken shelter.

"Huh?" I was definitely feeling slow on the uptake and had poured myself another mug of coffee, my fourth of the day.

"Smoking. I'm quitting. Have quit, actually, as of today."

"Congratulations!" Another notch of tension left my shoulders. "What brought this about?"

"Yesterday, if you must know." I waited. "It wasn't exactly like my life flashed before my eyes, but, you know, it made me think." She paused. Sibley jumped off the table and sauntered over to rub his gray-capped head on her shin. "And my throat was so sore, well, if I never taste smoke again I don't think I'll miss it."

"Well, good for you." I hugged her and she smiled. Sibley, for his part, was kneading the rug.

"Of course, I'm not promising I'll stay with it, but…"

"Violet!" She laughed and I joined her, but then her pixie-like face became serious again.

"I was thinking, Theda, about that woman. Denise."

I sipped from my mug and waited.

"You know how she was being so nice to me? You think she thought I wanted in on it? That I wanted to force my way into her scam?"

I remembered how the pet store manager had positioned herself as Violet's newfound friend, one who offered her discounts—and a place for any spare kittens at her next adoption fair. I shook my head.

"Not exactly. She thought she was smarter than all of us." I reached to pet the spotted cat's ears as I reasoned it through. "After they couldn't find the kitten at Rose's place, they must have realized they'd made a mistake. I think they may have searched my place, too." Violet's eyebrows registered her shock, but the more I thought about it, the more sense it made. "I think they looked in my apartment, but with my housekeeping....well, maybe we'll never know. When they couldn't find that last kitten there and I wasn't leading them to it, they must have figured out you still had it, somewhere—but that you didn't know what you had. That's why Denise started offering to help out with any new kittens that just happened to show up at the shelter. She thought she was shmoozing you."

"She did become all friendly after the cat show. Was it just the timing? Or do you think it was something about the way we were acting, or something she heard us say?"

"I don't know if we'll ever know, Violet."

"Yeah, I know." My friend leaned against the doorjamb and for a moment even her purple cowlick seemed to sag. "I just wonder if there was something I could have done earlier that would have kept them off Rose."

"Like not isolating a sick kitten?" I heard an echo of Bill in my own voice. "Or hanging a banner advertising your ignorance of show cats?"

She smiled sadly. I hugged her, and hefted Sibley up to place him in her arms. "C'mon, let's go back to the kids."

◇◇◇

By Monday, I was feeling more like a human. Or I would have been, if I hadn't been woken by the phone. It was Lannie: news of her photographer's arrest had shaken her already fragile confidence.

"Theda? Did you hear about this?"

I did not want to go into details about what had already transpired, so I passed along what I knew of her prospects. "She may get probation, Lannie. One of her victims is refusing to press charges." Cool had told the police that Sunny had done her a favor, forcing her to go public. Ronnie was working on her, though, so I didn't know how long that would hold.

"But blackmail! That's so..." She paused. I waited for her to say "tacky" or "low class." She didn't, letting silence complete her sentence, but in that moment I recognized my own sympathy for Sunny. I'd thought I wanted her to suffer, to do time for scaring Rose, and maybe she would. But I was a freelancer, too, and broke. It was a hard life at times.

"Hey, did you get my message?" Something good had to come of this.

"Yes, I did. I think that's a marvelous idea. Will the sister agree?"

"I think so. I was just about to call her," I lied.

"Well, set it up. I'll find somebody to send!"

It was after nine, so even before coffee I called the number for the Rose Blossom Cattery.

"Ivy?"

"No, this is Joy, the vet tech. Hang on."

As I waited, the endpiece I'd pitched to Lannie appeared in my mind: A full-page photo of Ivy and the new litter. A portrait of new life at the site of tragedy. Would Ivy want to do it, though? Would it seem too morbid or, worse, too cute?

"Theda. Sorry about that. There's just so much to take care of."

"Sorry for disturbing you, then." She must be cleaning out the offices at last.

"No, I needed the break. Joy has me practicing bandages on an old squeeze toy and it was getting pretty dull."

"Bandages?"

"She says that I need to know some basic emergency medicine if I'm going to take this on."

"Ivy?"

"Oh, didn't I tell you? I'm going to keep the cattery. The thought of some stranger coming in and carting all these beautiful animals away was simply intolerable."

I was speechless.

"And my children are basically grown. Dave has been saying I need a hobby. Well, this isn't a hobby. Far from it! But with Joy agreeing to stay on, I think I can do it."

"Would you like a little publicity?" I told her about my idea for a photo. She loved it, with two additions.

"Joy's got to be in it. She's going to be an employee, and she's really the expert. And, Theda? Can we shoot the kittens under a sign that says 'Rose Blossom Cattery'? We're keeping the name, of course. It's what people know, and we want people to remember her."

◇◇◇

Coffee was finally brewing when the phone rang again. Musetta was twining around my ankles mewing for her own breakfast, and I thought I'd let the machine take it.

"Theda? You there? This is Mathers. Tim Mathers."

My old editor, the youth-seeker. I waited and, strangely, Musetta did too.

"Theda? Please pick up. Please?"

How could I resist?

"Hi, Tim. I was off in the kitchen. What's up?"

"Theda, I know we got into it a bit when we last spoke, but I wanted to know if you'd consider writing for us again." I waited. "The column, Theda. Your column—'Night Lines'? If you still want to do it, we could use it. Every week. We could even put you on a retainer."

So baby Jessica was above writing now that she was an editor. Still, did I want to work for her?

"Would I be reporting to you, or Jessica?"

"Me. Can you believe the ingratitude of that girl?" Clearly I'd missed some gossip.

"What happened? She running the city room now?" I couldn't resist a little lip.

"Yeah, yeah, she is." I thought I heard him sputter, like he'd swallowed his own coffee the wrong way. "But not for us. Not anymore. She gave notice on Friday. She's been hired away by the *Washington Post*."

I laughed so hard I scared the cat, but by the time she emerged from under the sofa Tim and I had a deal: a one-year contract, renewable, that would pay enough of my expenses to keep us all in Fancy Feast. My first column would be on the Violet Haze Experience, due next Tuesday. I gave Musetta her belated breakfast after that, along with a good ear scratch that had her purring as she ate, left a message for Bill, promising him a celebratory meal of a different sort, and another for Bunny, telling her to look for me in the newsroom again. Then I pulled on some clothes and headed out for Violet's, planning my interview questions on the way.

Acknowledgments

Thanks to B. Iris Tanner of Silverlock Cattery, who first introduced me to Turkish Angoras, and the incredibly knowledgeable and generous members of the Cat Writers Association (including Wendy Christenson, Marva Marrow, Louise Holton, Steve Dale, Amy Shojai, and many, many others) for all the feline facts. All their info was solid gold, and any mistakes are mine. Fellow authors Caroline Leavitt, Brett Milano, and Vicki Constantine Croke provided boundless emotional support, writing advice, and caffeine. Frank Garelick and Lisa Jones, Sophie Garelick, Ann Porter, and of course, always, Iris Simon cheered me on. Ann Collette of the Helen Rees Agency lent an eagle eye to the manuscript, and numerous independent bookstore owners, particularly Kate Mattes of Kate's Mystery Books, have helped launch Theda Krakow in style. All the great people at Poisoned Pen, notably editor Barbara Peters, publisher Robert Rosenwald, Nan Beams, Marilyn Pizzo, and Jessica Tribble, made this book better— and possible. Jon S. Garelick, as always, read, supported, encouraged, and believed. Thank you all.

To receive a free catalog of Poisoned Pen Press titles, please contact us in one of the following ways:

Phone: 1-800-421-3976
Facsimile: 1-480-949-1707
Email: info@poisonedpenpress.com
Website: www.poisonedpenpress.com

Poisoned Pen Press
6962 E. First Ave. Ste. 103
Scottsdale, AZ 85251